Journey
TO THE
Pacific,

One Man's Quest

Published in the United States of America
ISBN   Paperback: 979-8-89091-340-1
ISBN   eBook: 979-8-89091-341-8

ReadersMagnet, LLC
10620 Treena Street, Suite 230 | San Diego, California, 92131 USA
1.619. 354. 2643 | www.readersmagnet.com

Cover design by Jhiee Oraiz
Interior design by Daniel Lopez

JOURNEY
TO THE
PACIFIC,

One Man's Quest

JUDITH A. PERKINS

ReadersMagnet, LLC

TABLE OF CONTENTS

DEDICATION

It amazes me that I have been able to write this story and create these characters. With the help of my family, it has been fairly easy. They have done nothing but encourage me in this endeavor. My grandchildren have been so excited about the project, my sons and daughters-in-law have been nothing but encouraging and my husband has been my rock, as well as reading over the initial manuscript and correcting my misspellings and punctuation errors. He has also been a great resource for dates and times of certain events in history.

To Jamaica, Cherry, and everyone at ReadersMagnet Publishing, a great big thank you for your kindness, your patience, and your advice throughout this whole publishing process. You are great people.

Most of all, I want to give my thanks and love to my son Jeffrey. His computer skills, his patience with a mother who does not understand computers and his amazing editing skills have been invaluable in preparing this manuscript for the publisher.

Judy/Mama

JOURNEY TO THE PACIFIC
ONE MAN'S QUEST
CAST OF CHARACTERS:

George Seevers .... Main Character

Daniel Seevers .... George's brother

Gregory Seevers... George's brother

Ira Seevers ....George's Father

Clara Seevers ....George's Mother

Mrs. Bennett .... Housekeeper for Clara

Mr. Wyler..Owner – Wyler Ranch

Fred Lewis............................... Chef at hotel restaurant Cheyenne, Wy.

Mary Lewis .... Fred's wife

Marie Lewis .... Fred's daughter.

Susan Lewis.. Fred's daughter.

Jane Lewis .... Fred's daughter

Doctor Stephens .... Doctor in Cheyenne

Pastor James Daniels ....Cheyenne Comm. Church

Anna Elaine Seevers.....................................George & Maries daughter

Clyde Rodgers ....owner of dry goods store in Portland

Irene Mae Seevers ....George & Marie's daughter

Charlotte Louise Seevers...........................George & Marie's daughter

Frederick David Seevers ....George & Marie's son

John Johnson .... owner of bakery in Portland

Isaac Sorenson .... Owner of Bank in Portland

Julia Sorenson... Isaac Sorenson's wife

Steven Taylor...clerk at Sorenson'sbank

Roy Collins... buys bakery from George

Jeff Jordan...buys land in Rawlings

Earl Jansen.. carpenter moved to Rawlings

Ray Clausen... blacksmith in Rawlings

Clyde Rodgers, Jr................... moves to Rawlings -opens general store

Daniel Johnson .... Pastor of Christian Church in Rawlings

Isaac Steven Taylor ....twin son of Steven and Jane

John Lewis Taylor.....................................twin son of Steven and Jane

Oliver Jordan .... Father of Jeff Jordan

Leo Gregory ....Works for Steven Taylor

Jake Leoni ....works night shift at hotel

Fiona MacGregor .... School teacher in Rawlings

Dr. Blake Stephens .... New Doctor in Rawlings

Otis Kingman... troublemaker in Rawlings

Virginia Kingman .... wife of Otis

Seth, Daniel, Bill and James......................... Sons of Otis and Virginia

Josephine, Margaret .... Daughters of Otis and Virginia

Jesse Chamberlain .... Grist Mill Operator

Joe and Cora Morrison .... Bunkhouse cook and

Housekeeper at main house

Bruce Williams... Buys Kingman farm

Jim Barnes .... New cook at Hotel

Will Jones .... Anna Seevers husband

William Henry Jones.. Anna's baby son

CHAPTER 1

George Seevers was born to Ira and Clara Seevers on June 8, 1859, in Streator, Illinois. He was a big happy baby boy with blue eyes and soft brown hair. He had two older teenage brothers named Daniel and Gregory. Clara was hoping to have a daughter but was happy with her boy. He was a surprise addition to the family and Clara being in her early 40's when he was born, made it hard on her physically to have him. It took her some time to recover from the delivery compared to the other two. Ira hired a wet nurse to come in so that she could feed George and a housekeeper, Mrs. Bennett, to cook and clean while Clara was recovering. Ira told her, "You need to rest my dear, and this is the best way for you to do it." "But I do not want other people in my house," complained Clara. "It will only be for about 6 months, then you will be on your own again," Ira reassured her.

Clara had to admit that it was very nice having someone else do the chores for her, but she knew that she would have to get back to them soon. Daniel, and Gregory were going to need attention. Both boys had jobs working at the livery stable in town caring for horses but would want their mother to cook their meals for them. Coincidentally, they both were unhappy with their new baby brother.

After the six-month recovery, Clara was able to resume most of her duties as a wife and mother. Ira dismissed the wet nurse but wanted to continue to have Mrs. Bennett come daily. It relieved Clara of much of the hard laborious work. Just the laundry for all of them was a daunting task.

There was much talk in the streets in 1859 and in the news about the possibility of the South seceding from the United States because of the states' rights issue. Both the older Seevers boys were hoping that a war would start so that they could get away and have some excitement in their lives. "As soon as I can, I am going to sign up for the Army," bragged Daniel. "I want to get away from this town and see some of the rest of the country." "If you go, I go," agreed Gregory.

Within the next six months, both the older Seevers boys joined the Army at the same time. Both Ira and Clara were upset at the idea of both of their boys being gone, but they knew it was the right thing for them to do. They wanted to escape from Streator and they both wanted to see more of the country. Both boys were being sent to Fort Leavenworth, Kansas for training and from there they did not know where they would be posted. They were just anxious to leave.

George was five months old when his older brothers left for Kansas in October of 1859. They, along with eight other young men from the Chicago area boarded a train for Fort Leavenworth. Ira, Clara, and George saw them off at the train station. Clara had tears in her eyes at the thought of her sons leaving but knew it would be good for them. Both she and Ira felt that it would keep them out of trouble and be good discipline for them. They only had an eighth-grade education and had no desire to continue with more schooling.

Life continued for the Seevers with Ira going to work as the assistant manager of the Illinois Bank in Streator every day. Clara stayed home to take care of George, but also continued with her weekly card games with her friends. Once a month, she hosted the game at her home. Most of her friends ignored George and could not imagine having another baby at their age. Clara did admit that it was not easy caring for an infant again, but he was such a sweet baby that she really didn't mind if he interfered with her social activities. That was what Mrs. Bennett was for. She was paid to take care of George as well as keep the house. Clara conceded that even though at first, she did not want anyone else in her home, she very much enjoyed the freedom that it gave her now.

In 1861, the South seceded from the United States of America and war was declared by the Union. Ira was compelled to join the Illinois militia and fight for the Union. George was barely 2 years old and it frightened Clara to be alone with the baby and household staff.

"I feel obligated to fight for my country," said Ira. "It is my duty."

"But what about your duty to George and me. We need you here with us as much as the country needs one more soldier," Clara complained. Ultimately, nothing she said though would change Ira's mind. He explained that his enlistment in the Army was only for six months. He was sure the insurrection would be over by then and the South would be put in its place.

Ira left in May 1861 with the militia, headed east towards Virginia to meet up with other units to fight the Rebel army. Clara was on her own with Mrs. Bennett and George. The gardener had also joined the militia. It seemed to Clara that all the men in the city were leaving. Life went on for Clara, but it was a struggle for her to get up every day and take care of George. More and more she left the duties of caring for him to Mrs. Bennett.

In August 1861, Clara received notice that both of her boys had been killed in the Battle of Bull Run in Virginia. She was devastated and tried unsuccessfully to notify Ira. She did not know where he was.

In September of 1861, Clara received word that Ira had died of dysentery while in Pennsylvania with his regiment. She was unable to function and had to rely on Mrs. Bennett completely to take care of George. She was incoherent and could not believe that she had lost both of her sons and her husband within a month of each other.

There were times when Clara seemed to snap out of her malaise and try to help with the chores and with taking care of the baby, but it did not last for more than a day or two. "Mrs. Seevers, please take care of your baby. He has been crying for a while and wants to have his diaper changed. I am busy with all the other chores in the house and trying to fix you some supper," Mrs. Bennett said. Most of the time, Clara ignored her and did not respond to George's cries.

Mrs. Bennett felt very sorry for Clara but was not hired to take care of the baby, its mother, and the household at the same time. And she was not being paid. Clara did not respond when Mrs. Bennett asked for her weekly pay. She was only staying because of George. She couldn't leave him alone with his mother.

One morning when Mrs. Bennett heard George crying very hard and Clara did not seem to respond, she picked up the baby and went into Clara's room. She was lying in bed in an almost catatonic state and did not respond to any sound. Mrs. Bennett was truly scared for George and finally called the authorities. The police came to the house to investigate and called for an ambulance wagon to take Clara to the hospital. Mrs. Bennett explained that she was not able to take care of the baby any longer and he would have to be placed somewhere else.

"Mrs. Seevers will not take care of her baby. She won't even hold him. She ignores him completely. I cannot keep taking care of her and the baby," explained Mrs. Bennett. "Where is the father of this child?" the policeman inquired. "He died of dysentery and both of her other boys were killed early on in the war." The policeman explained to Mrs. Bennett that they would get a doctor out to see Mrs. Seevers right away and the doctor would be the one who would recommend the baby be placed in the orphanage. "We cannot just take him since his mother is still alive."

The doctor came out within two hours and recommended that Mrs. Seevers be taken to the hospital and that George be placed in the county orphanage.

The police took him to the orphanage for temporary placement until his mother was better. Clara never did get better, and George was permanently placed in the orphanage until the age of 16, unless he was adopted, which during the war, was unlikely.

George was not allowed to be a baby very long after he was placed in the county orphanage. As soon as he could walk and understand simple directions, he was given chores to do. At first, he worked in the laundry area when he was two years old. He sorted clothes by colors and separated all the socks into piles. All the socks were black, so there was no color coordinating in the laundry room. His next assignment in the laundry was to sort the undershirts and underpants. This was an especially distasteful job even for a two or three-year-old. But he was forced to work if he wanted to eat. For two years old, he was a wise little boy and learned fast.

CHAPTER 2

George was growing up fast, not so much in size but in wisdom. He had learned to talk early and was very verbal. He learned very quickly that it was not advisable to talk back to the matrons or anyone very much older than he was. He was very careful who he talked to.

There was one matron that worked in the cafeteria that took a liking to George and pretty much took care of him. She taught him the alphabet and his numbers. He was a very quick learner and loved spending time with her. The other boys teased him about his closeness to the matron and he was embarrassed about it.

Because the head of the orphanage did not agree with his matrons becoming personally involved with their charges, the matron was moved to another part of the orphanage. George missed her personal attention but was resigned to the fact that he would not see her again.

George continued to grow and was quickly learning to read and do his numbers. He was not allowed to go to school but read every book that he could understand and learned his numbers by reading the books.

After working in the laundry, George was moved to the kitchen. He was getting taller and could stand on a stool and wash dishes. It was back breaking work, and he was tired most of the time, but he did the job so that he would not get into any trouble. If he was undisciplined, he would lose his privileges, one of those was being able to look at the books and magazines in the visitors' waiting rooms. One of his many jobs was to clean the visitor waiting room. There were not many visitors to the orphanage and the visitor waiting area never got too dirty or messy, but he was made to clean it anyway.

As George grew older and taller, he went to work in the fields. He weeded and plowed and cut hay eight hours a day and was exhausted by the time he got back to his room. He managed to eat a little food before he collapsed onto his bed and into a deep sleep. He was up at five AM the next day and back in the fields early that morning.

This life went on for years and George grew to be a large boy with strong arms and legs. He continued to read and learn as much as he could. Even though he was tired in the evening, he tried to read a few pages every night. There were always publications of some kind in the waiting room. He would pick them up while he was cleaning, take them back to his room and return them when he was finished.

George had read a story about the oceans and had a dream of seeing the Pacific Ocean. It started out as a dream, but quickly became an obsession. He started thinking about leaving the orphanage and somehow getting to the Pacific Ocean. He seemed to know that his life would improve if he saw the ocean.

He didn't know the area around Streator, so wasn't sure which way to go, but he could hear the train whistles at night when it was quiet and knew that if he could get to the train heading west, he could get to the Ocean. He did not know how far the ocean was, so he had no frame of reference.

One evening just before his 15th birthday in June 1873, he put all his belongings into a towel, stuffed it under his nightshirt and told the night matron that he had to go to the outhouse. She let him out, thinking that he was in real distress and that his stomach was swollen. He walked, hunched over to the outhouse, went inside, put his extra clothes on over his nightshirt and slipped out of the outhouse. He had heard the train whistle and knew what direction to head in. He kept close to the buildings and was not noticed by anyone.

As George made his way toward the sounds of the train whistles, he felt a profound sense of relief to be away from the drudgery of the orphanage. He knew in his heart that he would have to face drudgery again, but it would be of his own making and not forced on him by uncaring people.

He came upon the train depot very quickly, looked and did not see anyone milling around that could take him back to the orphanage. He did see a ragged old man sitting on the ground waiting for the train to come. George sat down beside him and asked him how to get onto the train headed West. He told him that he wanted to see the Pacific Ocean. The old man laughed and said to George, "You are crazy kid. It will take you forever to get there." As they were talking, they could hear the train whistle coming from the East. The old man got up, pulled George to his feet, and told him to follow him. George did as he was told and hid with the man until the train came in, unloaded the cargo for Streator and was ready to leave again. Then the old man grabbed George and ran for the open door of the freight car. Just as the train was starting to roll, George and the old man jumped aboard. George felt exhilarated. He had never done anything that exciting before and felt free for the first time in his life.

George had not even thought of bringing any food with him and would not have had any way of getting any. The old man offered to share a bit of jerky with him and told him to just eat a bite at a time, that it had to last awhile.

They stayed on the train for a couple of days and were still on when they got to Rapid City, South Dakota. George knew that he had to get off and get some real food. He did not know how but he knew that he had to try. He jumped off the train as soon as it slowed down enough and started running. He was weak from lack of food, but he was able to elude the inspectors.

It was early morning when he left the depot in Rapid City. He started walking up and down the streets looking for someplace that might take pity on him and give him a bit of food to eat. As he was walking up a street that was about 3 blocks from the depot, he saw a "help wanted" sign in the window of a laundry. If there was anything that George knew about, it was doing laundry. That was his first job in the orphanage.

He walked into the laundry and asked about the job. The owner hired him on the spot and put him to work on the scrub board doing sheets for the hotel. George was doing a good job of scrubbing but was obviously not concentrating too well on the job. The owner questioned George about his slowness. "I have not eaten a meal in three days and am very hungry," George explained. The owner pulled out a piece of bread and butter from his own lunch, gave it to George and said, "eat this and get back to work." George ate the bread very quickly, almost vomited it back up, but went back to work and felt much better.

George asked the owner if he knew of a room that he could sleep in and was told that there was an extra bed in the room in the back of the laundry. It was a room with six beds in it and five of them were occupied by other workers.

He fell into bed that night and slept like a baby. He was up again at 5 AM the next morning and after a piece of bread and butter was back on the scrub board.

The laundry was run like an assembly line with George and two other fellows using the scrub boards to get the clothes clean, two others to rinse the clothes and two others to hang the clothes outside on the lines.

On his Sunday afternoon off, George was walking down the main street of Rapid City and saw a sign in the general store window for a cook at the Wyler

Ranch outside of the city. Since George had learned to cook in the orphanage, he thought he could do the job. He went into the store to ask about the job and the clerk sent him to the back office. Mr. Wyler happened to be in the store at the time, planning with the store owner for a delivery to be made to the ranch.

George knocked on the door, was called in and waited for a few minutes before he was acknowledged. The visitor was obviously the rancher, wearing a cowboy hat, guns strapped to his hips and the most beautiful, expensive leather cowboy boots that George had ever seen. The store owner finally asked George what he wanted, and George said that he was inquiring about the sign in the window for a cook at the Wyler Ranch. Mr. Wyler responded to George's inquiry and asked him some questions about his experience cooking. George explained that he learned to cook in the orphanage in Streator, Illinois for about 100 boys from the ages of infant to 16 years. Mr. Wyler asked him to cook a meal at the ranch for the ranch hands that evening as a test of his skill as a cook.

George fixed steaks, fried potatoes and he made an apple pie for dessert. The hands were amazed at the taste of the food and loved having the pie for dessert. Mr. Wyler was impressed with George's abilities and hired him on the spot. "You are a good cook, George. I will pay you a fair wage for the work you do and give you a place to sleep in the bunkhouse. I run an honest place and my hands are all good men. I am counting on you to be the same." "Thank you, Sir. I will do my best for you."

George made a list of supplies needed for the menu for the week and Mr. Wyler's assistant ordered them for him. Beef was the main source of protein, but occasionally, there would be antelopes or deer and of course at least once a week they had chicken.

When George did go into town, he tried to avoid the saloons and the girls that worked there. He worked too hard for his money to spend it on women and liquor. He would limit himself to one beer and then would leave. He did not want to give up his dream of seeing the Pacific Ocean. His money was being saved for the trip to the Ocean.

George wasn't a creative cook, but cooked good, hearty meals that the cowboys loved. They looked forward to supper time every day and the meal that was served to them.

George worked at the ranch for 10 months. The winter was brutal with snow and ice and very cold, chilling weather. By February, he was ready to head West again.

This time, George was able to afford a train ticket to Cheyenne, Wyoming, and he rode inside the passenger car instead of the freight car. He even had a little money left over to buy some food along the way. Cheyenne was a rough cow and railroad town and was rowdy and loud on the nights the cowboys would come into town.

George knew that he had to find work very soon. He had very little money left and needed to eat. He walked the streets looking for a "Help Wanted" sign in a shop window. As he was walking past the hotel, he saw a sign that read "kitchen help wanted – someone to wash dishes and clean up." George felt his heart flutter with excitement. That type of job was exactly what he wanted.

He walked into the hotel and up to the desk. The clerk at the desk looked at George and sneered, "We do not rent rooms to vagrants. Please leave the hotel."

"I am inquiring about the sign in the window for the kitchen work," George countered. The clerk looked at him again, turned and went into the kitchen to get the head chef.

Fred Lewis, the head chef, came out of the kitchen, looked over at George and almost laughed. George was very rumpled and had not had a bath in several days. Plus, he was very weak from not eating recently. Fred did go over a talk to him though. "So, you are interested in working in my kitchen. What kind of experience do you have working in a kitchen?" Fred asked. George told him about working in the orphanage kitchen and cooking meals for all the children, of washing dishes and cleaning the counters, tables, and floors after each meal. He also told him about cooking at the Wyler Ranch for the cowhands who worked there. "Why are you so dirty if you are working in a kitchen?" Fred asked. "I have been riding on a train from Rapid City and I do not have a place to stay as yet, nor have I had a chance to bathe. I was walking along the street and saw your sign in the window and came in to ask about the job," George answered. "I don't have much money left and need to find a place to sleep for the night."

Fred looked George over and asked him to come back to the kitchen. George followed him back and Fred told him not to touch anything. He was too dirty. They walked over to the basin of water used for washing hands and Fred pointed to it and said "Wash!" George very happily complied with the request. Fred watched George wash his hands and was impressed with the way he used the soap and washed part way up his arms. Fred believed in a clean kitchen and clean employees. Fred then asked George to go to the counter and make a sandwich, reminding George that this was a restaurant kitchen, and the customers were waiting for their food to be served quickly.

George was nervous, but went right to the counter, pulled out the bread and the makings for a chicken sandwich. He made the sandwich, put it on a plate and added a dill pickle to the plate as a garnish. Fred was very impressed with the speed and the look of the plate. He ate the sandwich himself and complemented George on the taste of the sandwich. He offered him the job with the added request that he take a bath and put on some clean clothes.

George said, "I do not have a place to stay or a place to wash up, but I will see if I can find a room and a bath house."

Fred told George where the boarding house was and gave him a note to the owner explaining that he had just hired George. The note asked if he had a room and a bath for tonight and Fred would pay for it tomorrow.

The owner of the boarding house was reluctant to give George the room, but because Fred had such a good reputation in town, she agreed. George took his pack to his room, waited for the tub and hot water to be brought to his room and when it was, he sank into a hot bath with a sigh of relief. He had a job, would be able to eat on a somewhat regular basis and had a place to sleep. All was right with his world now. He would work here for a while and then board another train and head west again.

George went to work at 6 AM the next morning. He cleaned all the counters and prepared all the utensils for the chef to use to prepare the morning breakfast. He was kept busy doing odd jobs around the kitchen that no one else wanted to do or had time to do. George was a good worker, followed instructions and was quiet, and did not complain about anything he was asked to do.

On his break, Fred asked George, "Where did you learn to be so quick and efficient with your work duties?" George explained that he grew up in an orphanage and if he did not do what the matron or headmaster said quickly and do it correctly, he received a beating. "After three beatings, I learned to do what they told me to do. The practice has stayed with me George said. "They demanded excellence whether we were 5 years old or 15 years old," George added. "That is why I left at 15. I was not beaten anymore because I was a lot larger than the matrons, but I could not stand to see the younger ones beaten for some very small infraction. I had to get out of there," George explained. "No one deserves to be treated like that," he added. Fred was impressed with the way George handled himself and the fact that he knew his way around the kitchen.

Within two months, Fred had George doing some cooking for him. He would ask him to make some soup for the lunch meal or ask him to put together some sandwiches for a cowhand who was going out to the range for the day. George always did a good job and the meals that he cooked, even though they were simple meals, were very tasty. The customers would complement Fred on the soup or sandwich.

Fred did notice that George wore the same shirt and pants to work every day, but also noticed that they were always clean. He asked him one day if he had another set of clothes. George answered that he did not, but he washed out his clothes every night so that they would be clean the next day.

When George came to work the next day, there was a pair of pants and a shirt lying across a chair. Fred said that they were an old pair that he had that were not worn anymore. "I appreciate the clothes, but I am saving for a new pair of pants and will be able to get them with my next paycheck," George told Fred, but Fred insisted that he have them, so not wanting to insult his boss, George took the pants and shirt.

George did not like wearing other people's cast-off clothes. In the orphanage, he never had clothes that were his own. He always had to wear something that had belonged to someone else. He wanted his own clothes and would get them when he could afford to pay for them.

Fred Lewis was married and had three daughters. Marie was 17 years old, Susan was 15 years old, and Jane was 10. Marie had graduated from high school and was working as a housekeeper at the hotel. She was interested in learning all the aspects of running the hotel. Susan was ready to graduate from high school and was taking the exam to become a teacher. She was offered a job in Laramie, Wyoming with the provision that she passed the exam. Jane was still in school full-time, but occasionally helped Marie at the hotel. Fred's wife Mary stayed home and took care of their home and family.

Fred took a liking to George, thought that he had a lot of drive and ambition and wanted to make something of himself. He invited George to dinner on Sunday evening. The diner in the hotel closed at noon on Sunday so that Fred could have some family time. "George, would you like to come here for dinner tomorrow evening?" Fred asked. George was not sure what to say. He was not used to being in a family situation and had no idea how to act around women. He was only going to be in Cheyenne for a short time until he made enough to buy a train ticket West and wasn't really interested in having any attachments to people in the area.

"Come to dinner, George. You will enjoy it and my wife is as good a cook as I am, "Fred said. Not wanting to insult his boss or make him angry, he agreed to go to dinner. "What time would you like me there?" asked George. "About 5:00 PM. We will eat about 5:30," explained Fred.

George arrived right at 5:00. He knocked on the door and Fred answered and let him in. "Welcome George," said Fred. "The girls are in the kitchen helping Mary. They will be out shortly." Marie was the first one to come out. She was carrying a vase of flowers to put on the table. George looked at Marie and thought she was the prettiest girl he had ever seen. She had beautiful dark brown hair, blue eyes, and the softest, clearest skin. He wanted to touch her face it was so beautiful. "Hello!" Marie said, "Welcome to our home." All George could do was meekly say thank you and nod his head. He was tongue-tied. Both Susan and Jane came out next carrying dishes loaded with food to be put on the table. Mary was the last one out of the kitchen. He had a beautiful roasted chicken on a platter ready for Fred to carve.

When they all sat down at the table, Fred said a prayer of thanks for the food set before him and the guest that was with them. George had never heard a prayer said before eating before and was surprised at the idea of praying outside of a church. He had not been exposed to any religious training when he was a child and knew very little about it. He had read some books referring to the church but did not really understand it. It was something he wanted to read more about.

The meal that Mary served was one of the best that George had ever eaten. He was not often full after he ate, but he was so full after this meal that he could not eat another bite. While the girls cleaned off the table and washed the dishes, George, Mary, and Fred went into the parlor. Fred offered George a drink, but George declined. "I have never had a drink of liquor. I never had the extra money to spend on it and I never wanted to lose control of myself. When I was working on the ranch, I saw some of the cowboy's drink too much and get into fights and get beat up because they were too drunk to defend themselves. I never wanted to be that way," George explained. Both Fred and Mary admired George for his beliefs. The girls finished in the kitchen and came out to say goodnight to their parents and George. Mary also excused herself and went upstairs to do some needlework before going to bed.

"George, how would you like to stay on in Cheyenne and learn hotel business along with being my assistant in the kitchen?" Fred asked. "You would have free room and board and have the opportunity to learn a trade." George was stunned and flattered by the offer. He explained to Fred that he had a goal of seeing the Pacific Ocean and wasn't inclined to stay in one place for very long. "Can I think over your offer?" asked George. Fred said that he could but to think very seriously about the offer. It was a chance to have a future in a trade that was a good one and would offer him a good living for the rest of his life. With more people moving West, there would be a need for food and lodging for those people. It could be a very profitable business to be in. "I will think seriously about your offer Mr. Lewis," George said as he was leaving Fred's house to walk back to the boarding house.

As he was walking down the street from the Lewis house, George was stopped by several men who were obviously drunk. "You been visitin' the Lewis girls have you," one of them said. George said that he had been visiting the Lewis family, not just the girls. The men took offense to his comment and slugged him in the stomach. George went down on his knees in pain when another of the men kicked him in the side and kept kicking him. "You are not good enough for those girls – they belong to us. We got first crack at them," the man said. George had hit his head on a board in the road when he went down and was bleeding profusely from his forehead. The men were standing over him ready to kick him some more when they heard screaming coming from behind them.

Apparently, Marie had been watching George walk home from her bedroom window and saw the attack. She ran down the stairs yelling at her father to get help as she ran out the door.

George's attackers ran when they heard Marie screaming, leaving George crumpled in the street, bleeding and with extreme pain in his side.

Marie fell to the ground beside George and held him in her arms until help came. One of the neighbors saw the attack and ran to get the doctor. Doc Stephens was a tall, good-looking man with a wife and three children. He had been practicing in Cheyenne for 6 years and was liked by all the residents.

Doc asked Marie to gently place George on the ground so that he could see his cut forehead. She did as the doctor asked and Doc decided the cut was not too bad. A head wound always bled a lot. He would put a couple of stitches in his forehead so that it would not open up and bleed more. He was more concerned about the blows that George had taken to the stomach and side. He was concerned about a ruptured organ. He gently lifted George and carried him to his office where he placed him on an examination table. He gently felt around George's stomach and kidney area, asking him with each touch, "does that hurt there?" George answered "yes" to most of the inquiries. He was hurt everywhere. This was the first time he had ever been beaten up and was shocked at how much it hurt.

"You can go home now," Doc said to Fred and Marie. Marie was reluctant to leave George, but Fred took her arm and led her out of the doctor's office. "I will be back first thing tomorrow morning," Marie told the doctor. The doctor nodded as he was applying a liniment to George's bruises. He gave him a dose of laudanum to help him sleep for the night, covered him with a blanket and let him sleep.

Marie had seen the men who attacked George before and was able to give a description of them to the Sheriff. They have been causing problems in town a lot lately. They came in from the surrounding ranches to get drunk. They had had their eyes on both Marie and Susan for some time but had not had the opportunity to approach them. Fred was concerned about his daughter's safety in the light of what George's attackers had said.

Because of the description Marie had given to the Sheriff, the men were picked up at another tavern, still drinking and causing trouble with the other customers in the tavern. The sheriff took them all to jail to sober up. In the morning, they would have to go before the judge on a charge of battery, public drunkenness and causing a public disturbance. The Judge fined them each $50.00 and sentenced each of them to 5 days in jail.

Doc Stephens determined that George did not have any ruptured organs, but just had deep bruises on his side. Marie was at the doctor's office early the next morning to make sure George was okay. She had convinced her father to put George up in a room in the hotel so that she could look after him during his recovery. "Papa, I really like him," Marie explained to her father. She really wanted George to like her too. "I know girl! He is a very nice boy and would make you a good husband if he would agree to stay here. He has ambition and knows what he wants, even if it's to see the Pacific Ocean," Fred said.

Once Doc Stephens said it was okay to move George, he was put into a room in the hotel, not far from the kitchen. Marie went to see him several times a day and took him his meals. George had never had attention like this, even when he was very small. The matrons in the orphanage did not cater to any of the children, even when they were sick. They had to take care of themselves. George loved the attention that Marie was giving him, but he knew had needed to get back to work in the kitchen. He got up every day and walked around his room several times to get his strength back. Finally, he was able to walk into the kitchen. He was weak, but convinced Fred that he could at least stand and make sandwiches for the lunch crowd or stand at the sink and peel potatoes or carrots for the evening meal.

"George, are you sure you are well enough to stand and make those sandwiches?" Marie asked when she walked into the kitchen to check on him. "Yes, I am fine as long as I do not bend over," said George. "I need to work." "Okay, but please be careful," replied Marie. "I will," answered George.

After two weeks, George was healing nicely and told Fred that he would be willing to stay and work for him. "That doesn't mean I am giving up my dream of seeing the Pacific Ocean, but I realize that I need a steady job and I need to have a career. I like cooking and I like working for you and the hotel. Also, I like living here in the hotel. It is a much better room than mine at the boarding house. I need the job to be able to afford to stay here."

"You have made a good decision George. I am sure you will be happy here and I am very proud to have you as my associate," Fred commented. "You are a good worker and very reliable."

Marie was very excited when she heard that George was staying in Cheyenne and would continue to work in the hotel kitchen. Because of the attack on George and the threats that were made to the Lewis girls, Fred asked George if he would take the time to walk Marie home from work every day. It was not a long way to walk, but Fred did not want her to walk alone. Marie would come to the kitchen when she was ready to go home, and George would take a break from whatever he was doing to walk her home. After about a week of this, Marie started putting her arm into George's arm as they walked along. George was surprised but found it a very pleasant feeling to have her close beside him. After a while, he started holding her hand as they walked.

The hotel kitchen only served one meal on Sunday, the lunch meal at 1:00 P.M. It was usually a soup and sandwich meal made up of any leftovers from the week before, so the Lewis family was able to attend church on Sunday mornings. They went to the Cheyenne Community Church. The family enjoyed the service and talking with their neighbors afterwards, although George could not stay long because he had to get to the hotel to serve lunch.

One Saturday evening as Fred and George were cleaning up after the Saturday Supper crowd, Fred asked George if he would like to attend church with them in the morning. "I have never been to Church before, Fred," George said. "We did not go when I was in the orphanage, and I have never learned about the church. What do you do?" Fred was surprised that George had never been to church and explained that they sang some songs, listened to the preacher read some verses from the Bible, prayed, and listened to him give a sermon or a talk about a subject that he was interested in that day. Sometimes he talked about sin, sometimes faith, sometimes money. A lot of his sermons had to do with the teachings of Jesus. George was intrigued and said that he would go with them just to see what it was all about. He had never been around anyone who had talked about religion or faith. "I would like to go with you and your family Fred," George said, "but I do not have any good clothes to wear. I have only what I am wearing and my coat." Fred assured him that what he had on would be alright. He did not have to dress up to attend church.

The next morning, George met the Lewis family in front of the hotel and walked with them the rest of the way to church. As he walked into the church, people were surprised to see him with the Lewis's, but greeted him in a very pleasant way. As they sat down in the pew, Marie maneuvered herself so that she would be sitting next to George.

There was a piano in the church and a man was quietly playing as people were coming into the church and George enjoyed the music. He listened intently to all that was said, bowed his head when people prayed and responded to the prayers and hymns with the proper "Amen!" He didn't always know what it meant, but he figured someone would tell him if he was doing something wrong.

When the service was over, the congregation proceeded into a side room where cookies and coffee and juice for the children were served. People greeted each other by name and a lot of the people came up to introduce themselves to George. He shook hands with them but was very shy about answering a lot of their questions. The pastor came up to George after the service and introduced himself, "Welcome, I am James Daniels. Everyone calls me Pastor Jim."

"Thank you. I am George Seevers. I am here with the Lewis family. I liked the music," said George. Most of the time Marie stayed right by him and introduced him to some of the church members.

"George, there is going to be a dance here in the church next Saturday evening. Why don't you come and meet some of the young people from our community?" asked Pastor Jim. George was hesitant about going out in social situations. He was not comfortable around a lot of people but told Pastor Jim that he would try to be there. It would depend on his work schedule. He knew that Fred would not object to him going to the dance, but it was a good excuse if he didn't feel up to going. In any case, he did not know how to dance and was embarrassed about his clothes.

George said something to Fred about the dance on Saturday evening and Fred told him that the whole family was going. There were snacks served and Mary was planning on baking a cake to take with them. "I don't know how to dance, so I am not sure I will go," said George. "Don't let that stop you from going, George. There are plenty of people who go and don't dance. It is good music and Mary's chocolate cake is worth going," Fred laughed.

On Saturday evening, George washed up after work. Cleaned his clothes as best he could and brushed off his shoes and met Fred and his family in front of the church so that he could go in with them. It was crowded and hot inside the social hall and the band was playing a square dance tune. George was fascinated with how the people were dancing. Jane ran over to be with her friends, Susan joined some of her friends from school who were laughing at some of the boys in their class. Marie stayed with her parents hoping that George would ask her to dance.

When the square dance ended, the band played a slow dance and Mary asked George to dance. He shook his head, but she pulled him onto the dance floor anyway. "Fred told me that you do not know how to dance, but I will show you an easy way to slow dance." Mary put her hand in George's hand and put his other hand on her waist and said, "now just sway to the music. I know that you appreciate the music because you were swaying to the music in church this morning. Just do the same thing with me now," she asked. He did as she asked and thought it was a lot of fun to move with the music. When the music stopped, Mary led George back to Fred and Marie, then moved onto the dance floor with Fred to dance a faster square dance. George explained to Marie that he had never danced before and was not sure how to do the fast square dances. Marie was sure the next dance would be a slow one and maybe they could dance together. In the meantime, Marie sat down, and George got her a cup of punch.

They sat down and watched the dancers while they drank their punch. Unfortunately, two of the men who attacked George were at the dance and had been drinking again. They approached George and Marie and one of them said, "Remember what we told you? She's not yours. She's ours." George stood up in front of Marie so that they could not reach her, but just at that time the sheriff noticed the two men and grabbed their arms to lead them outside. They put up a fuss and said that they had not done anything wrong, but the sheriff pointed out that there was no alcohol allowed in the church and that meant no drunk cowboys allowed. "You have two choices," the sheriff said. "Either go to jail until you are sober or ride back to the ranch and sober up." He was going to report to their boss what they had done and that they were not going to be allowed to come to town if they continued to harass George and Marie.

Marie was shaking when she and George stood up to dance the next slow dance. George took her in his arms and swayed to the music the way Mary had shown him. Marie led him in a circle a couple of times, and he got the idea that you moved around the dance floor even doing the slow dances.

When the dance was over, they joined Fred and Mary near the punch table. Doc Stephens was there with his family and greeted George. After he saw the two cowboys approach George, he said that he was grateful that he did not have to patch George up again. He introduced his wife and then Doc took her out onto the dance floor for a square dance. George noticed that Doc was about the tallest man in the room. He was big and could probably take care of himself in a fight.

People headed towards the back of the room where cake, pie and cookies were being served.

George thanked Pastor Jim for the invitation. "I had a good time tonight." Pastor Jim was very glad to hear that. He always liked to have someone new in town come to his church and social functions. He was just sorry that George was put upon by those two men again. "It worked out okay. The sheriff was aware that they were here and took care of removing them from the hall."

George walked home with the Lewis family, Jane and Susan led the way with Fred and Mary following them. George and Marie brought up the rear. They talked very quietly about the incident with the two cowboys. Marie was frightened when she saw them approach. She was afraid that they would hit George again. She was very glad that the sheriff was there to remove them. Obviously, George was also. George said goodbye at their door and left to walk back to his room at the hotel. He went to bed and slept very well until it was time to get up for church on Sunday. He decided that he liked going to church with the Lewis family and he had met some very nice people at the dance last night. He had also decided that he liked Pastor Jim and wanted to talk to him about church and religion and praying. It was all very new to him.

George joined Fred in the kitchen of the hotel after church so that they could prepare the lunch menu. George was full of questions but did not want to disturb Fred while he was working. Both were busy serving the customers the meal and George was not able to talk to Fred about the church service. He was confused about some of the prayers and readings.

When all the diners had left and Fred and George were cleaning up, George said, "Fred, I am confused about some of the meaning of the readings and prayers that were said in church this morning. Can you explain them?" Fred said that it would be hard for him to explain them, that he should talk to the pastor if he had questions. "In the meantime, I will loan you a Bible so that you can read some of the passages." George thanked him and said that he would appreciate reading the Bible. He explained that he had learned most of what he knows from reading. That was his favorite past-time, but lately he has not had much spare time.

When they had finished cleaning up, Fred invited George back to the house for supper, but George was tired. He had a long day and had a lot to think about. His mind and thoughts seemed to be going in several different directions. The offer from Fred, church and religion, his growing feelings for Marie and his dream of the Pacific Ocean all were having a battle in his head. He had some decisions to make regarding his future and he wasn't sure which way to go. Right now, the road was not too clear.

CHAPTER 3

George had a restless night thinking about all his problems about deciding whether to stay in Cheyenne. Marie was foremost in his mind. He was falling in love with her and did not want to leave her. Sometime during the long night, he made the decision to stay in Cheyenne and work toward becoming an assistant chef in the hotel kitchen.

He also made the decision to ask Fred if he could court Marie. By her actions towards him, he was sure that she was in love with him. He was worried that Fred would not think him good enough for his daughter. He had no money or family name. He had nothing to give to Marie but his love. He had an abundance of that. He felt the religion dilemma would resolve itself with time.

When George went to work the next morning, he asked Fred if he could speak to him on a personal matter. Fred said, "We can take a break in about 10 minutes. Breakfast needs to be prepared first."

George nodded and went to work cutting bread to be toasted. He helped serve the customers and clean off empty tables. When he returned to the kitchen, there were dishes to be washed and vegetables to be washed and prepared for the lunch soup. Both Fred and George were busy all day and had no chance to have a private talk until just before it was time to close for the evening. Supper had been served and the kitchen cleaned up before they had a chance to have a quiet time to talk.

"What did you want to talk to me about George?" George was a little nervous but told Fred that he would like to stay and work with him in the kitchen and work towards becoming the assistant chef. "I am very glad to hear that." Fred answered. "You will make a very good chef someday." George thanked him, then added, "I also wanted to ask you if you would object to my courting Marie?" Fred was a little surprised at the request but was pleased by it. He felt that George would make a good husband for Marie. "What about your dream of seeing the Pacific Ocean?" Fred asked. "I still want to see the Ocean someday and I will, but I would like to see it with Marie." answered George.

"I see no reason why you cannot court Marie. She has been out of school for a year now, has been working at the hotel for all that time. She has good domestic skills and would eventually make a good wife for you." Fred smiled reassuringly.

"I would like to come and see her this evening, if that is alright with you." George asked. "Fine, fine. Come on over." Fred nodded as he answered. "I will go clean up and be over soon." answered George.

George arrived at the Marie's about an hour later and knocked on the door. Fred answered and George asked if he could see Marie on the porch for a while. Fred called her and she went to the door. "George, I did not know you were coming over." "Papa, let him come in," she pleaded. Fred said that he wanted to talk to her on the front porch alone. Marie had a puzzled look on her face but stepped out onto the porch with George. Fred closed the screen door but left the door ajar. George was very nervous, but just came right out and said what he wanted to. "Marie, I am falling in love with you. I would like to ask you if it was alright if I courted you. I have a lot of money to save and need to get more experience in my job before I can make it more permanent, but I would like to be your beau. Would you be my girl?" Marie had tears in her eyes when she said yes. "Yes George, I would be honored to be your girl. I am falling in love with you too and one day would love to be your wife and the mother of your children. But what about your dream of seeing the Pacific Ocean?"

"I have not given up on that dream but want to see it with you someday." George answered. They gave each other a quick hug and then went inside to tell the rest of the family who already knew because they were listening and watching through the window. They were all very excited and Mary served another piece of cake and a glass of milk to celebrate.

George had slept well the night before and woke up for work eager to get busy. He had a lot of plans to make and a lot to learn before he could afford to ask Marie to be his wife. He walked into the kitchen to a disaster. Half of the eggs they had ordered for the breakfast meal were broken and unusable and most of the milk for the gravy was sour. It had not been kept cold properly and Fred was in an uproar. He didn't want to close the restaurant, but how was he going to serve biscuits and gravy without milk and the eggs to go with it. George came in with a calm voice and suggested that they make flapjacks instead. They had enough milk for that, and they had the flour they were going to use for the biscuits and just enough eggs to make big fluffy pancakes. George explained that pancakes were a standby in the orphanage when they didn't have enough ingredients for a different kind of breakfast. Breakfast was the one good meal the boys had all day. They worked better on a full stomach. They could serve three giant pancakes along with butter and syrup or jam for the same price as the biscuits and gravy and not lose anything.

Fred was thrilled with the suggestion and put George in charge of pancake making. George even put a sausage patty on each plate of pancakes. The sausage was going to be used in the gravy anyway and they did not want it to go rancid on them. The revised breakfast was a big hit with the customers, and they asked Fred if it could be served again sometime soon. They really liked the taste of the pancakes. While they were cleaning up the kitchen after the breakfast crowd was gone. Fred asked George what he had put into the pancake batter to make it taste different. "I put in some cinnamon. I used to do that as a special treat for the boys at the orphanage, but the head chef never knew about it. He would not have approved of me giving the boys special treats."

The next day, Fred turned over the preparation of the breakfast meal to George. He had decided to make him the breakfast chef. He had experience in preparing enough food for a lot of people, especially hungry, growing boys.

Fred taught George all about ordering the supplies and where to get the best price for the merchandise. The eggs came from the farmer who would deliver the freshest eggs, the milk from the dairy who was the cleanest and the highest quality for the price and the flour came from the mill that would grind it fresh for them. They would get the meat from the ranch who would deliver the best quality available, but never purchased meat from the Three Bar Ranch where the drunken cowboys worked. The owner, Joseph Barnes, refused to fire them and continued to let them off to come into town and get drunk. They had been in jail several times for being drunk and disorderly and breaking furniture and glassware in a tavern. George refused to order from Mr. Barnes and the rancher didn't want to lose the business. He came into the hotel to talk to Fred about the lost orders, but Fred turned him over to George.

"I resent the fact that you will not order from me anymore and do not understand why. My beef is just as good as the stuff you are buying now." "I know that," said George. "But I will not order from you because you refuse to fire those three thugs who beat me up and they still come into town and threaten my girlfriend. The sheriff has had them in jail several times to sober up, but you keep them on your payroll. If they continue to be, I will not buy from you." Barnes was very incensed at the way George was talking to him and he looked at Fred for support, but Fred shrugged and said it was ultimately George's decision. The rancher stomped out of the kitchen very angry with both Fred and George, but with some big decisions to make regarding his business and his three recalcitrant employees. George was breathing very heavily after the rancher left, but Fred calmed him down and assured him he did the right thing. They were still using quality meat from the other ranches and were not compromising their meals. Fred was pleased with George's performance this day.

The restaurant profits were up since George had taken over the breakfast menu. The innovations he had made in the kitchen were part of the increase in profits. Fred had given George a raise in his wages, and it was put right into the bank for his future with Marie. He was a very happy man.

Marie was able to visit the kitchen a couple of times a day just to visit George. They would smile at each other but had no chance to talk because the kitchen was always busy. Marie was very proud of George and pleased that her Papa liked and valued him so much.

On a Sunday evening, a month later, George finally asked Marie to marry him. He got down on one knee and proposed, "Marie, I love you very much and would like to ask you to marry me. Will you?" "Yes, yes, yes." Marie answered. They hugged each other and went to tell her parents as they returned home from a walk.

Plans were started for a May 1878 wedding. Mary was busy sewing a dress for Marie while Marie was busy stitching linens for her hope chest.

On a Wednesday afternoon, George was in the kitchen getting ready for the lunch menu. Fred wasn't feeling that well that day and had gone home early, so Marie came in to help serve the meal. Suddenly, the two very drunk cowboys rushed into the kitchen and demanded a steak dinner immediately. George was surprised and said that they were serving lunch at that time and the steaks would not be ready until the evening meal. One of the cowboys unholstered his pistol and hit George over the head with it. Marie came rushing into the kitchen when she heard the noise and screamed when the other cowboy grabbed her and held her close. George was lying on the floor bleeding heavily from the back of his head. Some of the other customers came into the kitchen and ran back out to get the sheriff and the doctor. The Sheriff came running in with his gun drawn. The cowboy dropped his gun and the other one let go of Marie. The sheriff put hand cuffs on both men and took them away. Marie was on the floor with George in her lap, crying over his limp body. Doc Stephens came running into the kitchen and knelt to examine

George. He picked him up and took him over to his office to examine him. He had to put several stitches on the back of his head and was concerned because he was not waking up the way he should have. Doc knew he had a bad concussion and wanted him to stay in his office so he could keep an eye on him.

Fred was called to come back into the restaurant to manage the evening meal. One of the other maids came into the kitchen to clean up all the blood on the floor. Fred fixed a simple meal and Susan came in to help him serve. Everyone asked about George and sent their best wishes to him for a speedy recovery. They wanted him back into the kitchen.

The two cowboys were taken to jail and remained there until they saw the judge the next morning. The judge had read over their past record and sentenced them to prison. They would not be back on the streets of Cheyenne for some time. They were sent to the Federal prison in Laramie.

George finally woke up two days later, not knowing what happened to him. He was not allowed to be in the kitchen for a week. He needed to be off his feet and rest so that he could heal.

George healed quickly and went back into the kitchen within the week. He worked a little slower, but still got the meal prepared in his usual efficient manner.

On June 1, 1878, George Seevers and Mary Lewis were married in the Cheyenne Community Church. They moved into a small house close to the hotel that they were able to rent. The town's people were very generous with gifts for the newlyweds and Fred and Mary helped with furniture for the house. In February 1879, Anna Elaine Seevers was born at home. It was an easy birth for Marie, and she was sitting up feeding the baby soon after delivery. George was over the moon happy about his new daughter.

Three months after Anna was born, Fred made a trip to Denver to talk to some suppliers about dishes and silverware for the hotel. He wanted to see the items for himself, so he made the train trip south. He was in Denver for a week, then boarded the train for the trip home. About an hour out of Greeley, the train was speeding down the track and suddenly derailed and crashed down a mountain side. All passengers on board were killed. It was a tragic accident and everyone in the town of Greeley was shocked.

Telegrams were sent to the towns where passengers lived. The telegraph wires were in use in the Cheyenne office with notice of Fred's death. Doc Stephens took the wire to Mary and gently told her that Fred was killed in a train crash just outside of Greeley. Mary did not cry at first but asked that the girls be brought to her so she could tell them. Jane did not believe that she would never see him again, but Susan and Marie were in shock and then in bitter tears.

For some reason, the owners of the hotel did not want George to be the head chef so they hired another chef to take Fred's place. He and George did not get along.

George and Marie talked about it and Marie knew that George was not happy. They decided that it was time to move on. Marie talked to Susan and Jane about moving, but Susan had just been hired as a teacher in Laramie, so it was just Jane and Mary who decided to move with them. It was a bittersweet decision and they would miss all of their friends in Cheyenne, but it was a decision that they had to make.

CHAPTER 4

Susan left Cheyenne after she graduated from high school and received her teaching certificate. In August 1876, she moved to Laramie, Wyoming where she was offered a teaching job.

Laramie was a military town with soldiers stationed at Fort Laramie. It was also a railroad town with many of the workers and their families living in town. The men road the trains for their jobs, but their wives and children lived in town and the children went to the school there.

Susan began her school year with fourteen students scattered throughout eight grade levels. She had to be very organized and have lesson plans prepared for each grade level for every week. Most of the students were very eager to be there and to learn. There were a few of the older boys who resented the fact that their parents made them come to school every day. They wanted to be cowboys and didn't know why they had to be in school. It was not going to help them round up cattle. "If you do not know how to count, how are you going to know how many cattle you have got? If you do not know how much a dollar is, how are you going to know how much money you are being paid and if the amount is correct? If you cannot read, how are you going to fill out the reports needed for the owner of the ranch?" Susan asked. The boys shrugged and sat down in their chairs, but she could tell that they were thinking about what she said and wondering if she was right, and they should be there.

Fort Laramie had their own school for the children of the military personnel, so Susan did not have much to do with them. There was an ongoing rivalry between the two schools and sometimes there were problems in town with arguments and fights, but the military police usually took care of them and reported the incidences to Susan and the school board.

Susan met Gerald Carson shortly after arriving in Laramie. Gerald was the son of Gerald Carson Sr., the owner of the Carson Ranch, one of the largest spreads in the area. The Carsons and the Circle C ranch were known throughout the area as a good place to work and the Carsons were known as honest people and well respected in the town.

Gerald was in town one day purchasing supplies at the General Store. As he was coming into the store,

Susan came out and they crashed into each other. Susan fell and her packages flew all over. "I am so sorry" Gerald said. "Are you all right?" he asked. Susan looked up into the most beautiful blue eyes she had ever seen. She sputtered and said "Yes, I think so. My packages are all over the walk." "I will get them for you," Gerald said as he bent to help her up and pick up her packages.

"I have a wagon here and I could drive you home." Gerald said. Susan explained that she was the new schoolteacher, and she had a room behind the school house where she lived. It was only a short walk. Gerald offered to walk with her and carried her packages for her. They talked about Laramie and how she liked teaching. She explained that this was her first-year teaching, and she was nervous, but was enjoying it so far.

When they reached the schoolhouse, Susan realized that she had failed to introduce herself to Gerald. "Oh, by the way, I am Susan Lewis" Susan said.

"It is very nice to meet you, Susan Lewis. I hope to see you again. I am glad you were not hurt in the fall and that none of your packages were damaged" answered Gerald. Susan thanked him and went inside.

Gerald stayed in town for supper that evening. As he walked into the restaurant, he noticed that it was very busy and there were no tables available. Then he saw Susan sitting alone at a table near the back. She was reading a book while she waited for her supper to be served. He walked over and asked if she would mind if he joined her. She looked up from her book and was startled to see him and almost said yes, but looked around and saw there were no other tables available and nodded for him to sit down.

He ordered his dinner and then asked Susan what she was reading. "I am rereading "Pride and Prejudice" by Jane Austin," explained Susan. "I have read it several times but enjoy it more every time I read it" said Susan. Gerald said that he had never read it, but probably should so he would know what everyone was talking about.

Susan was curious about Gerald and what he did on the ranch. He explained that his father owned the Circle C Ranch and that someday his two brothers and he would inherit it. In the meantime, they worked on the ranch like any other cowhand. They mucked out stalls, fed the animals, went out on cattle drives the same as all of the other cowboys. He told her that his father wanted all three of his boys to know the ranch and the ranching business from the start to the finish. "Father is strict, but he is very fair. It is rare that we have a cowboy leave because of a dispute. Dad doesn't like to have feuds between the cowhands." Gerald said that he loved the ranch work and felt alive when he was out on the range riding his horse. They finished their dinner and Gerald walked Susan back to the school building. He was concerned about her being out on the streets in the evening alone, but she felt she would be fine. It was only a short distance to the schoolhouse.

Gerald managed to come into town at least twice a week to spend evenings with Susan. They were quickly falling in love with each other and were amazed at the speed in which their feelings were growing. Gerald had taken her out to the ranch one Sunday after church to meet his family. Gerald's mother had died when he was just a small boy, so there was just his father, Gerald Sr. and his two brothers, Robert, and Jerry. She met the Carson's' housekeeper, Tillie, and immediately fell in love with her. Tillie mothered all three of the boys and they did exactly as she said. She ruled the roost inside the house.

Susan said that she wished she could introduce all of them to her family, but they were too far away for a quick trip to Laramie. She explained that her dad was the chef at the hotel and couldn't get away. He had no one who could step in to help and was totally responsible for the running of the kitchen in the hotel.

One evening when Gerald was walking Susan home from dinner, he stopped, pulled her into his arms and kissed her. Susan was very surprised but pleased. Then Gerald got down on one knee and said, "Susan, I love you and would be so honored if you would be my wife." He held up a small diamond ring that had been his mother's. As the oldest son, he had asked his father if he could give it to Susan. Susan was stunned and started to cry but nodded her head yes. Gerald placed the ring on her finger. "I love you too and would be honored to be your wife." Susan finally was able to say.

Susan realized that once she and Gerald were married, she would not be able to teach any longer. She would move to the ranch to make a home for her new husband.

Susan had been writing to her family about Gerald and sent them a letter the next day telling them about the way that Gerald had proposed and about the diamond ring that she was now wearing. She was very excited and hoped that they could come to the wedding. She said that she would let them know as soon as a date was chosen.

The couple finally decided on a December wedding. The ranch was not as busy at that time, and it would give them time to get the little house on the property fixed up for their home. It was a small two-bedroom house that was originally built for a foreman and his family, but never used. It needed to be painted inside and some furniture added. Gerald let Susan pick out the furniture she wanted and ordered it to be sent from the East.

Susan heard from her family that they would not be able to come to Laramie for the wedding. It was not the time of the year when Fred could leave, and the weather was likely to be bad at that time. He hoped that Susan and Gerald could make a trip East to Cheyenne sometime in the Spring so that the family could meet Gerald.

Susan was disappointed that her family wouldn't be at her wedding, so a small ceremony was planned at the ranch. The big house would be decorated for Christmas and the ceremony would take place in front of the Christmas tree, next to the fireplace.

Susan seemed to glow all the time. She was so in love with Gerald, and it showed on her face. Her students teased her about it sometimes. Not only was she teaching every day, but she was busy picking out furniture and choosing linens, dishes, and silverware for her new home. She decided to make the curtains for the kitchen and bedrooms and bought the fabric from the general store. When she was at the ranch with Gerald one Sunday, she had him at the little house measuring windows. He was almost as excited as she was, but his mind was more on the week ahead. Animals or disease, something or someone was taking their cattle.

Just a few weeks before he and Susan were to be married, Gerald was out on the range with his brothers looking for strays. They had lost about 200 head within the last three months and that usually only meant one thing: rustlers.

Gerald heard a cow down in an arroyo and went in to find it and get it up to the level ground and back with the herd. As he was coming back out of the arroyo, a shot rang out and hit Gerald in the chest, knocking him off of his horse and killing him instantly. His brother Robert and the other hands heard the shot and rode to where they heard it. Robert saw Gerald's horse running away and then saw Gerald lying on the ground, covered in blood. Robert knew he was dead just by looking at him.

Robert yelled at one of the hands to catch Gerald's horse and bring it back. He gently lifted his brother onto the back of the horse and took him home. He instructed the other hands to be very careful, but to look for signs of someone being in the area.

Robert rode into the compound, up to the front of the big house. When Gerald Sr. came out of the door, he saw his first-born son lying over the saddle of his horse and knew for sure that he had lost his child. He was in shock when Robert told him what had happened. "Why would anyone shoot my boy?" he cried.

One of the cowboys was sent into town to let the sheriff know what had happened but was admonished to not say anything to anyone else for fear that Susan would find out. Gerald Sr. and Robert would leave right away to tell Susan themselves.

Harry Carson, Gerald's youngest brother, was still out on the range with the other cowboys searching for signs of any intruder or rustler.

School had just ended for the day and Susan was cleaning up the classroom when Gerald Sr. and Robert walked into the room. Neither one of them ever came into town at this time of day so Susan knew something was wrong.

"Where's Gerald?" she asked as she looked at their grim, tear-streaked faces. "There's been an accident," Mr. Carson said. "Gerald went out on the range looking for strays and was shot. We do not know who shot him or why, but it could possibly have been rustlers." "Will he stop by after he sees the doctor?"

Susan asked. "No dear. Gerald is dead," sobbed Mr. Carson. Susan screamed and fell to the floor.

Robert ran for the doctor while Mr. Carson tried to comfort Susan. The doctor's wife came along to help Susan into bed while the doctor gave her something to calm her and to help her sleep.

"How am I ever going to live without him?" Susan cried. "He is all I have ever wanted. I love him so much." She finally went to sleep with the doctor's wife sitting beside her and trying to comfort her. She whimpered in her sleep but slept until morning.

Gerald's funeral was torture for Susan. She had to sit through the service with people giving praises for Gerald's life and his accomplishments at such a young age. She sat and stared straight ahead and talked to no one. When the service at the graveyard was over, she went back to her room and locked the door. She would see nor talk to no one.

School was closed until after the first of the year. Susan was in no condition to teach and there was not another qualified person to take over for her. The chairman of the school board talked to the students and explained the situation to them. He assigned lessons for them to work on at home and to leave their completed papers at the schoolhouse. He picked their papers up to review them and returned them the next day. None of the children would lose time if they completed the work assigned. Because of the situation with Susan, most of the parents understood and tried to help their children as much as possible.

Susan did manage to send a message to her family to let them know that Gerald was killed. They were all very sorry that they could not be with her.

Susan was able to get back to teaching after the new year, but there was no joy in the classroom. Her heart was not in the job. Eventually the children brought a few smiles to her face, and she became more animated. She missed Gerald terribly and swore she would never love another man. She became accustomed to the life of an old-maid schoolteacher.

CHAPTER 5

Since the hotel did not want the services of George after Fred's death, there seemed to be no reason to stay in Cheyenne any longer. After a family meeting, it was decided that they would pack up and move west, possibly as far as Portland, Oregon. So, in May 1877, the Lewis and Seevers families packed two covered wagons with everything they could get into them and headed out of Cheyenne.

Just before the family left Cheyenne, Marie found out she was pregnant again. She was going to have another baby and he was just hoping they were not on the road when she had it. She was often sick in the mornings, and it would not make for a very pleasant trip for any of them.

The family stopped in Laramie to see Susan and try to convince her to come with them, but she refused. She was still in deep mourning for Gerald and did not want to be away from his family.

They had to stop often for several days at a time to let Marie rest. Although the delay was frustrating to deal with, it gave George a chance to hunt for game to preserve for the trip. They needed plenty of food for the family.

The family stopped in Boise, Idaho where they decided to stay for a while. Marie was terribly uncomfortable riding in the wagon and needed to rest. Both George and Jane found jobs in the same restaurant: he as a cook and she as a waitress.

When one of the ladies in the boarding house found out that both Mary and Marie were seamstresses, they had women coming to them to either repair, alter or make new garments for them. Both of them earned a few dollars to add to the money that George and Jane were making.

Because Marie was in the advanced stages of her pregnancy, they stayed in Boise until after Irene Mae Seevers was born in March 1878.

When Irene was two months old, the family packed up their wagons again and headed west towards the Columbia River. They went through some treacherous mountain weather in Northeast Oregon. It was beautiful country, but not what he was looking to settle his family in. They decided to follow the

Oregon Trail route to the west, which by that time was well established.

The ride along the Columbia River was breathtaking. They marveled at the sight of Celilo Falls, an Indian fishing mecca.

As they rode further West, George was amazed at the difference in the climate. They had passed through a mountain range in Northeast Oregon, then into a desert terrain as they came upon the Columbia River. For miles the land was arid and had rolling hills, on clear days, they could see tall mountains to the West.

After riding past Celilo Falls, they again came upon lush green terrain with giant trees and high mountains right up to the river's edge. They had to climb to the top of some of the hills just to head West. The rocks went right down to the water line. They saw some spectacular views of the river and mountains.

Hidden among the trees were several enormous waterfalls. The water cascaded down the mountain side into pools that flowed into the river. George thought he had never seen anything so beautiful.

As they drove further, they drove through a grove of trees so thick they could barely get the wagons though. Marie was nervous the whole time as they were traveling through the trees. She did think it was pretty, but she preferred the flat country or living in a city.

As they got closer to Portland, the land broadened out along the river and George noticed lumber mills and granaries along the waterfront. The industry seemed to be centered along the river.

As the family got nearer to the city of Portland, they drove along another river flowing into the Columbia. It was called the Willamette River and was the first river George had ever heard of that flowed from the South to the North. The Willamette River flowed into the Columbia River and formed a large estuary at its mouth. There were large ships moving up the river to the docks in Portland.

As they drove South along the river, they had to take a ferry across to the other side. The west side of the city was where commerce was, and George felt there were better opportunities for a job there.

George needed to find a place for his family to live quickly and get his family settled and then find a job. He had a little money left, he hoped enough to find a room for everyone and a meal to fill their almost empty stomachs. They found a spot along the river to set up camp in their wagons. Marie started a fire and heated some stew that she had left over from the night before. She had a few slices of bread left. Mary and

Jane each ate a little bit but were very tired and went to lay down in their wagon right after they cleaned up the supper dishes. Marie settled the babies down for a nap and sat by the fire for a while. George walked up the hill away from the river to some buildings he saw. Maybe there would be notice of a job on one of those buildings. He walked up one street and down the other side looking for "Help Wanted" signs in the windows.

On the second street he was walking along, he saw a sign in the window of a dry goods store. George didn't know much about selling dry goods, but he was willing to learn and at this point, was willing to try anything if it was a paying job.

Fortunately, before he left his wagon by the river, George had changed his shirt to a clean one and combed his hair, so he looked a little more presentable. He walked into the shop. "I saw your help wanted sign in the window and wanted to inquire about the job." George said. The owner of the store was a portly man who looked George over carefully. "Have you had any experience working in a store?" asked the owner. George told him he hadn't, but he was willing to learn, and his wife was a very talented seamstress and could help him with that part of the store. "Oh, I couldn't employ both of you," the owner explained. George said that he didn't mean that he should hire her for the job, just that she had knowledge of dry goods merchandise and could assist him in identifying different things in the store. The owner was very anxious to hire another employee. He was working long hours and his wife was complaining that he was never there with her, always in the store. He decided to take a chance on George and hired him. He felt he had an honest face. "Do you have a white shirt and tie?" the owner asked George. George answered, "No sir, I don't." The owner went to the men's shirts, pulled a white shirt out of the stack, and handed it to George. Then he found a black bow tie and handed it to him also. "The cost of these will come out of your first two paychecks." The owner explained.

George raced back down the hill to his camp and told Marie, Mary, and Jane that he had a job working in a dry goods store. He showed Marie the white shirt and tie and explained that he would have to wear that every day. They were all very pleased that he had a job, now they had to find a place to live that wasn't their wagons. They found a livery stable about a quarter of a mile down the waterfront and walked down to ask if they knew of any place for rent, but they did not.

The owner of the dry goods store was Clyde Rodgers. He had a wife and a grown daughter teaching school in a small-town south of Portland. When George reported for work the next morning, he asked Mr. Rodgers if he knew of any houses or apartments nearby that he could rent for his family to live in. They had been living in their wagon for several months while moving from Cheyenne and were ready for a normal bed.

Clyde said, "There is a small apartment upstairs that I have not rented out for a long time. I did not want the noise above the store, but you are welcome to look at it and see if it would meet your needs. How many of you are there?"

"There is my wife, my mother-in-law, my 13-year-old sister-in-law and my two baby girls." Clyde was skeptical but said there were two small bedrooms and a kitchen sitting room combination. Clyde took George up the back stairs to look at the apartment. It needed some cleaning up, but George was sure that it would be just what the family needed at this time. Grandma Mary, and Jane would use one bedroom and he, Marie and the babies would use the other. They could make it work. There were beds and a table and chairs in the rooms. With what they had in the wagons, they would be able to be comfortable until they could afford something larger. "This will be just right for us. We have some dishes and things with us in the wagon that we will be able to use here. My wife is a very good seamstress and can make curtains for the windows." George commented.

After completing the arrangements with George about the apartment, Clyde took him downstairs to show him where things were in the store. George only hoped that he could remember without looking like a fool when people asked for things that he didn't recognize.

The store opened at 9AM and was busy right from the start. A lot of ladies came in for sewing notions and men came in for shirts and ties. George quickly learned how to measure and cut fabric, how to pick the best color thread to go with the fabric. He learned where men's collar stays were located and what size were needed for what shirt. He could find a certain size tablecloth or towel and learned the difference between a kitchen dish towel and a bathroom towel. Clyde also carried some dishes and bathroom accessories in the store. There was not a lot of call for those, but on George's first day, he had two customers ask for a pitcher and bowl and a chamber pot for their bedrooms.

It was a very busy day, and his body and mind were exhausted by the time the store closed. He still had work to do before he could go home. He had tables of merchandise to straighten and bins and tables to restock to be ready for the next day's business. The store was open six days a week and George would be working every one of those six days.

As he was walking back to the camp that evening, he was pleased to be able to tell the family that they had a place to live. Marie had used the last of their food to make another stew for supper that evening. George ate his meal and started organizing their things to move them to the apartment. Clyde had given him the time in the morning to move in and he did not have to go to work until noon that day. As soon as they moved in, he and Grandma Mary took the horses and wagons to the livery stable to board them. The cost of boarding them would take a chunk out of his paycheck, but he did not want to sell the wagons yet.

When Clyde found out that Marie was an accomplished seamstress, he started telling some of his women customers about her. They were always looking for someone to make their dresses and children's clothes. She hadn't thought of sewing for other people. She usually only made her own and her family's clothes. Clyde explained to her that there was a level of society in Portland and the ladies were very conscious about what they wore. They all wanted to be very fashionable. The ladies got copies of the fashion magazines from the east and wanted clothes like the ones worn there.

Marie was astounded at the amount of money the ladies would pay would pay for a high-fashion dress.

She knew that she could make them and asked George if it would be okay if she tried. "Certainly, it would be okay. You are an accomplished seamstress. Use your talents. It will also add to our income, and we will need it." George said. Grandma Mary agreed to watch the little girls and do the cooking while Marie was busy sewing.

George had asked Mr. Rodgers about a church in town. He wanted his girls to grow up with a religious education and wanted that outlet to meet people. "There is a Community Christian Church only three blocks from here." explained Mr. Rodgers. "A lot of the people in this community go to that church." George thanked him and on Sunday, the Seevers/ Lewis family walked to the Community Christian Church. They were greeted warmly by Pastor Silas Jacobsen and welcomed to the congregation. After the service, there was the usual social hour in the social hall with cake and coffee. George met several people who had seen him in the dry goods store, and he introduced Marie and Mary to them. Jane was off talking to some girls her own age and both Anna and Irene were asleep in their mother's and father's arms.

Marie had mentioned that she was doing some sewing for ladies in the community and several of the women from the congregation said that they did sewing also. "I have got a lot more work than I can handle with the two little ones to take care of also. How would you like to join forces and work on some of the projects together?" Marie asked the ladies. They were all very excited about the idea. The Pastor's wife volunteered the parsonage for a gathering place. They would be able to meet there and not be disturbed by other church activities. The women said that they would check with their husbands and let Marie and Mrs. Jacobsen know. Marie explained to them that she would be glad to share the profits from her sewing with them, depending on how much they did. They were all very happy to help increase the family income and sewing was one way that a married women could help.

Shortly after settling in Portland, Marie discovered that she was going to have yet another baby. This would be the third child in three years. She would welcome another child but wished that they were not so close in age. She figured the baby would be born in February or March of 1879. George was hoping for a baby boy this time so he could pass on the Seevers name.

Because the room above the dry goods store was already cramped, with four adults and 2 babies, George knew that he had to find something larger for them to live in. He asked his customers to keep watch for "For Rent" signs but hadn't found anything yet.

This was not an easy pregnancy for Marie. She was sick a lot of the time and was not able to do a lot of her sewing. Her sister Jane offered to help, but she was not a very good seamstress and Marie did not want her sewing some of the more complicated outfits.

George worked long, hard hours at the dry goods store, but missed cooking. He loved the creativity of cooking a good meal and the satisfaction of doing a good job and of people enjoying his meals.

He thought of an idea to satisfy his urge to cook and bake and to increase their income some. There was a bramble of blackberries behind the store, and he thought that the children could pick the berries and he could bake some pies to sell in the store. He would have to bake them in the stove in the apartment, but he would love to do it.

"Clyde, would it be okay if we picked the blackberries behind the store and made pies to sell in the store?" asked George.

"I love blackberry pies!" said Clyde. "You can sell the pies in the store if I can have one of them." George laughed and said that he certainly could have one of the pies.

The blackberry pies were a great hit. They were sold almost before George could get them onto the counter. The success of the pies only reinforced George's desire to cook again.

Jane helped the little girls pick the berries and made sure they did not eat too many. She had one more year before she would graduate from high school, but she really didn't care if she graduated or not. All she wanted was to be married, have babies, and make a home.

George was working long hours at the store, but couldn't save much money towards getting a larger place to live in. Marie was generating some income from her sewing, but just enough to buy food and some other essentials for the family. She was sharing the profits from her sewing with the other ladies at church and since she wasn't feeling well because of her pregnancy, she was not able to sew that much.

George was flattered by the attention he got from his pie baking abilities and wondered about working in a bakery – learning to bake bread and other pastries besides pies. It was a possibility if he could find a bakery that would hire him and teach him the business.

On a rare Sunday afternoon when the family was all together, they went for a buggy ride. They wanted to explore Northwest Portland. They were driving along Burnside Street when George saw a "Help

Wanted" sign in the window of a bakery at 21st and Burnside Street. George stopped the wagon, jumped off the wagon seat and told Marie that he was going to check with the bakery owner about the sign. He saw a light on in the back of the shop and knew someone was there. The shop owner finally opened the door to George's insistent knock and invited him in after George inquired about the sign in the window. "Hello, my name is George Seevers. I am interested in the job you have available."

"I am John Johnson. I have owned this bakery for six years but am ready to pass it on to someone else. I am looking for a competent person to train and pass the business to."

George told John about his background and how he had learned to cook and bake. John agreed to hire George on a temporary basis to see how fast he learned the business.

George's only concern now was where his family would live. The baker said that there was a spacious apartment above the bakery that needed a lot of cleaning to make it livable, but it had two bedrooms and an alcove area that would be ideal for a nursery. The kitchen was small, but they had the ovens in the bakery downstairs to use.

So, in October 1878, the Seevers family moved into the apartment above John's bakery and started a new phase in their lives.

The bakery was a demanding place to work. George had to get to work by 3:30 AM every morning so that the bread would be baked and ready for sale when the bakery opened at 6 AM. When the bread was in the oven, George would start working on the other pastries that would be for sale that day. He always had a great surge of satisfaction when he looked at all the baked goods for sale. John Johnson was impressed with how fast George was learning and what a good worker he was.

Mr. Johnson was very strict about keeping the bakery clean. He demanded that every counter and work surface be cleaned several times a day and that at the end of the day, they be thoroughly cleaned and ready for the next morning. He was also strict about washing hands often during the day. George would not only do the baking but would do the cleaning as well.

The family was settling into their new home and loving the fact that they had more room. Jane and Grandma Mary each had their own beds now and did not have to share. They were still in the same room but were able to sleep in their own beds.

Marie was still not feeling well because of her pregnancy but was able to stitch together some curtains for the windows and was able to do some of the cleaning. Mr. Johnson supplied some paint for the walls in the apartment, but Marie could not be in the rooms when they were being painted. She would take her daughters for a walk or sit out in the back yard with them until the heavy smell left the rooms.

Marie lived further away from a lot of the customers she had before and was not able to take in as much sewing as she did before, and their income went down because of it. Mr. Johnson let her put a sign in the window of the bakery advertising her sewing skills and she had a few people inquire about her making garments for them or their children. She was also busy repairing some of the baby clothes that Anna and Irene had worn. It was a constant chore to keep their clothes in good repair.

Christmas in 1878 was a special time for the Seevers family. George baked some special breads and pastries and Marie made new outfits for all of them, Grandma Mary included. George went into the nearby woods and cut down a tree and Jane and the little girls made decorations to adorn it. The bakery was closed on Christmas day, so George was able to spend the entire day with his family. They had a great dinner and spent time playing games, reading, and singing songs.

The New Year was ushered in with great fanfare and a lot of noise. They were looking forward to a new baby in a month. George was hoping that it would be a baby boy. He wanted a son to continue the Seevers name. George had a very short night's sleep because he had to be up at 3:00 AM to get the bread baked in time.

In February 1879, Marie gave birth to Charlotte Louise Seevers. She weighed a little over 9 lbs. and was a hard birth for Marie. Charlotte was a fussy, demanding baby and needed more attention than the other two. She would not eat very much at a time and never seemed to be sated. She did not sleep more than an hour at a time. Marie was tired all the time now from taking care of Charlotte. She grabbed sleep whenever she could and worried constantly about the baby. George was worried about Charlotte also but was busy at the bakery. Unfortunately, Marie was not able to do any sewing and ultimately their income went down.

George was trying to figure out ways to increase business at the bakery. He asked John Johnson what he would think of putting some tables and chairs in the bakery and serving some soup and sandwiches for the noon meal. "George, as long as you are willing to do the extra work, I have no objection to you serving lunch. I think I can find some tables and chairs that can be cleaned up and used. Just remember, this is a bakery, and we need to make sure that we have enough baked goods to sell." George asked Jane if she would be willing to come into the bakery during the lunch hour and help with serving the meals. "I can come in to help if Marie and Mama don't need me to help with the babies," said Jane.

George baked enough extra loaves of bread in the morning to make sandwiches for the noon meal. Business was slow at first until word got out that John's Bakery had a lunch meal, then businessmen started to come in to have a quick sandwich before they had to get back to work.

Jane was a very pretty girl and attracted a lot of attention from the men in the neighborhood. She had a very pleasant manner when she served the customers. She attracted the attention of Steven Taylor, a clerk in the bank. Steven would come into the bakery almost every day for lunch and became very taken with Jane and she in turn was very smitten with Steven. They began seeing each other on a regular basis with the blessing of Mary, George, and Marie.

It wasn't long before both John Johnson and George knew that they would have to expand their menu. They decided to add soup to the lunch menu. They could make a good, hearty vegetable soup for a little amount of money. As the weather got warmer, they added a green salad to the fare. The word was out that John's Bakery was serving lunch every weekday. They had people waiting in line for soup or salad and sandwiches. The building was not large enough to add any more seating space, so people were ordering their sandwiches to go.

John was amazed at the increase in his business. He was very pleased with George and his innovative ideas about the bakery. "George, I am ready to retire. How would you like to buy this bakery?" John asked George one morning as they were getting the bread ready for the oven. George looked at John as if he had not heard him correctly. "What did you say Mr. Johnson?" asked George. "I said, how would you like to buy this bakery?" George just looked at him with a stunned look on his face. "I can't afford to buy this bakery Mr. Johnson." George answered. "I have no money saved to afford something like this. What savings I have is put aside for an emergency." "Just something to think about George." Mr. Johnson said as they continued to put the bread pans into the oven.

George was in a fog most of the day. His mind would not get off the idea of being a business owner instead of an employee. But then he would realize that he could not afford to own the business. He had no money and no one or no bank would ever loan him enough money to buy a business.

When the bakery closed that afternoon, George asked Marie to go for a walk with him. The only time they could have any time alone was to get away from the apartment and take a walk. "Mr. Johnson offered to sell me the bakery this morning." George told her. Marie looked at him in stunned silence. "Well, there is no way we could buy it. We have no money and nothing of any value to put up for collateral for a loan. No bank in their right mind would give us a loan. All we own outright are two wagons and four horses and two of the horses are Mama's." Marie said. "I know, but wouldn't it be fun to be the business owner instead of the employee of the owner?" George said.

The days continued to be busy. There seemed to be new customers in the store all the time. They were not just there for lunch. They were also buying bread and pastries to take home. At the end of the month when John was going over the ledgers, he was amazed that even after the added expenses of the lunch menu, the profits were up by six and a half percent.

John showed the figures to George one morning and asked him if he had thought about the offer to buy the bakery. "Sure, I have thought about it. I would love to own the bakery, but no one in their right mind would loan me the money to buy it. All I own are my wagons and horses. That is not enough collateral to cover a loan the size that I would need to buy this business." George said.

"George let's go visit Isaac Sorenson at the Citizens Bank this afternoon. I want him to meet you and see these sales figures. He might have some ideas on how you could get a loan." George was skeptical but agreed to go meet Mr. Sorenson. He ran upstairs to let Marie know that he would not be home right away after work. He explained that he and Mr. Johnson were going to the bank.

George was very nervous as he and Mr. Johnson walked into the bank. Mr. Sorenson came forward to greet them. "Hello John. How are you doing? I haven't seen you in a while. Julia was asking about you just the other day," said Mr. Sorenson.

"I am just fine, Isaac. I would like you to meet George Seevers. George works for me and is the one responsible for the sandwich shop now in the bakery," answered George. The men shook hands and sat down at Isaac's desk.

"What can I do for you John?" Isaac asked.

John explained the whole situation to Isaac and showed him the ledgers. "Would you, with the information here in these ledgers, consider giving George a loan to buy the bakery?"

"Probably not, John," answered Isaac. "But I would possibly consider it with another six months of figures like this. John, if you would be willing to wait another six months before you retire and during that six months, the bakery's profits continue to rise at or about the same pace and teach George the basics of running the business, I would consider giving him a loan to buy the bakery."

George sat there in stunned silence. He could not believe that someone would consider giving him a loan.

CHAPTER 6

Both Mr. Sorenson and his wife Julia had eaten lunch at the bakery and were impressed with the quality of the food and the cleanliness of the shop. They found that a lot of the restaurants in the area were not as diligent about keeping their places clean. Julia Sorenson also had small children and wanted to meet other ladies with children their ages. She was lonely and wanted another female to talk to.

Julia stopped by the bakery every morning to buy some bread and asked George if it was possible to meet Mrs. Seevers. Jane was in the bakery helping that morning and said that she would go up and ask Marie if she would like to come down and meet Mrs. Sorenson, the banker's wife. Marie was a little startled at the request, but she asked Jane to show her up the stairs and into the sitting room. The little girls were playing with their toys on the floor, but the room was tidy, and Marie thought it was presentable enough for a visitor.

Jane introduced the two ladies and then excused herself to go back downstairs and help George in the bakery. Mr. Johnson was not working that day, so it was just George and Jane in the shop.

"I am sorry for just dropping in on you this morning," said Mrs. Sorenson. "I did want to buy a loaf of bread, but I also wanted to meet you. I miss having other women to talk to. I thought it would be nice for our children to get together for some play time. I also have two little daughters," said Mrs. Sorenson.

"I am so glad you stopped by. I, too, miss other female companionship, even though my mother and sister live with us. Occasionally it is nice to have the point of view of someone outside of the family." Marie added, "Mrs. Sorenson, would you like a cup of tea. The kettle is hot on the stove, and it would just take a minute to brew it?"

She answered, "I would love a cup of tea and please call me Julia."

George and Isaac became good friends and the couples, and their families spent many evenings at a park along the Willamette River with a picnic supper. Isaac and Julia were about ten years older than the

Seevers but had a lot in common with them. Isaac also grew up as an orphan but was raised by an aunt and uncle. They were not a real loving couple and did not pay a lot of attention to Isaac, but they did see to it that he had a good education.

The holidays were a very busy time at the bakery and the restaurant. Holiday treats were baked, and apple pies were in great demand. The shop still closed at 3:00 PM so it could be cleaned and be ready for the next day's baking. Marie was feeling much better, and Charlotte was settling into a routine and becoming a much happier baby now that she was eating some solid food.

On New Year's Day 1881, Jane and Steven Taylor became engaged. They wanted to get married in April. That wasn't a lot of time for Mary and Marie to plan a wedding and for Marie to sew a dress, but they would manage.

On April 18th, 1881, Steven Taylor and Jane Lewis were married at the Community Church before about 30 people. A luncheon was served to the guests at the Seevers bakery. Steven and Jane went east along the Columbia River to view the waterfalls. They took George and Marie's wagon and horses and had a great honeymoon camping trip. They had four days of good weather and fun viewing the scenery along the river.

When they returned home, Steven went back to the bank and Jane went back to the bakery. They had the room at the boarding house but knew that they needed a place of their own. Both were afraid they would have to move further away from the family and get different jobs. There were no houses or apartments available in the northwest part of Portland. In the meantime, they made do with the boarding house, eating their meals with George and Marie, Mary, and the children.

In late March of 1881, Marie gave birth to Frederick David Seevers named after Marie's father. They finally had their son. Freddie was a robust baby, and he ate well. He was a big baby but bright-eyed and aware of all the things going on around him. Freddy's older sisters loved him although Charlotte was a little leery of him. She wasn't the baby anymore. Anna was five years old; Irene was three years old, and Charlotte was two.

When Anna turned five, she was expected to do small simple tasks in the bakery. She wiped off the tables, took empty plates to the kitchen and generally relieved Jane of some of the little chores that needed to be done.

Anna would start school in September so her services would be drastically reduced. She was a very smart, resourceful little girl and both of her parents knew she would do well. Her Mama was teaching her the basics of sewing and she was learning fast. She was able to sew a straight seam, although the stitches were uneven. She did try to do good work and sat and listened to instructions very well.

Irene was a curious little girl and wanted to know "why" all the time. She loved books and loved to have stories read to her.

Charlotte became very possessive of Freddie and didn't like it when other people held him or paid any attention to him. He was her baby. She was too little to pick him up by herself, but she tried. The family had to watch her very carefully so that she did not drop him. She did not like it when Mama would feed Freddie. She wanted to feed him and didn't know why people would not let her. She had a tantrum when Freddie was taken away from her. Her constant tantrums were becoming a concern for her parents. They were not sure how to deal with them. Grandma Mary thought that she should be ignored. "She has the tantrums to get attention. If she finds they don't work, she will stop," commented Mary. It was hard for George and Marie to ignore Charlotte. They did not want her to hurt or be angry, but they did as Grandma Mary suggested and it seemed to work after a couple of weeks. Charlotte realized that she was not getting the attention that she was hoping for, and it did not get her any more time with Freddie. In fact, it gave her less time.

Life became a little more peaceful around the Seevers house when the tantrums slowed down.

George was thinking about getting a larger place for his family to live. The apartment above the bakery was getting much too small with he and Marie, Grandma Mary and four children. Jane and Steven spent most of their time with the family. They slept at the boarding house but ate all their meals with the Seevers.

George looked for housing ads in the small weekly paper he received. There was nothing available within a reasonable distance of the bakery. He noticed an advertisement for 160 acres in a small town in Eastern Washington called Rawlings. The advertisement said there was a hotel and small home on the land and several other outbuildings. George was intrigued by the fact that there was a hotel on the property. He wrote to the agent listed in the paper with questions about the property and the town of Rawlings.

The answer came within a week that Rawlings was a town of about 150 to 175 residents, mostly farmers and ranchers in the surrounding area. It was a railroad town and was the end of the line. The trains reversed direction and went back the same way they came.

The hotel had 16 rooms, eight on each floor. There was a diner with a good-sized kitchen. The lobby was large with sofas and easy chairs placed around the room. The post office was in the hotel, but with a separate entrance from the front porch. There were two saloons in town but were located across the road and railroad tracks from the hotel and were not part of the 160 acres for sale.

George was very interested in the place and the fact that it was a smaller town than Portland. He was becoming concerned about raising his family in a large town with all the bad influences that were around. There was a schoolhouse on the property but was not used at this time for lack of a qualified teacher.

He and Marie discussed the possibility of relocating again. Marie grew up in the hotel business and loved it. George would like to get back into the hotel kitchen along with learning all aspects of the hotel business.

They talked to the Sorenson's about the possibility of purchasing the land and the hotel. Isaac said that he would do some research on the financial viability of the area and if a hotel could or would be a profitable business for his friends. Because of George's success in the bakery and sandwich shop and the fact that the shop had been in the black since he bought it, there was no doubt that he would make a success of a hotel and diner.

After making some inquiries about Eastern Washington and the growth in the area, Isaac said that he felt it would be a good investment for George and Marie. Isaac knew that George would have no trouble selling the bakery. It was a good business and drew in a lot of customers daily.

When Isaac was doing some investigation in Rawlings and the hotel there, he learned that the hotel was making a profit because of the railroad business but needed some upgrades. The diner was not operating at a profit because of poor management. Rawlings was the end of the line for both the Northern Pacific and Camas Prairie lines.

Rawlings was also a steamboat town. The boats would dock at Rawlings, then head down the Snake River to the Columbia River and West to Portland. The steamboats were an essential vessel in shipping goods into and out of Eastern Washington, and Rawlings benefited from the trade route.

George and Marie wrote to Susan in Laramie about the possibility of moving to Rawlings and opening the school. They were sure that there were other children in the area that needed a formal education. The county school district would pay a small salary to a qualified teacher and the teacher was provided with an apartment to live in behind the schoolhouse. Since the death of Gerald, Susan had been very lonesome in Laramie and missed her family. She had been in Laramie for eight years, five without Gerald and was ready for a change. She wrote back to George and Marie that she would be very pleased to move to Rawlings and open the school and be with her family again.

Jane was upset that her family was leaving Portland. She and Steven were living in the boarding house but spending most of their time with George, Marie, Grandma Mary, and the children. George suggested that Steven and Jane move with them to Rawlings. Possibly Steven could get a job working for the railroad or working for some business in town. Jane would be a great help at the hotel. Since Steven had no family in the Portland area, he and Jane agreed to move with the Seevers.

As arrangements were being made to move, a "For Sale" sign was put in the window of the bakery. Customers were sorry that George was leaving. They would miss his baked goods and his lunches.

About a week after the sign went into the window, a stranger walked into the bakery for lunch. He ordered the vegetable soup and chicken sandwich and sat down at a table to wait. His food was served by Jane, and he began eating. He was impressed by the taste of the food and asked Jane if he could speak with the owner of the shop. Jane was afraid she had done something wrong but went into the kitchen to get George. George came out wearing his white apron and a net over his hair and introduced himself to the stranger as the owner of the bakery. "I am George Seevers. What can I do for you sir?" asked George. "Hello. I am Roy Collins from Streator, Illinois and I saw your for-sale sign in the window and would like to ask you some questions about the business." George did a double take when he said he was from Streator. "I am also from Streator. What a coincidence." commented George. Collins told him that he also grew up in the county orphanage and remembered George's name because of the ruckus that was made when he ran away. He was one of only a few that they did not find and return. He said that he did not know George personally, but always admired the fact that he got away. George was astounded that someone would show up in Portland that was raised in the same place he was. The kicker was that Ray Collins was interested in buying the bakery. He had become a wealthy man in business and wanted to establish himself in the West. What better way than to own a bakery and diner that was well received by the public in a large city like Portland.

George was amazed but answered Ray's questions about how he got to Portland. Ray was fascinated by George's adventures west and asked many questions about George, his family, and the bakery.

George felt that he was getting a little too personal in his questions and tried to steer him back to the sale of the bakery. "Have you run a bakery before?" asked George.

"Yes, I have several throughout the country. We started in Texas with the original Collins bakery and now have stores in Denver, Chicago, and San Francisco. I would like to add one in Portland."

Ray made a generous offer. One that would allow George to purchase the land and hotel in Rawlings and leave him some money to make the improvements necessary to the hotel and the diner. The sale was contingent on the addition of the recipes George used for his baked goods. "I am not willing to give you my personal recipes but will add the ones that the previous owner passed on to me. When I purchased the bakery, it did not have a soup and sandwich shop. I added that later and all those recipes are mine," explained George.

"That is reasonable. The offer stands with the addition of the original recipes for the bakery items," answered Ray.

"Let me discuss this with my wife and if you will come in about the same time tomorrow, I will let you know."

"Good. I will see you tomorrow at about the same time," said Ray.

George talked to Marie about the offer, and they discussed it with Mary, Jane, and Steven. They also talked to Isaac and Julia Sorenson. They all thought it was a very generous offer and that they should accept. The Sorenson's did not want the family to leave but understood the reasons for it.

The next day when Ray Collins came into the bakery, George and Isaac Sorenson were there to greet him. The offer was accepted, arrangements were made through Isaac's bank for money to be transferred and the title to be in Ray Collins' name. It would take about two months for all the paperwork to be finalized and the transfer of title to take place. In the meantime, George continued to run the bakery as usual and Marie, Mary, Jane, and Steven were busy packing up all their belongings. George would pack his personal cooking equipment at the last minute.

Horses and wagons were purchased. The ones that were used to travel from Cheyenne to Portland had been sold after they arrived in Portland. Three wagons were purchased. One for George and Marie and the children, one for Steven and Jane and one for Mary. Mary was experienced in driving a team and wagon and it was decided that she and Jane would drive one wagon and Steven would drive the wagon with most of their belongings in it. George would drive the other with Marie and the children. With bed rolls for all the children, there was not much room for additional items.

The money was deposited into George's account at the bank in June of 1884 and the title to the bakery was cleared and put into Ray Collins name. Isaac Sorenson sent the money to the county assessor in Dayton, WA for the purchase of the 160 acres that the Seevers were buying. George and Marie said goodbye to all their customers and friends with a special, tearful goodbye to the Sorenson's and left for their journey to Rawlings, Washington.

In June of 1884, the Seevers family set out from Portland, Oregon to Rawlings, Washington in three wagons with all their worldly goods packed inside. A ferry took each wagon across the Columbia River at the mouth of the Willamette River, where it flows into the Columbia. It would be easier traveling along the

Washington side of the river than the Oregon side. They were all nervous about moving to a new area, but all were ready for a new adventure. It took them seven days of hard travel to reach Rawlings. They had to wait on the other side of the Snake River for the ferry to come and pick them up and take them across. The ferry was only big enough for one wagon at a time, so it took a while for all of them to cross.

They could see the hotel from across the river and it looked like it was in pretty good shape from a distance. But they were anxious to see it up close and to get inside to see if the hotel and their home were livable. They knew that extensive cleaning would have to be done before they could move their belongings in. As soon as the last wagon had crossed the river, they all headed for the hotel at the same time. They all felt that the diner would be their main source of income to begin with but wanted to get the hotel rooms ready for occupancy as soon as possible.

The hotel was a 2-story structure with a wide covered porch all the way across the front. The entrance was in the middle with the dining room on one side and a separate door to the post office on the other side. George had been told that the hotel was closed, and no one was using it, but there were people going in and coming out. The children stayed with Grandma in the wagons while George, Marie, Jane, and Steven went into the building. There was no one at the desk, but there were men sitting around the lobby and a few coming down the stairs. They could hear women laughing upstairs.

George asked one of the men where the owner was and was told that she was upstairs in one of the rooms with a gentleman. Marie muttered to George, "some gentleman." George demanded that she be called downstairs, explaining that he was the new owner of the building and that he wanted her downstairs now. Eventually she came sauntering down the stairs dressed in a flimsy dressing gown. She sidled up to George and asked what she could do for him. George replied, "You can get all your possessions, your ladies and the gentlemen and get out of my building. This is my hotel and not a brothel."

It took two days to get her out of the building. After much sputtering and crying and pleading, she admitted that she had just moved her girls into the empty building and set up business. No one objected. The men in the lobby complained bitterly, but George explained that he had a family, and he would not have his children exposed to that kind of behavior. Most of the men worked for the railroad, but some of them were cowboys from the surrounding farms and ranches.

After everyone was gone, George and Marie were able to inspect the hotel. The building was structurally sound but needed a lot of scrubbing and painting to brighten it up.

Their priority though, was the house they would live in. They had to get the family settled and into someplace other than the wagons. They looked through the house and found that it was a spacious place, but the sleeping arrangements were going to be cramped. Mary and the girls would share one room, Steven and Jane would have a room and George and Marie would have Freddie in with them. It would be tight, but they would make it work. They were just happy to have a place to live.

Mary and Marie unpacked all the cleaning supplies that they had brought with them. Steven hauled water from the well while George made sure that the wood stove was cleaned and ready to use. As soon as they had some hot water, they all got their rags and started scrubbing. Even the little girls tried to help with the cleaning. George was sure that by tomorrow, they would be able to move in.

Several of their neighbors came over to introduce themselves and bring food for them to eat. They were all very welcoming and were grateful that George and Steven had moved the ladies out of the hotel and back across the tracks to the saloons. George explained to them that they were going to open the hotel and diner as soon as they possibly could.

Several of the men offered to help George and Steven unload their wagons and get the furniture into the house.

It seemed that the residents were excited about the Seevers being here and bringing some life back into the town.

Susan would be arriving soon. She had her own place to live behind the schoolhouse. It was in good condition and clean. Some of the ladies had cleaned both the school room and the little house behind when they learned that there would be a teacher coming to town. Susan would be having her meals with her family but would live in the house.

Marie set the children up on the front porch of the hotel with their toys and strict instructions not to leave the porch. She was not sure whether there were poisonous snakes in the area and did not want the children exploring until they were aware of what was around them. Grandma Mary was on the porch with them doing some mending of linens to be used in the hotel. Until they had a chance to order new linens, they would have to make do with what they had.

Anna and Irene were very content to stay on the porch and play with their dolls, but Charlotte wanted to explore and was trying to climb down the steps. Anna had to holler at Grandma several times that Charlotte was leaving the porch. Either Grandma or Marie had to interrupt what they were doing to keep her on the porch. Finally, Marie brought her into the house to entertain Freddie. She would try to sing to him, which amused Grandma and Marie greatly. Eventually, both Freddie and Charlotte fell asleep and there was some uninterrupted time to get some serious cleaning done.

Within two days, the house was ready to move in. The whole family was anxious to get out of the wagons and into their own home. Marie had brought some fabric with her and started making some curtains for all the windows. Mary set out vases and knick-knacks so that the house looked like home.

Meanwhile, George and Steven were getting the hotel ready to open again. They found some ladies in town that were willing to help clean. Each of them worked about an hour a day for four days and had all the rooms and the common areas clean and ready for guests to come. They realized that the guests in Rawlings would be different than in a big city.

The guests here would be people coming through on the train with only a one night stop over or cowboys moving from one ranch to another. A lot of the guests would be railroad workers with a layover and would be leaving the next day.

The previous owner had left all the ledgers behind, and Steven went over them carefully. It gave them an idea of the number of guests that they would have, which helped George plan meals for the diner. He knew that the diner would be his most profitable part of the business, but only if he served good nutritious food and plenty of it. He would also have to provide some type of boxed meal for people to take with them on the train. It would be a daunting task and he knew that he would need the help of all the adult members of the family. The children would need supervision, so one of the ladies would have to be available for them. He might have to find someone to hire as a dishwasher and to clean off the tables.

Steven was not very experienced in any of the jobs that George needed help with, but he could keep the ledgers for both the hotel and the diner and that would be a major help to George. He did not like keeping books. Steven could also learn to do the ordering of supplies for both the hotel and the diner. The post office was in the hotel and the town needed a postmaster. Steven applied with the county for that position and received it. The county would pay him a small stipend for his work.

Steven also volunteered to feed and care for the horses in the barn behind the hotel. He felt inadequate to do much more but was willing to learn. He wanted to make Jane proud.

There were several fruit trees close to the river and they were overloaded with fruit: apples, pears, cherries, and peaches. It looked like the previous owners wanted an orchard, but only planted a few trees. Steven found several boxes of canning jars in the barn. Mary suggested that they can the fruit. One morning, the whole family picked fruit. The children picked up the tree falls to be used to make jam and jelly. Before the diner even opened for business, the ladies were in the kitchen canning the fruit and making jam. When they were finished with the work, they looked at the filled jars and were excited that they had their first supplies for use in the diner. "It feels so good to fill the shelves with food that we canned. In the Fall, I will order seeds to plant a garden next Spring. It will be good to have fresh vegetables to serve and maybe there will be enough left over to can for Winter use," explained Marie. Both Jane and Susan volunteered to tend the garden and to help with the canning when the time came. "I love being with you again. I was very lonely after Gerald died without family around. It was hard being alone," explained Susan. Marie gave her a big hug and said, "We are glad you are home."

CHAPTER 7

Jeff Jordan had arrived in Rawlings by train from the East. He was a young man on a mission. He had received a substantial inheritance from an uncle the previous year. His Uncle John was his mother's brother and Jeff was very close to him, especially after his mother died. He was her only relative, and since John had never married and had no children, Jeff was his only heir. Jeff's father was also in Chicago and even though he loved his father dearly, he was never as close to him as he was to his Uncle John. The inheritance allowed Jeff to travel and find the area of the country he wanted to make his permanent home.

He was a young man with a lot of money and wanted to buy land in the West. He was a tall man with piercing blue eyes that seemed to cut into you when he looked at you. As he walked across the road to the hotel, he saw Susan Lewis on the porch washing the front windows of the hotel. He was stunned by her beautiful looks. "Excuse me ma'am," he asked. "Can you tell me if there is a county land agent in town? I am interested in buying some ranch land in this area."

"I don't believe there is a land agent here in town, but you can talk to my brother-in-law, George Seevers. He owns this hotel." Susan answered.

He talked to George Seevers about his land and whether he would be willing to sell. "No, I just purchased the land and hotel six months ago. My wife and I are here to stay. We want to make this town our home. I'm sure there are other sections of land available if that is the amount you are looking for. There are not many places that are for sale that already have buildings on them. You would probably have to start building from the beginning. You might want to go to the county seat and ask the assessor what is available in this area."

Jeff rode all around the area looking at the terrain and the land in proximity to the river. Some areas were interesting, but he decided to take George's advice and take the train to Dayton to the county seat. He asked the assessor what land was for sale in the Rawlings area. "I have three sections available just South of Rawlings, but it is not posted yet. The current owner wants to be away from the area before it is listed," the assessor mentioned.

"If you will give me a map of the area that is for sale, I will inspect it as soon as I get back and let you know if I want to buy it," explained Jeff.

Jeff caught the next train back to Rawlings but didn't get there until 7 P.M. He was exhausted from all the train travel. He fell onto his bed at the hotel and was asleep within minutes. The next morning, after a good hearty breakfast, he went to the barn in the back of the hotel and saddled his horse for a ride out to inspect the land for sale.

He rode all over the sections for sale, inspecting the land and looking at the terrain in relation to the river and other water sources. There was an old shack that could be fixed up to be a comfortable place to live until a ranch house could be built. He would also have to build a barn and corral area for horses and cattle.

He rode back to town and bought another train ticket to Dayton and the county assessor's office. He let the assessor know that he was interested in the sections discussed previously. A purchase price was agreed upon, transfer of funds was completed, and Jeff left the assessor's office with a deed in hand. He was jubilant! He had the start of his long-awaited ranch in an area that he felt would be his permanent home.

After returning to Rawlings, he sought out George to thank him for the suggestion about asking the county assessor about available acreage for sale. "I have purchased three sections just south of town. It is a beautiful piece of land and will make a great cattle ranch. The only problem is, there is no place to live. There is an old shack that can be made into a comfortable cabin, but it will take about 2 months of construction to make it livable. I would like to make arrangements with you to rent the hotel room for at least 2 months or maybe more until I can move onto the ranch," Jeff explained. George assured him that there was no problem in renting the room on an extended basis. "I will also need to find someone who is familiar with carpentry and is willing to stay in the area for a while."

"Your luck is holding," George laughed. "A young man checked into the hotel last evening and said he was looking for work. He is a carpenter by trade but said that he would be willing to do any job. I don't know how good a carpenter he is, but he had a whole satchel of tools with him, so I'm assuming he knows how to use them. He is in room 9 on the second floor. His name is Earl Jansen." Jeff thanked George, shook his hand, and left in search of Earl Jansen.

Susan walked into the hotel while Jeff was speaking to Jane about keeping his room for an extended period. "Hi, Jane." Susan called out as she was headed for the diner to see Marie. She saw that

Jane was busy with Mr. Jordan and did not want to disturb them, but Mr. Jordan called to her, "I have a question to ask you Miss Lewis. I have asked Steven and Jane to ride out with me and see the land I just purchased. I was wondering if you would like to join us?" Susan looked briefly at Jane for confirmation. "George will fix us a picnic supper to take along. Do come Susan. It will be fun," Jane said excitedly.

Susan had not been out with anyone since Gerald was killed, but she felt that if Jane and Steven were going to be with her, then it would be okay. "All right, Mr. Jordan. I would enjoy seeing your land and a picnic supper would be fun. Thank you for asking me."

Jeff, Susan, Steven, and Jane set out in George's wagon for Jeff's ranch. It was beautiful rolling hill country ideal for raising cattle and if the soil was good, for planting wheat. Jeff could see the potential of owning land in this area.

"This is the shack I want to upgrade into a cabin to live in until I can get a house built. I will build a barn and corral in that area over by the creek. It should be easy to dig a well and reach water close to the top," Jeff explained. "Steven, I am going to need some supplies ordered and some building materials shipped in, and I understand you are the man who knows how to do that." "George has asked me to order supplies for the hotel and the diner and occasionally someone will ask me to add something to that order. Just give me a list and I will take care of it for you. If you have a line of credit with a bank in either Dayton or Colfax, it makes the process of ordering and receiving your merchandise a lot easier and quicker," Steven explained. "I do have a line of credit at the Dayton bank, and I will figure out what I will need to get this shack ready for me to move in," declared Jeff.

Jeff noticed that Susan was quiet most of the time and said very little unless asked a direct question. "What do you think of the place Miss Lewis?" asked Jeff. "It is very nice," Susan answered. She was looking around and remembering Gerald and the Circle C Ranch in Laramie. Even after all these years, she missed Gerald and the life they could have had together. "I assume with this purchase, you are planning on staying in the area," Susan commented. "Yes! I plan on making Rawlings my home," Jeff answered.

As they were leaving, Jeff noticed a grove of trees near the creek that he thought would be a great place for a picnic. They had an excellent meal and sat and talked for a long time after eating. At last, they decided to leave. It took about 40 minutes to drive back to town and they wanted to get back before it got too dark, and they wouldn't be able to see the road. They all helped pack up and headed back to Rawlings.

Jeff took Susan directly to her room behind the school. "Thank you so much for coming today. I really enjoyed myself and enjoyed getting to know you." Jeff said. "Thank you for asking me. I too had a very good time. You have a lovely piece of land, and I am sure you will make it a very successful ranch," answered Susan.

Susan unlocked her door, went inside, and locked the door again. She went directly to her room, changed into her night clothes, crawled into bed, and sobbed from missing Gerald. Today reminded her so much of him and she felt guilty being with Jeff when she had made a promise to Gerald that she would never be attracted to anyone else.

Jeff let Jane off at the Seevers home, then he and Steven drove the wagon to the barn behind the hotel. Steven unhitched the team and led them to their stalls. Both he and Jeff gave them a good rubbing down and a fork full of hay. "Jeff, George wanted me to tell you that you were welcome to use the wagon and horses anytime you need them until you can get some of your own." "Thanks Steven. I will thank him personally tomorrow. I will also get you that list of supplies I will need."

"Hey Steven," Jeff hollered as Steven was leaving the barn. "Did I do something to offend Susan today?" "No, I don't think so. I just met Susan the other day when she got off the train from Laramie. She taught school there for 7 years. She was engaged to a rancher, but he was killed. They think it might have been rustlers. There were some cattle missing. Susan's fiancé was out rounding up strays when he was shot. She might have been uncomfortable with all the ranching talk," Steven explained.

"Thanks for the explanation, Steven. Susan is a very pretty girl, and I would like to see more of her." "Tread lightly, Jeff. Jane says she still misses her fiancé after all these years," Steven warned. "Thanks, I will. Have a good evening," Jeff commented.

Jeff went up to his room thinking about Susan Lewis. He would like to see her again. She was one of the prettiest women he had seen in a long time. He wanted to know a lot more about her; what kind of music she liked, what she liked to read, her favorite subject in school and what kind of food she liked to eat. Besides the ranch, she was going to become a priority in his life.

Steven and Jane were looking for a small house of their own to either rent or buy. They wanted to move out of the hotel and have more room. They had found a small house 2 ½ miles from the hotel that was for sale and perfect for them. Because Steven was thrifty and spent his money wisely, he had saved enough money to buy the house. It had been abandoned for some time and needed major cleaning and repair work. Earl Jansen was helping Steven with the carpentry work. A new front porch was added as well as a new door and a new roof was put on. The inside was painted throughout, and the ladies were busy making curtains and braiding rugs for the floor. The stone fireplace was cleaned and repaired so that it was safe to use. George and Marie gifted them with a new wood stove.

Jeff walked into the dining room at the hotel wanting something to eat. He had been visiting the Palouse Indian camp and had purchased horses from them. He was building a good stable of horses for his ranch.

He noticed that Susan was just leaving the dining room. He had been thinking way too much about Susan latcly. Being in that close proximity to her was a disaster for his wellbeing. He had tried to reach out to her several times, but she rebuffed him every time. Mary saw Susan walking out of the dining room and said, "Susan, please come in here and sit down for a bit." It was warm outside, and Susan was tired from not sleeping very well the night before. She had been dreaming about Gerald and what their wedding would have been like, but when she woke up, it was Jeff that she was thinking about. "Susan, I am worried about you. I don't want you to be alone for the rest of your life. You are a lovely young woman and deserve to have someone to share your life with. Jeff Jordan is a very nice man and is interested in you. Why won't you open up to him?"

"Mama, when Gerald died, I swore I would never be interested in another man. He was the only man I would ever love," Susan explained. "I can't imagine living my life with someone else." She didn't explain to her mother that Jeff was filling her thoughts more lately than Gerald was. She did not want to admit that she was interested in Jeff.

"Just please think about what I have said, Susan. Jeff Jordan is a very nice man. Do not close yourself off to the possibility of a future with him. You are too special to be alone."

"Thank you, Mama. I will figure it out in my mind. I had removed the thought of another man from my mind the minute Gerald asked me to marry him and haven't put it back yet."

"Maybe that is because there was no other man who could possibly replace him," whispered Mary to herself.

Instead of going into the diner for dinner with the family, Susan walked back to her room to think. She took out pen and paper and started to write, "Dearest Gerald, I made you a promise the day you were buried that I would never love another man. You were my one true love, and I could never be attracted to another. Well Gerald, there is another man who has moved to Rawlings. His name is Jeff Jordan. He bought a large plot of land and is starting to raise some cattle. He asked me to go on a ride with Jane, Steven, and him to see his land. Gerald, it is beautiful land, and I did have a very good time, but I felt so guilty being there because of you and my pledge to you. Sweetheart, you know that I will always love you, but I need to be released from the promise I made to you. I need to be able to live and love again. I am starting to see that life for me did not end that terrible day. It just took a different turn." Susan cried as she folded the letter and put it in the back of her bible. She slept for several hours, woke up and fixed herself something to eat and felt that life could be good again.

It was a week before Jeff came back into town. He walked into the hotel lobby and saw George talking with Jane and Susan. He hadn't seen Susan in over a month and was stunned at how pretty Susan looked. During the school summer break, she was helping in the hotel and was on a break from cleaning some of the rooms. "Hello George; ladies. How is your day going?" Jeff asked all three of them but was looking only at Susan. George answered for all three of them. "Fine," he muttered. "I must get back to the kitchen. Thanks for all your hard work girls. See you later Jeff." George was chuckling as he walked back to the kitchen. He knew that Jeff wanted to talk to Susan alone. "Goodbye Jeff. See you later Susan," Jane said.

Would you like to take a walk with me after you finish work?" asked Jeff. "I have a question to ask you."

"I would enjoy a walk. It has been a beautiful day and I have been inside all day. I am finished with my work now. I will go home and change, and you can meet me in front of the school in about 30 minutes," Susan explained. Jeff nodded and went into the kitchen to see if George could fix a quick supper basket for Susan and him.

Jeff met Susan in front of the school with the basket of food. "I hope you don't mind, but I asked George to put together a picnic supper for us. I thought we could walk down by the river and find a place to sit and eat."

"That will be fine," said Susan. They walked to the river and found a grassy place to spread a blanket. Jeff opened the basket and found that George had sent along some chicken, fruit that the ladies had canned and a piece of cake for dessert. He also had packed a pitcher of lemonade. "This is a treat. Thank you for thinking of it," commented Susan.

"I want to know if I have offended you in some way," asked Jeff. "Every time I have tried to talk to you lately, you have avoided me. I don't understand why," questioned Jeff. Susan was astounded but understood why he would think so. She realized it was time to tell him about Gerald and her promise to him.

Susan proceeded to explain to Jeff her love for Gerald and the devastation she felt when he was killed. She told him about the promise she had made to him at his funeral, that she would never be attracted to or love another man. "My Mama made me realize the other evening what an unrealistic promise that was," explained Susan. "I haven't felt alive for seven years and I want to have a normal life again."

Jeff took her hand and said, "Susan, I am very attracted to you and would like to spend a lot more time with you. You are one of the prettiest women I have ever seen, and you deserve to have a happy life. I would hope that it could be with me." All Susan could say was thank you. She was afraid she would start to cry. Life was going to be good again.

CHAPTER 8

Rawlings was growing as a town. There were new businesses starting and old ones being revitalized. Ray Clausen came into town from Lewiston and checked into the hotel. He was inquiring about a job as a blacksmith. "We do not have a blacksmith shop in town," explained George. "Well, I am a blacksmith, and I am looking for work. I wanted to come to the Northwest to get away from Texas. Every town I tried to live in was rowdy and noisy. I thought maybe it would be a little less wild here."

"Do you have your own tools?" asked George. "I do. They are in a crate over at the railroad office. All I need is a forge and I am ready for work. I would like to live here. It looks like a nice peaceful town," answered Ray.

"Let me take you out back to the barn. I think it could be modified to become a blacksmith shop and a livery stable. Would you be willing to manage both?" queried George.

"Sure. I have done both. I might need someone to work with the horses and wagons," Ray commented.

The men looked over the barn area and decided where to put a forge and how to modify the barn to provide room for wagons and buggies to be stored.

"I would like a list of places where you have worked and some sort of guarantee that you would stick around for a while. I don't want to invest money in renovations if you are not going to be here in six months," George commented rather forcefully.

"That is only fair. I have all the information that you will need in my pack. It is also at the railroad station. I did not want to haul it around if you had no job available in the town," Ray said.

George arranged for Ray's crate of tools to be brought to the barn. He offered Ray a room in the hotel for the night, but Ray said he preferred bedding down in the barn. He was used to it. George let Ray know that he would get ahold of a carpenter to help with modifications on the barn. They needed a tack room and a room behind the blacksmith shop for Ray to live in. He would get ahold of Earl Jansen to see if he knew of anyone who could help on the project. Earl was busy working on Jeff's cabin. Ray told George that if it was okay with him, he would like to build the forge himself. He noticed a lot of concrete blocks alongside the barn and the hotel, and they would be just the thing for building a forge. That was certainly okay with George. It was a perfect way to get them away from the buildings and to use the materials that they had on hand.

George went back into the hotel diner while Ray unpacked some of his tools and made plans to build the forge. He made a passable bed in an extra stall for himself, laid down and promptly went to sleep.

The next morning, Ray was up early and had a lot of his equipment unpacked. George came out of the diner carrying a cup of coffee for Ray. "Thanks so much. This will wake me up this morning," Ray said gratefully. George noticed that Ray's equipment was of good quality. "Where did you learn the trade?" George inquired. "From my Pa. This was his equipment. He and my Ma lived in Lincoln, Nebraska and died last year. He left me all his tools. I did not want to live in Lincoln or Texas and had heard about the Pacific Northwest and was told that it was a nice place to live. It is dryer and there are less trees than I thought, but it looks like a place I could settle down in," explained Ray.

George asked a couple of young boys that were sitting on the steps of the hotel if they would be willing to help the new blacksmith unpack his gear. They were eager to help. It was something different to do.

With the boy's help, Ray thought he would be able to start building a forge and get it ready to fire up. He needed something heavy to put the anvil on. One of the boys knew of a large stump down by the river that he thought would be perfect. They took Ray down to see what it looked like, and he said it would be perfect. All they needed to do was haul it up to the barn and set it up. The boys suggested using a horse to haul it up. Ray was amused at them and their thought process. He knew that was the only way to get it up to the barn, but decided to let the two boys take the lead and figure it out. The two boys, Jeremy, and Danny Smith were proud of themselves for thinking up the idea of a horse pulling the stump to the barn.

George saw Earl in town the day after Ray started working on the forge and asked him to stop by the barn when he had a chance. "I can come right now if you want," answered Earl. "What's up?" George explained the idea of turning the barn into a livery stable and the need for a tack room and an area to park buggies and wagons.

"We will also need a room for the new blacksmith to live in. I know that you are working on Jeff's cabin, but do you know of anyone around who would be willing to help with this job?" asked George.

"Let me talk to Jeff and see what he would say if I took a little time away from his project to work on this one. I know that he has mentioned the need for a good blacksmith in the area. He will probably be very willing to help get him started."

George introduced Earl to Ray Clausen. Together, they made arrangements to get started on the work needed to turn the barn into a livery stable. Ray got the forge fired up, the anvil placed on the stump and the bellows positioned correctly and almost before the fire was hot enough, he had horses lined up to be shod. He could tell that the shoes were put on by amateurs. He had a lot of repair work to do on the hoofs for the shoes to fit correctly. He was working from dawn to dusk and had little time for the remodel of the barn but tried to get at least 2 hours of time in the very early morning hours.

Jeff had walked into the hotel lobby one morning about a week after Ray had started working on the forge. George was in the lobby talking to some guests when he motioned to Jeff to wait for him. George walked over to him and told him about Ray and wanted Jeff to meet him.

They walked out back to the stable and Jeff was impressed with the work that had been done already.

"It's good to meet you Ray and welcome to Rawlings. We needed a blacksmith in town. Would you be willing to make visits out to my ranch to work on my horses? It would be much easier that way."

"Sure, I have no problem with that at all. Just let me know when, so I can make the time," answered Ray.

CHAPTER 9

Since school was out for the summer months, Jeff was able to spend more time with Susan. One Saturday morning, he hired a horse and buggy from Ray at the livery and took Susan out to his ranch to see what progress he was making with his cabin and the barn and corral.

Earl had built a porch onto the cabin and Jeff had two wicker chairs sitting on it. He and Susan sat relaxing enjoying the view of the horses in the corral. He explained to Susan that when he built his ranch house, the cabin would be turned into a bunkhouse for the ranch hands.

As they were sitting on the porch, Susan said, "tell me about yourself Jeff. What was your childhood like?"

"I grew up in Detroit. My mother died when I was very young, and I was raised pretty much by nurses and nannies. When I was old enough, Father sent me off to boarding school. The school was a horrible place. There was no affection shown to us at all. We went to classes, studied, and exercised for 16 hours a day. The rest of the time was spent on eating meals and sleeping."

"My Father owned a steel mill outside of Detroit. I rarely saw him except on holidays. I would come home, but he did not spend time with me. Instead, my Uncle Leo did. He is the one who taught me to fish and climb and to get dirty. He was terrific and I adored him."

"When I was 12, Father sent me to a military academy. The war was over, but the officers were still fighting it and treated us all like we should be on a battlefield. It was a miserable way for a boy to live. Between classes, studying and drilling on the field, we had no time for any fun activities."

Susan was fascinated listening to him. His upbringing was so different than hers. She grew up in a loving, caring family with both a mother and father and sisters to love and care about her. She wondered what kind of a parent he would be. Would he be like his father, or would he be the opposite? "What did you do after you left school?" she asked. "I worked in the mill office for a while, then my Uncle Leo got sick and wanted me to come and live with him. He lived in Chicago. I loved it!

His house was so different than my Father's. He would plan fun things for us to do. Even though he was sick and wasn't well most of the time, he still managed to spend time with me. I believe he truly loved me, and I felt the same for him. I stayed with him until he died a year later. Father was not happy that I didn't come home and take over the mill for him, but I was not going to be under his thumb for the rest of my life. That is when I decided to come West and do what I wanted to. Uncle Leo left me a sizeable inheritance, so I have been able to use it to accomplish my dreams."

"You have lived a life that is so different than mine. I am amazed that you want to live in a town as small as Rawlings," commented Susan.

"Being small is the reason I want to live here. People care about their neighbors, and it is so refreshing to walk down the road and have your friends and neighbors greet you with such enthusiasm. I love it!" answered Jeff.

It was getting late, and Jeff wanted to get Susan back to town before it started to turn dark. They had spent the whole day exploring Jeff's property and talking. They both felt that they knew each other a lot better now.

As they were riding back into Rawlings, they heard gunshots coming from the saloon across the road from the hotel. Jeff stopped the buggy in front of the hotel and told Susan to go inside and to tell people to stay off the street until he found out what had happened. Jeff ran across the road and carefully approached the saloon. Men were coming out saying that there was a dead man in there. He looked in the door and saw that the bar was all shot up and there were two men lying on the floor. One man was obviously dead, the other was on the floor, propped up against the end of the bar bleeding from a leg wound. He kept yelling that the dead man had accused him of cheating at a game of cards.

Susan ran into the hotel to get George, but George was on his way out to see what was happening. Susan told him that Jeff was over there, and George went running across the road to make sure Jeff was okay.

The railroad depot had a locked room that the town used as a jail cell. The city did not have a jail or a sheriff. They sent a wire to the county seat for a Marshall to come anytime there was a crime committed. Even though witnesses said that it was self-defense, for his own safety, they locked him in the room. Both men were from out of town and had a layover in Rawlings and decided to sit in on a game of poker. They were both more than a little drunk when the shooting occurred.

As Jeff and George were walking back to the hotel, Jeff asked, "Does this kind of thing happen often?"

George explained, "I haven't been here that long, but this is the first killing I have heard of. There has been gun fire, but as far as I know, no one has been killed. I will send a wire to the Marshall in Dayton and ask him to come and do an investigation."

Earl was busy working on the barn at Jeff's ranch. He had hired two men from town to help him. He hoped to get it finished by the time the cold weather set in. Jeff wanted to buy more horses and would need additional space in the barn for them.

While Jeff was visiting surrounding ranches and meeting the owners, he learned that the best place to buy horses was from the Palouse Indians. They had superior quality stock and were willing to sell them at a fair price. None of the local ranchers had any trouble with either the Palouse or the Nez Perce Indians. They were all very friendly to the white men. To begin with, Jeff wanted about 15 horses. He wanted to have horses available for his ranch hands if they did not have their own. Most cowboys had their own saddle and tack, but not always the horse.

Jeff and Earl were walking around the property one afternoon discussing fence lines and where they needed to be placed. Jeff was anxious to get started on a larger ranch house and needed to pick a site for it. He wanted to be sure that the house was easily accessible from the road. Earl suggested building on a rise about 400 feet away from the barn and corral. The road could be extended to the front of the house and a side road off the main one could be made to the barn and bunkhouse. They walked up to the rise and looked out over the landscape. Jeff walked around in a circle to decide where the front of the house would be. He decided the front of the house would be facing East and the back facing West. In the back would be the living area with large windows overlooking the valley below and a view of the setting sun. The barn, corral and bunkhouse would be over to the right side of the house.

Jeff had big dreams of buying more land and more cattle and building one of the largest ranches in the area.

Not only were the Palouse and Nez Perce Indians a great resource for buying horses, but they were also great hunters and were asked to hunt on rancher's land. The herds of deer and antelope sometimes would over graze the land needed for cattle. The landowners did not want the wild animals gone completely, but the herds thinned out. By allowing the Indians free access to the land, they were making friends with the natives. None of the locals were interested in any discord with them.

The Indians would also canoe down the Snake River to Rawlings and board the tugboats heading toward Celilo Falls on the Columbia River. Celilo Falls was a prime place for the Indians to fish for salmon. There was a long-house there and the Indians were able to dry their catch and easily take it back to their village near Rawlings. They would spend months at the falls, fishing and drying their catch and then board another boat heading back up the Columbia and Snake Rivers to Rawlings, the supply of dried fish would last them most of the year until they headed back to the falls the next year.

Very rarely did the Indians cause any trouble in Rawlings. Occasionally, one or two would go into the saloon and drink too much and get into fights, but that occurred rarely. Both tribes that lived in the area were peaceful and caused no problems.

Earl Jansen was impressed with the vision Jeff had for his ranch. "Earl, my biggest priority as far as building is concerned is to have a place to house the men that I hire to work the ranch. I need a bunkhouse with all the necessary additions to make the men comfortable. To begin with, I would like to have seven to ten men to tend to the cattle and maintain the property around the ranch house," Jeff explained.

"Mr. Jordan, I really like what you are doing here and am happy you asked me to help with your building projects," Earl stated. "When the building is completed, I would like to stay on and work for you."

"I would be pleased to have you stay, Earl. You will be my first full-time employee," replied Jeff. Both men shook hands enthusiastically.

Earl was smiling all the way back into Rawlings. He was relieved that he would be staying here and not have to move again. He liked Jeff Jordan and would enjoy working for him.

Jeff tried to make it into town at least twice a week to purchase supplies and to get his mail. Mainly, he came into town to see Susan. He would get to the hotel before school was out so he could get cleaned up before he saw her. He still did not have adequate bathing facilities at the ranch. They would usually go for a walk then have supper at the hotel and he would walk her back to the school. He would always come in on Saturday, spend the night at the hotel and then go to church with the family on Sunday.

Susan was becoming more attracted to Jeff the more she was with him. It was hard not to compare him to Gerald even after all these years. They were so much alike in temperament. Both were calm in stressful situations, and both were kind and solicitous towards her. She appreciated that trait in a man. She was learning to respect Jeff for his integrity and honesty. He also respected the fact that she had been in love before and did not hold that against her. Her mother and sisters liked him a lot and were very happy about the budding romance.

In September 1885, Steven and Jane announced that they were going to have a baby the next April. They would continue to live in the hotel. As postmaster, Steven was at the hotel all day and Jane worked at the front desk, along with doing some work in the diner to help George when it was busy. When trains arrived at night, both Jane and Steven were available to help the travelers check in.

Rawlings was considered a way station for the train. The passengers would leave on the next train headed in the direction of their destination. The town was growing. Businesses were being added that made living in Rawlings more comfortable. The addition of the livery stable and the blacksmith shop added the possibility of people having transportation while they were visiting. It also gave visitors a safe place to board their horse for an overnight stay if they were travelling by horse instead of train.

The addition of Susan Lewis as the schoolteacher had brought children from outlying ranches into town for school and therefore their parents came into town more often. The diner at the hotel had never been busier and the added business had forced George to place ads in newspapers in Portland, Seattle, and Spokane for a cook to help him.

There was also talk of opening a general store in town. When something was needed, it had to be individually ordered and the person ordering had to wait until it arrived either by train or steamship. There was a building available for a general store. The building was on George's land, but he was willing to offer a long-term lease for very little money to anyone who would be willing to open and run the store. If the ads that he placed did not produce results soon, he would branch out to other towns. Both Cheyenne and Denver were possibilities.

In August 1885, a young man stepped off the train in Rawlings and headed to the hotel. He had a suitcase with him and was dressed in a suit and tie with a fedora on his head. "Hello! I am looking for George Seevers. I understand he works at this hotel," said the young man.

Jane answered him saying, "George owns this hotel. I will get him for you." She walked through the lobby into the diner and then into the kitchen. "George, there is a man in the lobby asking for you. He is wearing a suit and tie." In the meantime, Steven had stepped out of his office to see who the new guest was.

Just then George walked up to the stranger and introduced himself. "Hello, I'm George Seevers. What can I do for you?"

"My name is Clyde Rodgers Jr. and I believe you used to work for my father in Portland."

"Junior? You were just a little guy the last time I saw you," George said with a surprised look on his face. "Excuse me a moment," George said to Junior. "Jane, would you please ask Marie to come help in the kitchen for a few minutes while I talk to Junior?"

George turned back to his guest, then asked "How is your father doing?"

"He is well and no one calls me Junior anymore. I go by Clyde."

"Okay. What brings you to Rawlings, Clyde?" George asked, somewhat taken aback by the young man's curtness.

"This advertisement brings me here. I am interested in opening a store in this town and my father mentioned that you were a hard worker and could show me how to run an effective and profitable business. I'm sure he did not know that you owned this hotel. He told me that you worked here."

"I do work here. I am the cook for the diner. I just happen to own the hotel also."

George invited Clyde into the diner for a cup of coffee. They sat down and Clyde proceeded to tell him about working for his father and how much he wanted to get out of the city. "Father is not happy with me for leaving. He wanted me to take over the shop, but I do not like the city and wanted to leave. When I saw your ad, I thought it was the perfect opportunity to see if I would like to live in a small town and to start my own business."

"So, you want to open a General Store. This would not be just a dry goods store. You would need to stock farm equipment, canned and fresh food when available. You would have the dry goods also and you would also have to have school supplies and books. My sister-in-law Susan would like to have some books available for loan. She is trying to promote independent reading among her students. I would propose starting out small and growing as the need arose."

Clyde was nodding as George was explaining what would be stocked in the store. He agreed with almost everything except starting out small. He thought that they could start a little larger than George proposed but decided to stay quiet for the time being.

"If we reach an agreement Clyde, I will want you to commit to running the store for at least 5 years. I do not want to get a store up and running and then have you decide that you do not like living here and decide to move," George declared.

"I would commit to running a general store for a minimum of 5 years. I will not pull out on you," Clyde affirmed.

As George and Clyde were walking down to the building that would be used as a general store, Clyde was looking around at the people. He realized that they were not as sophisticated as he was used to and that he would have to change his way of dressing to fit into the community. The building that was to be used as the store was good sized and would work well. There was a large porch across the front that would be where large merchandise could be displayed and there was good storage in the back of the building for extra merchandise. There was also an apartment on the second floor that would become his home. It had an entrance both inside and outside.

"How do you propose to finance this store, Clyde?" George inquired. "My father gave me half of my inheritance when I left Portland. I will use that as collateral to purchase the stock needed. I am hoping that sales will support the balance."

Clyde got busy right away and cleaned up the store and apartment above. He would stay in the hotel for a week in order to get things ready to move in. Earl had found some barrels in the stable that could be used for display in the store and on the porch. Clyde knew how to order supplies for the dry-goods store but knew very little about farm supplies and school supplies. Steven Taylor ordered the supplies for the hotel, diner and blacksmith shop and was well informed as to where to order almost anything needed.

By the end of September 1885, the store was ready to open on a limited basis. Some of the larger items, especially farm equipment, had not arrived yet, but the soft goods and some food stuffs were on display and ready for sale. Clyde arranged with some of the townspeople who had gardens to purchase some of their extra produce at a reduced cost to sell at the store. There were people in town who did not have gardens or had very small ones who wanted to buy fresh produce.

The store became a big success right away. People would come in and purchase something, then suggest another item they could use that Clyde did not have in stock. The possibilities of increasing inventory and customers were endless.

Clyde was thriving with his new responsibilities and couldn't have been happier. Steven was reviewing all the orders that Clyde was making and thought that he was ordering too much at a time. Because George was still technically the owner of the business, Steven went to him with his concerns. "He is ordering way too much at a time and will have to hold the merchandise for too long before it sells. He is ordering like he would in Portland. It is not the same for here."

"How about taking an inventory now and using it as a guide for additional orders," George suggested.

"I will suggest it to him. That is a good way of inventory control," Steven commented.

One day, after the store closed, Steven sat down with Clyde to discuss the ordering procedures and the inventory. "Clyde, I would like to take an inventory of the merchandise in the store now and use it as a guide for ordering in the future. I am concerned about the amounts you are ordering. It is not good money management to have a lot of extra inventory on hand, especially if it is not selling. I am not sure why you need 10 spools of pink thread. You only have 1 piece of fabric that would call for pink thread. You would be ahead if you only had ordered 2 spools. At 5 cents per spool, you have 40 cents sitting in inventory and not selling."

"Why are you questioning my ordering practices?" demanded Clyde. "I learned to order dry goods supplies from my father and he ran a very successful, profitable business."

"Yes, he probably did. But he ran that business in Portland, a much larger city than Rawlings. He could have had 3 or 4 ladies into his store in 1 day asking for pink thread. If you look around at the ladies in town, there are not many wearing pink. They dress mostly in blue, grey, and brown. You need to familiarize yourself with the needs of the people who live here, not in a big city like Portland."

Clyde was incensed at being reprimanded by Steven. But because George was a part owner in the store, he had to abide with what he wanted. They arranged a day when the store would be closed an hour early so that an inventory could be taken. Steven would ask Jane to help him, and they would come in one afternoon and count and record all the merchandise for sale in the store.

Before the inventory, Steven and Jane made charts so they could name every item in the store and keep track of the count.

While counting the items in the store, both Steven and Jane noticed that there were more vegetables than were needed for a farm community. Most people had small gardens and either canned the produce themselves or bought fresh if they did not have them in their garden. It was a waste of money and space to have 10 cases of canned corn, when corn grew so well in Eastern Washington, and it was readily available for home canning. What Clyde needed to stock were more canning jars and lids and he had very few of those in stock. The ladies were going to be asking for them very soon as harvest was about to begin.

Steven went over all the figures with George and they both went to see Clyde. "We have inventoried all the merchandise for sale in your store. There are some concerns we have about the quantities of different items that you are ordering. As I told you before, this is not Portland and the items used here are very different than in a big city," Steven explained. He had spread all the papers out on the store counter for Clyde to look at. He explained about the canned goods and the need to immediately order a quantity of canning jars. When Clyde saw the numbers in print, he realized that he was not ordering for the housewives in Portland and had to modify his way of doing the ordering. Steven proposed that he help Clyde with the ordering for a while until he got used to the quantities needed. Clyde agreed with that idea and planned to sit down with Steven and go over the ordering process.

"Clyde, I must say that the store looks very good. You have done a great job of arranging the merchandise and displaying the items very effectively," George said with sincere pride.

Anna, George, and Marie's 9-year-old daughter went into the store after school almost every day to visit Clyde and to look at all the pretty things on display. Clyde had purchased some fancy hair ribbons and shoe clips for young girls. He also had an elegant looking doll on display. Anna wanted that doll! She would stand and stare at it until Clyde told her it was time to go home.

The other Seevers children usually followed Anna home but did not go into the store. They thought it was silly to stop at the store every day. Nothing was that interesting and anyway, Papa had usually baked something special, and they were allowed to have a sweet for an after-school snack. Irene would go right home, do her homework, and start reading. "If Mr. Rodgers had books in the store, then I might go in," said Irene. "How disgusting," Anna commented with a sneer on her face and went back to dreaming about the doll.

Charlotte was only interested in getting home to Freddie. Since the day Freddie was born, she considered him her baby. She resented anyone who paid attention to him. She would get upset when her Mama fed him. She would throw tantrums until Grandma Mary would take her out of the room. As both got older, she realized that Mama had to take care of Freddie, but she was always protective of him. When she got home from school, the first thing she did was check Freddie and see what he was doing and who he was with. If she was satisfied, she would go to see her Papa and have her snack.

Both George and Marie worked very hard to make sure the children were not underfoot at the hotel. They did not have free access to the place. Most of the time, Grandma Mary would look after them at their house. Grandma Mary was living with George and Marie in their home. She shared a room with Jane until she and Steven were married, then Anna moved into the room with her. Anna was not happy about the move. She didn't want to have any adult watch over her all the time.

"George, I would like to have a permanent room here in the hotel," Mary asked. Both Marie and George had stunned looks on their faces.

"But why Mama?" asked Marie. "Aren't you happy living with us?"

"Yes, I am my dear, but I would like to have a little privacy now. I have had one or more of the girls sharing a bedroom with me for years and would like one of my own. Anyway, you could use the extra room. Anna, Irene, and Charlotte could share a room and Freddie could have his own "boy" room. He will need it, being the only boy in the family. The stuff stored in that room can be boxed up and stored in the stable until we can have Earl build us a storeroom beside the barn."

"Please don't think I won't be available to watch the children. I will always be here for them, but I would like to put some of my things out without fear of them getting broken and I would like to read in the evening without disturbing Anna's sleep."

That same day, the hotel room was cleaned out and ready for Mary to move in the next day.

At supper that evening the children were told about the new living arrangement for Grandma Mary. Anna and Charlotte were not at all happy with the plan. Anna was not happy because she would have to share a room with her two sisters. Charlotte flatly refused to move into the other bedroom. Freddie would not be there. She firmly stated to her parents that she would not move. "You will start moving your things this evening and you will be ready to sleep there tomorrow evening. There will be no discussion or arguments," George asserted. Charlotte went into full tantrum mode with kicking and screaming. She had done this before and her parents had always given in to her before, but not this time. "Freddie will have a room of his own and you three girls will share one. End of discussion!" Charlotte's tantrum continued for a short time, but it was not accomplishing what she had hoped it would and she called down a bit. No one was paying any attention to her.

Charlotte's tantrum calmed to sobbing instead of screaming and kicking. The girls were then sent to their room and asked to prepare their belongings to move to the other bedroom. Grandma Mary would have her things moved by that evening and Anna would make room for Irene and Charlotte to move in.

Marie's thought was that she was very glad they were eating at home instead of at the diner. Charlotte was acting like a two-year-old. Grandma Mary said that she felt bad about causing such problems with the girls, but George countered, "No – Mary! It is time you had some private time and a place that you can call your own."

When Charlotte woke in the morning, she found Irene busy getting her books ready to move. All of Charlotte's clothes and toys were in a heap on the floor because the chest of drawers was being moved. Charlotte was told to get up because the bed was to be moved next. Since there was a bed, dresser and washstand in the hotel room, Grandma Mary did not have to take hers to her new room. She could leave them for the girls to use. Irene and Charlotte would still have to share a dresser. George assured Irene that he would have some shelves made for all her books.

Charlotte still refused to move her things from the floor. She was told that there would be no breakfast until all her belongings were moved to the other bedroom. Since her temper tantrum the night before started prior to eating her supper, she was very hungry this morning. Even being as young as she was, she knew when Papa meant business.

Since it was Saturday and there was no school, Jeff had driven the buggy into town. He and Susan were planning another picnic on the ranch. Susan asked Marie if Freddie could come with them. "Oh yes Susan. Please take him," Marie pleaded. "I really don't think he needs to be exposed to all of Charlotte's drama right now. She had another tantrum last night about moving in with her sisters. She thinks she needs to be with Freddie. We must find a way to deal with her and her obsession with Freddie. She thinks he belongs to her and resents anyone else who tries to spend time with him. Any suggestions teacher?"

"Let me think about it. Maybe I could keep him overnight on Saturday and you could pick him up after church on Sunday," Susan suggested.

"That sounds like a great plan. I don't want to break the bond between brother and sister, just stem that possessiveness of hers."

Freddie's bed was moved into his parent's room for a few days so Charlotte couldn't crawl into bed with him without being heard. Then on Saturday afternoon, he went for a ride with Jeff and his Aunt Susan. After their picnic, Jeff took both back to the school building so Freddie could spend the night. Freddie was a little scared about being away from his Mama and Papa and sleeping in a different place, but his Aunt Susan read him two bedtime stories and he had a cookie before he went to bed. Irene had tried to read him stories at night, but Charlotte objected and said that it was her job to read to him. The only problem was that Charlotte was not very good at reading and gave up trying to read to him.

On Sunday morning, Jeff rode into town to church and sat with Susan and Freddie. When the Seevers family came into the church, Charlotte started to go sit with Freddie. Marie held her back to sit with the rest of the family. After church, Freddie was busy telling his Mama, Papa, Grandma and Sisters about his adventure the day before and the two bedtime stories that his Aunt Susan had read to him. He was excited to be the center of attention for a change. Charlotte wasn't speaking for him.

George and Marie knew that it would take time for Charlotte to adjust to the fact that Freddie was becoming his own person and could have a life separate from Charlotte's.

CHAPTER 10

Steven and Jane were spending most of their time alone. They were getting used to living with each other and learning to be a married couple. They also learned that they would have a baby in about 8 months. It was a daunting feeling for them to realize that they would be responsible for another human being.

While Mary was moving into the hotel to gain some private time, Jane and Steven wanted to find a house that they could afford to buy or rent close enough to the hotel so they could get to work easily. It wouldn't be long before Jane would not be able to work. By Steven and Jane moving, George would gain a room to rent to a paying customer. Mary's room had been a storeroom and was not rented.

The Taylor's finally found a little house about 2 miles from the hotel that had been vacant for 2 months and needed a little work done to make it comfortable. The bank in Dayton held the loan on the property and was willing to rent the place to Steven and Jane for the amount of the payment, with the agreement that when the delinquent payments were made, their payments would then go towards the purchase of the house.

The house had most of the furniture and a lot of kitchen utensils left. It looked like the previous owner left with just his personal belongings. There were even some cans of food left in the pantry.

A lean-to was built at the side of the house where they could stable their horse and park their wagon out of the weather. A well had been dug and there was a pump inside the house. The out-house had to be moved farther away from the house and Steven would hire someone to do that for him. He made sure that the cookstove was vented properly. He wanted things perfect for his new baby.

Again, the women of the family were busy sewing curtains for the new house, and they had started sewing little garments for the baby. Steven had ordered a bed and dresser for the baby and surprised Jane with the gift. She was excited about making blankets for the bed and filling the dresser with baby clothes.

While the Taylor's were moving into their new home and getting ready to have a baby, the romance between Susan and Jeff was blossoming. They spent time together almost every weekend. Jeff usually spent

Saturday nights at the hotel and accompanied Susan to church on Sunday.

On Saturdays they were either working on the remodeling of Jeff's cabin and barn or out riding, exploring the area around Rawlings. A couple of times, they rode into the Palouse encampment near Rawlings. Jeff wanted to negotiate the purchase of 5 more horses. He also wanted the Indians to meet Susan. He was making some friends among the Palouse, and he wanted Susan to be included in that friendship.

Jeff still thought that Susan was one of the most beautiful and sweetest women he had ever met and was deeply in love with her. He just didn't know if she felt the same for him. One Saturday afternoon, they were riding beside the stream when Jeff stopped and got off his horse to get a drink of water. He helped Susan down and walked both horses to the edge of the water where they drank also. Susan knelt to scoop up a handful of water. Jeff knelt beside her, then took her hand to help her get to her feet. He did not let go of her hand and said, "I have fallen in love with you Susan and want to marry you, but I have no idea how you feel. I do not want to embarrass either of us by making unwanted gestures."

"Oh Jeff, seven years ago Gerald was killed, and I made the pledge at his graveside. I thought I would never love again, but I was wrong. I do love you. When you first asked me to ride out here with you, Steven and Jane, I was very hesitant about going. I was afraid I would betray Gerald. After I got home that evening, I realized I had a good time. It was a revelation that I could enjoy myself with someone other than Gerald. I realized then that I could have a life with someone other than Gerald. You are that someone Jeff. I am in love with you. It is a different kind of love than my love for Gerald. We were so young, and I think now that we were in love with the idea of being in love. I do feel released from the pledge I made and know that the love I feel for you is a more mature, adult love," Susan said as she smiled at him.

Jeff grinned down at her, let go of her hand and took her face in both of his hands and kissed her. "Will you marry me, Susan?" Jeff whispered to her.

"Yes! I would be honored to be your wife."

"Who do I ask for permission to marry you?" inquired Jeff.

"I guess it would be George. He is the head of the household now," answered Susan.

"Okay, I will ask George. When would you like to get married?"

"Both Marie and Jane were married in June. I would like to continue that tradition and I would be able to finish out the school year. After we are married, I will not be able to teach."

"Are you going to be okay living in the cabin until we get the house finished? It could be through the winter months before it is finished enough to move in."

"I think it will be fun living in the cabin with you. It will be an experience I will remember forever," answered Susan.

"You have seen the start of the building of the house. I would like your input also. It will be as much your house as mine," commented Jeff. "I want us to have a lovely home to raise our family," added Jeff. He kissed her again and then helped her mount her horse for the ride back to town.

They rode slowly back to town, stabled the horses with Ray at the livery and walked into the back door of the hotel. Susan went to see her mother while Jeff went into the kitchen to talk to George.

Jeff walked into the kitchen and asked George if he could speak to him alone for a few minutes. George answered by saying, "Yes Jeff. You have my permission to marry Susan." Jeff was taken aback at what George said.

"How did you know what I was going to say?" questioned Jeff.

"We could all see in both yours and Susan's eyes how much you loved each other. You have a way of looking at each other that shows you love and value each other."

"When will you get married?" asked Marie.

"Probably sometime in June. That will give the school board enough time to find a new teacher and it will give us more time to get the house closer to being done. In the meantime, Susan is looking forward to staying in the cabin. It will be a new experience for her."

Susan had Freddie stay with her again that Saturday night. After supper in the diner, Jeff walked both back to the school, then went back to the hotel for the night. He would be with them in church the next morning where their engagement would be announced.

Jeff sat at a table in the lobby of the hotel looking over the plans for the house. He wanted to get Susan's ideas for the house but knew that he would add one room that he knew she would be pleased with. He would add a library. Susan had a large collection of books all packed away in crates and stored at the hotel. She would be so pleased to have a place to display them and have easy access to them. Jeff fell asleep in the lobby of the hotel with his plans all around him. He dreamed of houses, books, and Susan.

Freddie loved spending the night with his Aunt Susan. He was the only one she paid attention to. He liked having Mr. Jordan there too but being alone with Aunt Susan was special. She read him the best stories. He didn't always understand them, but just listening to her read gave him a goose-bumpy feeling. She was reading Tom Sawyer to him now and he loved the adventures that Tom had. Sometimes he wished that he could be Tom.

Susan had asked Clyde to order some books for the store. She hoped that there could be an area where people could borrow a book and return it when they were finished. It would be a mini library and would be a benefit to the older students who like to read. Clyde said that he would order the ones she requested, but he never did. He only ordered what she needed for her students like paper, pencils, chalk, slates, and ink. He ordered the readers that were needed for the grade levels but did not order the extra books. She decided to talk to George about the books. She had an idea for a reading area in the lobby of the hotel. There was an alcove at one end of the lobby, close to the door to the diner. If there were some shelves on the walls, books could be displayed, and people could sit in a comfortable place and read. They would not have to take them out of the hotel. There could be a section for newspapers and magazines also.

George thought the idea was terrific. He was an avid reader and had been since her first learned in the orphanage. He would encourage anyone and everyone to read for their own pleasure. Books could transport you to places and events that would never happen otherwise. "Susan, give me a list of the books and magazines you would like to have, and I will ask Clyde to order them. I will find someone to build some shelves to display the books and we can move the chairs into a more comfortable position for reading. We do have plenty of chairs available."

"I think Clyde is a little sweet on you and is jealous of Jeff," commented George.

"Goodness, I have never given him cause to think that I was interested in him," Susan answered indignantly.

"I know, but I think he thought that you would pay attention to him because he was becoming a successful business owner. If he does not order the books for me, I will ask Steven to do it and we will bypass Clyde all together."

"Thanks brother-in-law! Marie is one lucky lady." Susan said with a grin on her face.

"No, I am the lucky one to have married into this family," George answered chuckling as he went back to the kitchen.

George stopped at the store the day after he talked to Susan about ordering books. He looked around and hollered out to Clyde, "Looks good Clyde. You have a good assortment of merchandise here. I'm impressed with your displays. I don't see any books though. I was hoping to pick up a couple of new books today. Are they just late in coming in?"

"No, I don't think there will be that much call for books that are not part of the school needs. I don't have the extra shelf space and they would be wasted on most of the people in this town," Clyde declared.

"Clyde, I'm astounded at your feelings about the people in this town. There are many of us who read for pleasure and would like to have new books to read and discuss. If you don't want to bother with them, I will have Steven order them and we will set up a corner in the lobby of the hotel as a reading area. I'm sorry you don't feel that we are sophisticated enough to read good books."

"It's not that George, I just don't feel that I can carry that much extra inventory."

"Okay, I will have Steven order what we need, and we will sell them through the hotel. Susan, I understand, has been asking you to order books for her older students to read for extra credit." Clyde turned beet red at George's statement. He finally admitted that he had Susan's list and would order the books she wanted. "Never mind Clyde. I will include them with my order. Her students can come to the hotel to get the books they want," George said with sadness. Clyde had lost out on some good business because he felt that the residents of Rawlings were not capable of enjoying a good book and because he was angry at Susan for not noticing him.

Steven ordered a variety of books to be placed in the reading alcove of the lobby. Marie and Susan arranged comfortable chairs and put tables between the chairs so that they could be used for coffee or other drinks. It was a custom for some of the men from town to come into the hotel, have a cup of coffee with an evening cigar. The books, magazines and newspapers were an added treat for them.

Within two weeks, a crate of books arrived at the hotel. Susan and Marie unpacked them and set them on the shelves that Earl had built for them. If someone wanted to buy the book, George decided that the money would go into a fund to purchase more books. The long-term goal was to make this into a lending library. There should be no reason anyone should be deprived of reading just because they could not afford to buy the book.

The reading corner became a huge success. Many times, after school some of Susan's students would come in to read uninterrupted by younger brothers and sisters. During the day, some of the women would come in, borrow a book to read at home or sit and do their needlework and discuss the books they were reading. In the evening you could find men enjoying their cigars and a cup of coffee while reading the newspapers that were sent daily by mail.

Usually, George would spend a couple of hours a week reading. It was much quieter than trying to read at home when the children were clamoring for his attention. Ever since he was a small boy and the matron at the orphanage had taught him his letters and he had learned to read; he had wanted to read everything he could get his hands on. Reading about the Lewis and Clark expedition when he was young contributed to his obsession with seeing the Pacific Ocean. Even though life has gotten in the way lately, he still had the strong desire to see the ocean.

Irene had her nose in a book most of the time. She was as passionate about reading as her Papa and Aunt Susan were.

Anna, on the other hand, could care less about reading or schoolwork. She was interested in pretty dresses, new hair ribbons and gossiping about the other girls in her class. Marie was always admonishing her about comments she made about her fellow classmates. She made fun of their clothes, their hair, or the fact that they had to wear the same clothes every day because they didn't have any others.

Marie was very upset one day when she heard Anna talking to a friend and criticizing another girl for the clothes she wore and making that girl cry. Marie went to Anna's chest of drawers and found the oldest dress she had. "Anna, you will wear this dress to school tomorrow and every day for the rest of the week," Marie said with authority.

"But Mama," Anna cried, "that dress is ripped and too small for me. I can't be seen in that."

"You will be seen in this dress. For now, it is the only dress that you have. You seem to think that you are better than the other girls."

"You don't seem to realize that you have been blessed with a Papa who works long hours to give you what you want and need. You have been blessed with a grandma and two aunts who love you like you were their very own child and make sure that you have what you want. And you have been blessed because you are able to eat three meals a day. Some of the children in this community are lucky if they get one meal a day. Tonight, you will go to bed with just a piece of bread and butter for supper and learn what it feels like to go to bed hungry and get up in the morning hungry. Maybe you will learn how some of your schoolmates must live and you won't tease and bully them."

Anna went to bed that night with only a piece of bread and butter and a drink of water to wash it down. She was very hungry in the morning, but she had to go to school without any breakfast. She resisted putting on the old dress, but her Mama would not back down, and she put the dress on. She left for school without a ribbon in her hair and wearing an old pair of shoes. She walked very slowly with her head down, not wanting anyone to see how terrible she looked.

Marie walked the girls to school that morning so that she could let Susan know what was going on with Anna. Susan greeted her as she did all the students, seemingly not noticing the difference in her dress. As Marie walked back to the hotel, she hoped and prayed that a lesson would be learned today.

The other girls looked at Anna askance and laughed at her dress and shoes. They would not sit with her during recess or lunch. Susan sat beside Anna during lunch and noticed that Anna had tears in her eyes. "What's up sweet girl?" Susan asked.

"Mama made me wear this awful dress and these terrible shoes and would not let me put a ribbon in my hair. She would not let me eat supper last night. She is being unfair," Anna stormed.

"Well honey," Susan answered calmly. "I think she is trying to help you realize that just because someone doesn't have the prettiest dresses or isn't able to have three meals every day, doesn't mean that they are any less of a valuable person. They still deserve your friendship. I think your Mama is being very kind in showing you how the less fortunate feel."

While Susan called the rest of the students into the classroom, Anna thought about what she had said. She supposed she could be nicer to the other girls. Not even her own sister would sit with her.

Anna was very quiet that evening. She ate a good supper because she was very hungry, but she did not talk very much. When Marie asked her how her day was, she answered with one word, "Fine."

"Are you sick, girl?" Grandma Mary asked. "You are not your usual peppy self."

"No, I am fine, just tired. I think I will go to bed after dinner."

"That is certainly not like you." Grandma Mary said with concern in her voice.

After Anna excused herself from the table and had taken her plate to the kitchen, she went off to bed. Marie explained to her mother what had happened with Anna last night and today at school. Mary then understood Anna's mood. "I hope she learned something," Mary commented.

The next day, Anna was much friendlier at school and did not tease anyone and did not brag about the new hair ribbon she wore, but she still thought some of the girls were not worth having as friends because of the way they looked. She apparently had not learned much of a lesson from her day of looking bad and being hungry.

CHAPTER 11

In late November, the town was gearing up for the Christmas season. Clyde was busy ordering special things for the holidays and getting ready to decorate the store. George had already chosen the tree that he would cut down for the lobby of the hotel. The children would pick out a smaller tree for the house. Anna, Irene, and Charlotte were busy making decorations for both the trees. Marie had made some pretty centerpieces for the tables in the dining room.

There definitely was a festive feeling in the air. Jeff and Susan were eagerly anticipating their wedding in June. They were waiting for the house to be finished, enough for them to move into. Right now, however, the weather was not cooperating with them. It had been cold and icy, and the men had not been able to work on the construction. Most of them were busy making sure the cattle were safe and fed. They both spent hours going over the plans and making modifications when they had a new idea. Jeff still had not told Susan about the library being added. He wanted that to be a surprise for her. He was also seriously thinking of having indoor plumbing installed in the kitchen and bathroom. One of the first things he did before starting construction was to have a well dug, so water would be close at hand. He wasn't exactly sure how it was going to work, but the idea of not having to get up in the cold of winter and walk outside to the privy was beyond belief. Jeff was besotted with the idea of giving Susan all the modern luxuries that he could. Lord knew she did not have many during the time she was in Laramie.

During the second week in December, it started to snow, and it kept coming down for a week. Jeff was busy making sure that his cattle were safe. In anticipation of more bad weather, he had brought the herd closer to the cabin. He had six cows who were going to deliver in the Spring, so he put them in the corral. They were going to be the continuation of his herd.

Steven and Jane were having fun decorating their little home. Jane was almost five months pregnant at this point and getting very large. She was over the "sickness" time, but none of her clothes fit and she was getting tired very quickly. She was still working at the front desk at the hotel and was able to sit down most of the time. She spent her down time sewing baby clothes. Steven was watching over her like a mother hen. Mary and Marie were concerned about how large she was getting so early, and Mary mentioned that she thought she might have twins. Marie shuddered just thinking about having two at the same time.

George was planning menus for meals he wanted to make during the holidays. The Palouse Indians rode into town with two large deer for George to serve during the holidays. Because it was winter and the weather was below freezing at night, George was able to preserve the meat so that he could use it in a timely manner. After butchering the meat, he used the scraps and made mincemeat that Marie and Mary canned. He made pies out of mincemeat for the holidays. He and Marie wanted to do something special for the town this Christmas and decided to have a holiday party at the hotel for all their guests and neighbors. They would have music, dancing and sing Christmas Carols along with a buffet supper. It would be a big project for them, but they wanted to thank the community for their support during their first year and a half in Rawlings.

With the snow falling, the town looked like a fairyland. Even the railroad office had a tree in the window. The only home that had no decorations or signs of Christmas was the Kingman farm. Otis

Kingman wouldn't let his wife or children participate in any activities other than work on the farm.

The Saturday before Christmas was the day of the Seevers party. It had stopped snowing and the roads were passable. The neighboring ranchers started arriving in town about noon, far too early for the party, but Clyde had opened the store earlier and would leave it open later so people could purchase last-minute items for Christmas. Susan opened the schoolhouse so the children would have a warm place to play while they waited for their parents to take them to the party at the hotel.

Ray had the blacksmith shop open and was busy all day. Between the livery and the blacksmith, he needed help. He recruited one of the teenage sons of a rancher to help him in the livery while he was busy shoeing horses.

The party was a huge success. The townspeople and a lot of the ranchers and farmers from the surrounding area were there to thank the Seevers for bringing life back to Rawlings. Because of the hotel and dining room, the blacksmith and livery stable, the general store and the school opening up again, people were feeling that Rawlings was more than just a city for whiskey and women. It was becoming a place where families could shop, have a good meal out, go to church on Sundays and have their children get a good education.

Several of the Nez Perce and Palouse Indians stopped by to give George and Marie presents of antelope and deer that they had smoked and dried and small trinkets that they had made. They felt that George and Marie had helped them by settling in Rawlings also. It gave them a chance to sell their horses and to receive some of the benefits that the white man could provide them.

Both George and Marie thanked them profusely and asked them to stay for the festivities. Some of the townspeople were nervous about having the Indians there, but soon learned that they meant no harm. They clapped their hands to the music and especially enjoyed the carol singing. Freddie was very excited to see them. He had been to their village with his father, Aunt Susan and Jeff, and had made friends with some of their children.

On Christmas eve, the Seevers family went to church, then went home and attempted to get the children to bed at a reasonable hour. Jeff walked Susan home and then went back to the hotel. He would get up bright and early, go to pick up Susan and walk to George and Marie's for Christmas breakfast and gift opening. Mary would walk over from the hotel. Steven and Jane would also make an appearance. It would be a crowded little house on Christmas morning, but very joyful.

The children were up and very excited to see if their stockings had been filled with goodies or pieces of coal. There were hair ribbons and trinkets for the girls, some tin soldiers for Freddie and candies and nuts at the bottom of each stocking. Each child had a wrapped package under the tree. The girls all had pretty dresses for school and Freddie had a new shirt and pants. Marie had been busy sewing. George had several new chef's aprons and Marie's gift was a length of cloth she had admired at the general store.

Jeff surprised Susan with a carved sign to go over the gate at the entrance to the ranch. It said, "JSJ RANCH" for Jeff Susan Jordan Ranch. Susan was astonished that he would add her name to the ranch. He explained that the brand on his cattle would be JSJ also. In addition, he gave Susan a beautiful diamond ring that had belonged to his mother. It had a single solitaire diamond mounted in a gold band. She had tears in her eyes when he put it on her finger. Everyone else in the room was tearing up also.

Susan asked the whole family to bundle up and walk over to the livery stable. After they all crowded into a stall, she surprised Jeff with a large crate that he had to open. Ray was there with the necessary tools to open the crate. Jeff was at a loss as to what Susan would give him that was so big. He opened the crate to "oohs and aahs" from the rest of the family. Inside was a very large, beautiful oak desk and a chair for his study. He was without words at the gift he had been given.

After Jeff saw the desk, he made the decision to make the library that he was planning a combination library/study for both and to make the desk the centerpiece of the room. He would ask Susan to choose some occasional chairs to place around the room.

The day after Christmas was a quiet day with the dining room open in its normal hours. People came into town to shop and get their mail or to visit with friends and neighbors. That evening, it started to snow again and didn't stop for several days. After the snow stopped, the temperature went down to below zero and everything froze.

There was a New Years dance scheduled for the young people at the school, but it was cancelled because of the weather. Parents did not want their children out in the sub-zero weather.

Jeff was not able to come into town to see Susan. He was busy trying to keep his cattle fed and safe from predators. There were coyotes, mountain lions and wolves all looking for food. They were hungry and would go after any animal that they thought they could get.

Jeff and Earl managed to herd most of the cattle into a fenced area closer to the barn, but they had to be vigilant in watching them. The predators would come right into the area if they were not stopped. Either Jeff, Earl or one of the hands would stand watch all night long.

The harsh winter weather made Jeff more determined than ever to grow hay and alfalfa for winter feed. He also wanted to talk to George about building a grist mill along his stream. He thought that he had an ideal spot for one and the water in his stream flowed fast enough that only in the worst conditions did it freeze. The idea of being able to grind the wheat into flour locally was appealing to Jeff and he figured it would be to other growers also. It would save the month it took to get an order delivered from Portland.

Jeff missed Susan terribly. He was used to seeing her at least every weekend and sometimes in the middle of the week when he had to be in town to pick up supplies. She was quickly becoming the other half of him.

He did manage to get into town once to pick up supplies. He saw Susan for a few minutes but did not want to take too long. He wanted to get back before dark and the temperature went down even further.

The new year brought even more snow to the area and all the farmers were concerned about their livestock and their crops. Susan closed school for several days for fear the students would get lost in the snow and cold either on the way to school or going home. The hotel was still open, but with a skeleton crew. George wanted to be available in case someone got stuck in town or the train brought passengers in. He only prepared minimal food so any guests could have something to eat. He almost always had a pot of soup on the stove.

By the first of February, the snow had stopped but it was still very cold. Earl got back to working on the ranch house. Because the train didn't stop running because of the weather, the building supplies were arriving on a regular basis. The walls were up, and the beams were ready to be installed. Jeff had hired some additional hands to help with construction.

The barn and the corral were made larger and a bunk house was added to the side of the barn big enough for 10 hands to sleep. Jeff was living in the cabin. It was warm and comfortable, but he was hoping that the house would be finished enough to move in soon. Susan was willing to live in the cabin with him, but he hoped that she would not have to. He wanted to carry her over the threshold of their new home.

Jeff had written to his father inviting him to the wedding, but his father answered that he was not well enough to travel that far.

The next Saturday when Jeff was in town, he asked Susan, "How would you like to go to Chicago for a honeymoon? Dad's health isn't good enough for him to travel here for the wedding and I want you two to meet."

"That would be a great trip. I have never been east of Cheyenne and have never seen a big city," Susan replied.

"If it is okay, I will go ahead and make the arrangements," answered Jeff. Susan nodded and took Jeff's hand and kissed his fingers. "What was that for?" Jeff asked, smiling at her.

"Just because I love you and thank you for thinking of such a nice honeymoon."

March was a month of cold and rainy weather, but had days of clear, bright sunshine. Jeff and Susan's house was being built in record time. With the help of the extra men that Jeff had hired, Earl was able to accomplish a lot more in a shorter amount of time.

Jeff had hired some cowboys to help manage the herd. All of his pregnant cows had delivered successfully with only one calf in distress, but one of the cowboys was able to assist and the calf was fine.

Steven and Jane were getting anxious for their baby to arrive. Jane was very large and was having a hard time getting around. By the end of March, she was so large she needed help to get up from a chair. She was being kicked constantly and could hardly sleep at night. She just wanted the baby to be born.

On the third of April, Jane started going into labor. Mary, Marie, and Susan were called to Jane's house. The labor pains went on and on. After 14 hours, the ladies were getting worried because the baby wasn't anywhere near being born. They soothed Jane as much as possible and when she was finally ready to push, the baby popped right out at the third push. It was a baby boy but was fairly small for Jane being so large. All of a sudden, Jane screamed at another fierce pain, and she said she had to push again. She delivered another baby boy. Both babies were laid on her stomach and she cried with joy at the sight of her sons.

Marie went to the hotel to let Steven, George and Jeff know that Jane had safely delivered twin boys. They were not identical twins. One had blond fuzz on his head and the other had a full head of soft brown hair.

Steven was in shock at the idea of having two sons. George and Jeff were very pleased for him, slapped him on the back and said, "Good job, Brother!"

The boys were named Isaac Steven Taylor and John Lewis Taylor. They were good babies, ate well and only woke up once during the night. Jane recuperated quickly and seemed to be a natural mother.

The babies were the talk of Rawlings and a curiosity to the citizens of the town. Many of them had never seen twins before.

The month of May was very busy for Jeff and Susan. The school board had hired a new teacher to start in August. Susan was relieved that the children's education would not be interrupted. Their wedding was coming up very soon and all the women in the family were rushing to finish their specific projects for the ceremony. Marie was altering her wedding dress for Susan; Mary was completing some of the linens for the new house and Jane was putting together decorations for the tables at a reception to follow the ceremony.

The ranch house was finally ready to move in. All the rooms were not complete, but the master bedroom, the kitchen and the study were done to the point that

Jeff and Susan could live in them. Most of Susan's belongings had been moved to the ranch, along with the many crates of books. Jeff's desk had been moved from the livery stable out to the ranch and put into the study. It looked perfect in there. Susan had ordered some occasional chairs to be placed around the study. The rug for the floor was still to be ordered. Ray had made some andirons and a screen for the fireplace as a wedding present to them. They were a great addition to the room. Susan couldn't wait for her wedding and her first night in her new home.

Earl had crafted a beautiful mantle for the fireplace and Steven and Jane had given them a mantle clock.

The day of the wedding was finally here, and Susan was more relaxed than she thought she would be. Her sisters helped her dress, and her mother presented her with the pearl necklace that she wore the day she married Susan's father. The ceremony was about to begin when two Palouse Indians came in the door. They were dressed in all their ceremonial regalia. Some of the people there were shocked to see them there, but Jeff smiled at them and bowed a welcome. They stayed at the back of the room and watched their friend marry the lovely lady, Susan.

There was a reception at the hotel after the ceremony where everyone toasted the happy couple and ate some of the magnificent wedding cake that George had made. There were gifts given, both store bought, and handmade. The two Indians had given them a beautiful handwoven blanket. It was a special gift that meant so much to them because it was made especially for them. It was early in the evening when Jeff and Susan left the reception and headed for their new home.

Jeff had another surprise for his wife as they drove onto the property. The arch was completed across the road. He hung the "JSJ RANCH" sign on the arch above the road. It was now really their home. Jeff had officially registered the brand with the State, so their cattle would be branded and identified.

After an idyllic night in their new bedroom, Jeff and Susan were up early the next morning to drive into town and catch the train to Chicago. The whole family was there to see them off and wish them well on their trip. Jeff had ordered a sleeper room, so they would not have to sit up the whole way.

Susan was excited because Jeff had planned the trip with a stay in Cheyenne. They stayed at the hotel that her father worked in. It was fun to be nostalgic for a bit, but she was soon ready to move on.

When they arrived in Chicago, they were greeted by Jeff's father, Oliver Jordan. He was a very distinguished looking gentleman with white hair. He did not get out of his carriage, but when they got in the carriage, he greeted them both warmly. Jeff was astounded at the difference in his father. When Jeff was growing up, he always saw him as stiff and uncaring and never willing to listen to his opinions. Now he seemed to be the complete opposite. He wanted to know all about the ranch and how Jeff found the land to buy. He was impressed with what Jeff was building on the ranch. "I envy you that freedom Jeff," commented Mr. Jordan. "You are very wise to buy land. It is always a good investment."

Oliver was enamored with Susan, as she was with him. She fell in love with him immediately. It was obvious that Oliver was not well. Jeff remembered him as tall and always standing ramrod straight. Now he was bent at the shoulders and walked with a cane. He had a live-in caretaker and a housekeeper/cook who also lived in. It was rare when Oliver came downstairs to eat a meal, but while Jeff and Susan were there, he was down for supper every evening.

Jeff and Susan were to be home toward the third week in July but stayed two weeks longer. Jeff wanted to spend as much time as possible with his father. Susan was glad that they stayed longer. She got to know her father-in-law and learned about the family history. She learned to admire Oliver greatly. His wife,

Martha, had died when Jeff was four years old, and Oliver raised him with the help of a housekeeper. He had never remarried.

Susan had fun shopping for her mother, sisters, nieces, and nephew. She and Jeff also picked out some furniture for their home. Oliver offered her the pick of several pieces of furniture that were in Jeff's mothers' family. There were also porcelain China dishes and a beautiful silver tableware service that were a wedding present to Jeff's parents. "They will belong to Jeff when I am gone, but I want you to have them now. I have no further need for them," Oliver said with a tear in his eye. "Martha and I used them every Sunday while she was alive, but they have been used very few times since then. I will have someone come in and pack them safely for you. Perhaps it would be best for you to take the silver table service with you when you leave. It is not a very large box and should not be too cumbersome for you. They do need to be in your home now." Susan sat there with tears in her eyes as she listened to him speak of his wife and their life together. She thanked him and gave him a kiss on the cheek. He was tired and needed to rest after a long day of talking to Susan.

She supervised the packing of all the items they were taking home. There were crates of furniture and barrels of dishes. Jeff planned for the shipment to be on the same train that they were on going home.

On the day Jeff and Susan were leaving, Oliver presented them both with a leather bound first edition of Robert Lewis Stevenson's "Treasure Island." Susan was stunned at the gift and proclaimed it to be the best gift she had ever received. Jeff had told him how much she loved books and that he had a library room added to the house. Susan was overwhelmed at the generosity of her father-in-law.

Oliver made the effort to go with them to the train station. Among hugs and kisses, and a few tears, they boarded the train for Cheyenne. They would spend two days there and then head to Rawlings and their new home.

CHAPTER 12

The family came out in full force to greet the newlyweds when they returned to Rawlings. Jeff had wired George to ask that arrangements be made for all their crates and barrels be transported to the ranch. They would be stored in the barn until ready to unpack.

George had prepared a special meal for them and arranged for them to spend the night at the hotel. Mary and Marie had gone to the ranch to put new linens on the bed and arrange some flowers in the kitchen and study, but it was late when the train came in and Susan felt better getting a fresh start in the morning. She also wanted to spend a little time with her mother. After talking to Oliver and seeing Jeff interact with him, she wanted to make a connection with her mother again.

Steven, Jane, and the twins joined them for supper. The boys were happy babies and at almost five months old were sitting up by themselves and starting to cut teeth. Jane had gone back to work at the hotel desk. She was able to take the boys with her most days. Steven had set up a bed for them in his office for nap time and Mary took them for walks when the weather was not too hot. They always attracted a lot of attention when they were out and about.

The morning after their arrival home, Jeff and Susan piled up their wagon with their bags and some fresh food from the general store and headed to the ranch. Susan got a thrill when she rode under the "JSJ RANCH" sign at the beginning of the drive to their home. As they headed up the knoll to the house, they were amazed at the progress made to the exterior. The walls had been finished with brick up to the second story and painted to the roof line. It looked beautiful to Susan. Jeff pulled the wagon up to the front porch, got out and went around to help Susan down. He promptly picked her up in his arms and carried her over the threshold again. "Welcome home Mrs. Jordan," he said as he gave her a big kiss. "Welcome home yourself my love," Susan answered and kissed him right back.

Right about that time, Earl walked around the corner from the kitchen and laughed happily at seeing them there with their arms around each other. "Welcome home you two. Glad to have you back!"

"Earl, the place looks great. You have really outdone yourself while we were gone.yourself while we were gone. Thanks for the excellent work. Could you ask a couple of the boys to help carry in our bags from the wagon? Beware, there are a lot of them. They can put them in the room next to our bedroom for now. We will unpack from there. We will be having a couple of wagons coming out this afternoon with crates and barrels of things from my father's house in Chicago. Those will be stored in the barn until we decide where the furniture will go. Susan and I will take a walk around and see where we want things."

Jeff and Susan wandered into the kitchen and saw an almost completed room. There was a brand-new wood stove with a warming oven attached. The counters were beautifully finished oak and there were oak cabinets ready to be filled. A round oak table sat in the middle of the kitchen with eight matching chairs. They had ordered the table before they left, and it was delivered three days ago. As a surprise to Susan, Jeff had ordered a water pump for the kitchen so she would not have to haul water. She was overwhelmed at the additions made to the original plans.

From the kitchen, they walked into the study. They were pleasantly surprised to see the mantle installed over the fireplace and the andirons and screen that Roy had made for them all in place. There were long windows on each side of the fireplace and Jeff's desk was on the opposite side of the room. The walls were lined with shelves ready for Susan's books to be placed. Some of the occasional chairs that Susan had ordered would be replaced with the ones Oliver had given them and Jeff would ask Earl to build a special stand for the special book that Oliver had given to them.

They walked into their bedroom and saw what Mary and Marie had done. They put new linens on their bed and put the beautiful quilt that Mary had made for Susan years ago and not had the chance to give to her. The whole room looked beautiful. They started unpacking their cases when Susan said, "Jeff, I know you are anxious to get out to see the progress on the rest of the ranch and to see your herd. I can take care of this unpacking. You go ahead and inspect your land. If I have any questions, they will wait until you get back. Also, I will see what I can make for supper. I will cook our first meal in our new home."

"Thank you. I am anxious to get out and see what progress has been made on the barn, bunkhouse, and corral. Also, I wanted to ask you what you thought about my asking Earl to be the foreman of JSJ. I trust him to make the right decisions about the ranch. He and I have the same vision for it. I also would ask if he would like to move into the cabin."

"I think that is a great plan. He has done a great job of overseeing the property while we were gone and I see no reason for that to change," answered Susan.

Earl had brought to the kitchen the box marked pots and pans and cooking utensils, so Susan was able to unpack what she needed for the evening's supper. She was excited about fixing her first meal for them.

Jeff wanted to ride up to the cabin to clean out the last few personal things he had in there before he offered it to Earl. As he was coming out of the house to walk to the barn and saddle a horse, he noticed Earl walking down to the barn also. "Hey, wait up Earl!" hollered Jeff. "I'd walk with you. I have something I want to discuss with you."

"Did I screw up boss?" asked Earl.

"No, not at all. In fact, you did an outstanding job of overseeing the ranch and the building of the house. We do appreciate your efforts. To show you how much we appreciate you and your dedication, we would like to ask you to be foreman of the JSJ."

Earl stopped walking and just looked at Jeff. "You're kidding, aren't you?" Earl questioned.

"No, I am very serious. Susan and I talked about it, and we think you are the best person for the job. We know you and trust you," Jeff told him.

"Boss, it would be my pleasure to be foreman of your ranch. I feel that I have a stake in it, what with building the house and overseeing the ranch while you were gone. Thanks so much!"

"Come ride to the cabin with me. I need to pick up a few things and move them to the house," Jeff said.

When Jeff and Earl reached the cabin, Jeff went in to get his things. Earl stayed outside looking at the porch that he had added to the cabin earlier in the year. One of the steps needed a couple of nails to make it more secure. He would have to make sure that it was done. When Jeff came out, he said, "Earl, how would you like to live in this cabin. The foreman of a ranch needs a place to do his paperwork uninterrupted. This would be a great place for you to live and work and it is close to the bunkhouse, barn, and corral."

"You are full of surprises today. I would love to live here. It gets pretty noisy in the bunkhouse, and it is hard to read and concentrate. Again, thanks boss!" said Earl.

One afternoon when Jeff and two other cowhands were riding the perimeter of his property, they came to the stream, dismounted, and let the horses drink their fill and rest awhile. They had been discussing where to plant hay and alfalfa for winter feed for the herd. They needed an area that had good irrigation and easy access to a road to facilitate harvest and getting it to storage. They would have to build some sort of structure for storage.

At the same time, Jeff remembered his idea of building a grist mill on or near the stream. The stream was large enough and flowed fast enough to dam it and make a pond below to support a waterwheel that would generate the power to run the grinding wheel.

Jeff wanted to talk to both George and Earl about his idea. George was a big user of flour in the restaurant. He had heard George complain about the time it took to get a shipment from Portland. He also wanted to talk to Clyde about purchasing flour locally instead of from Portland.

The head of the school board in Dayton had finally notified Susan that a new teacher had been hired for the Rawlings school. Fiona MacGregor is a 29-year-old widow from New York City. She was in Cheyenne visiting relatives and read the advertisement in the paper about Rawlings needing a full-time teacher and decided to apply. The school board approved her application sight unseen. She was due to arrive in town any day.

Fiona Mary MacGregor arrived in Rawlings via train from Cheyenne in August 1886. She was like a whirlwind, full of energy and ready for any adventure.

Susan, Jeff, George, and Marie were at the station to meet her. She was to stay at the hotel until her belongings arrived. A small house on the edge of town was purchased by the county to accommodate the teacher. The extra room at the school that Susan lived in was being incorporated into the classroom. It would also increase the space for church services on Sunday and for dances and other get-togethers. The townspeople were excited to have the extra room.

Fiona was escorted to the hotel, where her luggage was waiting in a room for her. She would move into the little house when all her belongings arrived. She was a small, petite woman with a huge personality. She talked all the way across the street to the hotel. As she came into the hotel, she took off her hat and revealed bright red hair and the bluest eyes the group had ever seen. She was tired from all of the traveling. She had been in Cheyenne visiting some of her deceased husband's relatives when she read about the job in Rawlings. With her husband gone and no ties to New York, she decided to have an adventure. She was also ready to settle down and teach again. When she got married, she had to quit teaching and she missed the challenge and joy of molding children's minds. It was good to be back in the classroom.

"I am very anxious to see where I will live and teach, but I am very tired. It has been a long trip," Fiona said.

"The school should be in good shape. They have taken the room that I lived in and incorporated it into the school. Your house is about a half mile away from the school building. A horse and buggy will be provided for your use. We do have some pretty cold weather during the Winter months. Last Winter, school was closed for over a week because of weather," Susan explained.

Mary brought her grandchildren to meet Mrs. MacGregor. The three girls all shook her hand and whispered hello. Freddie held back close to his grandma. "This is my son Freddie. He will be starting school in September," Marie explained.

"Hello Freddie. I am very pleased to meet you," Fiona said with a very soft smile on her face.

Susan explained to Fiona, "There are about 20 students now. Some of them don't come on a regular basis. It depends on what time of year it is. Work on the farm or ranch comes before school."

Fiona was glad to get to her room, take off her traveling clothes and relax. She had been on a train for a long time and had not had a chance to rest well since her stay in Cheyenne, so she was ready for a hot bath and a soft bed.

After a good night's sleep, Fiona woke early, dressed and went in search of coffee. She needed her black coffee to get her started in the morning. She wandered into the dining room, found it empty, so went through the door to the kitchen. She found George and two of his assistants taking freshly baked bread out of the oven and putting more into the oven. The smell was heavenly.

"Excuse me, Mr. Seevers," Fiona said. George jumped and almost dropped a tray of bread.

"Yes, Mrs. MacGregor, what can I do for you?"

"I would love a cup of coffee if you have it made this early," Fiona asked.

"We always have coffee on the stove. If you give me a minute, I will pour you a cup."

"Point me in the right direction and I can pour myself a cup," answered Fiona. George nodded to the back of the large stove. The coffee pot was there with a row of cups on a shelf beside it.

She poured herself a cup, thanked George with a nod and wave and went into the lobby to look around. She noticed the reading alcove and went over to see what it was. She was impressed with the variety of books that were displayed, from nursery rhymes to old masters to some new authors making names for themselves. Fiona set her coffee cup on the table and picked up a book of poetry by Lord Byron. She was amazed when she saw the variety of poetry books available. Not only Lord Byron, but Longfellow, Poe, Thoreau, Walt Whitman and several others. She wondered if the books were there for show or if people really sat and read them. She looked at the rows of other books and found Dickens, Washington Irving, Herman Melville, Mark Twain, James Joyce and many others. Who in this little town would have put together such a library. There was also a shelf of children's books; Little Women, Heidi, Treasure Island and more.

George found her standing and staring at all of the wonderful books. "Do you like my reading corner?" he asked.

"You did all this?" Fiona said, stunned and amazed that a hotel owner and cook would have such an interest in good literature.

"Yes! I have been an avid reader since I was a small boy and want to surround myself and my children with the best available. Susan, my sister-in-law, was the driving force behind this reading corner. It works very well for some of the people on outlying farms and ranches. They are able to take a book with them to read, but must return it before they take out another," George explained.

Fiona just shook her head in wonder. "I have some time free now. If you would like to gather your things together, I would be happy to show you your new home. The rest of your belongings should arrive by train later today," George explained. Fiona nodded and rushed up to her room to pack her things.

CHAPTER 13

When George got back from taking Fiona to her house, Marie was waiting for him with tears in her eyes. "Sweetheart, what's wrong? Why have you been crying?"

"Because, I am pregnant again," Marie wailed and dissolved against George in sobs. "How am I going to handle the four children we have plus another one?" she cried.

George kissed her and wiped away her tears. "My darling, we will handle this precious baby the same way we have the others, with patience and lots of love. There is nothing you and I cannot handle as long as we are together," George assured her. Marie snuggled in his arms and wondered how in the world she was lucky enough to have found her precious husband.

Mary came into the room and saw George holding an obviously distraught Marie and instantly thought something had happened to one of the children. "What's wrong?" she cried.

"Nothing's wrong," said George. "Marie was just telling me we are going to have another baby!"

"Oh, how wonderful. I did think it would be Jeff and Susan next, but I am so thrilled for you."

"Mama, how am I going to manage five children?"

"You will, my daughter, you will," Mary said with emphasis on the "will".

It was quickly known around town that Marie was expecting another baby. She was still dismayed at the idea of having a fifth child but was feeling well and able to do her normal activities without any discomfort. She tried not to think about it too much. It would become a reality soon enough. Irene and Charlotte were excited about having another baby in the house. Anna was mortified and embarrassed that her mother got pregnant again. She wanted nothing to do with a new baby.Freddie could have cared less. His only comment was that it would be nice to have a brother. They were all old enough to realize that they would have some responsibility for taking care of the baby. The girls were hoping for a brother so that he could share a bedroom with Freddie. Their room was already too crowded.

George thought that it was time to build an additional room onto their house. It would be very crowded with one more person in the house, even a very little one. He talked to Jeff about asking Earl to come and see what needed to be done to the house to add a room.

Earl made a trip into town for supplies and came to the hotel to see George. "Earl, as you might have heard, Marie is going to have another child and our house is bursting at the seams now. We need another room added on. I know that you probably don't have the time to do it yourself, but could you recommend someone in the area?"

Earl shook George's hand and said, "Congratulations, George! Let's go over to your house and look to see what you have in mind."

As they walked, Earl told George that he would not be able to do the work himself, but he could probably recommend someone who could. It did not sound like a very complicated job.

The town of Rawlings continued to grow. New people were arriving all the time and were looking for property to buy. There was still land available in the town of Rawlings and the surrounding area. With more railroads making Rawlings a stop, the availability of services was growing also.

Jeff was still thinking about the possibility of building a grist mill but had not found anyone willing to run it. He needed to build the mill itself and a water wheel to power the grindstone. There had been an old steamboat blown up on the Snake River and it was towed to Rawlings for salvage. Jeff thought maybe if the engine was still in decent shape, it could be used as alternate power for the mill. He talked to both Earl and Ray Clausen about the idea. They thought it would work but had to examine the engine to see if it was still able to be used or how much repair was needed. Jeff needed to talk to a few more of the people around the area and especially the wheat farmers to see if this was an idea that they could and would support. He knew some of the ranchers were interested in growing corn. Maybe it could be ground into corn meal for human use. Jeff had a lot of things to think about and decisions to make. Right now, he needed to talk to his wife about some of these ideas.

Susan and Jeff discussed some of the ideas that he had and decided that maybe a town meeting would be in order. Neither one of them knew if a town meeting had ever been held, but the thoughts and ideas of the farmers were needed to help make the town grow. If the farmers and ranchers were not behind the idea of a grist mill, it would not pay to build one.

Jeff asked George what he thought about a meeting of the entire population. "I think it is a grand idea. The input of everyone is important in helping to make a town grow. I will see if the girls will make some notices to put around town," George stated. "Let's make it at 6:30 PM on Friday, September 17th. The weather should still be good at that time, and it will be light enough for people to get home. I will arrange for some refreshments to be served after the meeting."

George would plan to double the volume of food in the dining room that evening. He thought that many people would come into town early. He also anticipated that the hotel rooms would be full. Activities would be planned for the children so they would not disturb their parents during the meeting. Susan agreed to keep a record of what was said at the meeting so that, if decisions were made, no one could deny the facts.

On the 17th of September, people started coming into town early. Clyde was doing a brisk business at the store. Some of the outlying ranchers did not get to town very often and it was exciting for them to see what was new in the store. Steven kept the post office open past the 3 PM closing time so that people could pick up their mail or post letters to go on the next train. Ray was busy tending horses at the livery. There was not enough room for all the animals, so many of them were tied to the rail outside the hotel.

Many of the ranchers and their families came into town to meet the new schoolteacher. Jeff thought that he would introduce her before the meeting started. Fiona was so bright, active, and engaging that he thought it would be a good ice breaker for the beginning of the meeting. Fiona, in turn, was anxious to visit with the parents. It could answer some questions that she had about their child's attitude towards school and the need to attend.

The dining room at the hotel was very busy from noon on the 17th. Fortunately, George had asked three boys from town to come in to help him. Anna and Irene helped to serve the meals as well as Marie and Jane. George had made a good, hearty venison stew. The carrots, onions and potatoes were just harvested, and the venison came from the Palouse Indians. Along with a large slice of fresh bread, the meal was delicious. Everyone praised George's expertise in the kitchen.

People started coming into the school at 6 PM. They were visiting with friends and neighbors that they had not seen for a while and talking about these new people in town. The Seevers and the Taylors and the Jordans had moved into town within the last two years and really stirred things up. Most of the townspeople thought it was for the better.

At precisely 6:30, Jeff got up and asked the people to find a seat or line up against the walls. "Hello! My name is Jeff Jordan and I have purchased and founded the JSJ Ranch just south of town. It was my idea to call this town meeting. But before we get into the business at hand, I wanted to introduce you to the new schoolteacher especially since I took the previous teacher off the teaching market by marrying her," Jeff explained among the laughter of the audience. "Ladies and Gentlemen, may I present Mrs. Fiona Mary MacGregor. Mrs. MacGregor comes to us from New York City."

Fiona stood and acknowledged the clapping of the crowd. "Thank you so much Mr. Jordan. I also want to thank you everyone for your interest in your children's education. It is vital for their future that they have as good an education as can be presented to them. I do require a lot of work and dedication from the children, and we work hard, but we also have a lot of fun. Please feel free to come to me at any time if you have questions about your child's progress or about the way I am teaching them. I look forward to meeting all of you." Fiona sat down then, and Jeff proceeded with the reason for the town meeting.

"As most of you know, there was a damaged steamboat hauled into the yard and will be scrapped for salvage. We ranchers and farmers could purchase the steam engine at a reasonable price. Ray Clausen and Earl Kingman, both assure me that the engine is repairable and can be used again."

"Let me give you a little background on my idea. As most of you know, there is a good-sized stream on my property that flows into the river. I propose that we build a grist mill there and use the steam engine as a power source to run the mill." There was a lot of murmuring in the crowd and a lot of questions were asked, but Jeff said, "Let me finish and I will be glad to answer your questions. The stream on my property has enough down slope to it and the current is strong enough to power a backup water wheel if necessary."

"Yea, but you would own the mill. What would you charge us to have our wheat ground into flour?" came a question from the back of the crowd.

"I would charge you nothing because I would not own the mill. I propose to lease the necessary portion of the land to either the city of Rawlings or whoever owns the mill with a 99-year lease for $1.00 per year."

"Why would you do that? What is the trick?" came another question.

"No trick," said Jeff. "I am thinking of growing a few acres of wheat and think it would be more financially feasible to ship the flour itself than ship the raw wheat. Also, our lovely wives would have a steady supply of flour to bake with."

"What do you think Clyde?" asked Jeff. "Wouldn't you rather have a steady supply of local flour to sell instead of relying on your orders to get here before you run out?"

"Sure would, Jeff!" answered Clyde.

"Who would run the mill?" asked someone else.

"We would have to advertise for someone who would be willing to move here and run the mill. That someone would have to be knowledgeable about the whole business including what kind of stone or stones we would need."

"I did not want to proceed with this project without knowing whether you ranchers who are growing wheat would want to sell locally. Let me see a show of hands from those in favor of me proceeding with the steam engine and placing an advertisement in large city newspapers." There were some people who did not raise their hands, but most of them did. "If it is the consensus of the majority of those present, I will contact newspapers to run an ad for someone who would be interested in running a grist mill. I will also contact an attorney to draw up papers to lease the area needed to either the city or the owner of the mill, whichever is decided at the time, for 99 years at $1.00 per year."

"The logistics of building the mill will come if we can find someone who knows something about running a grist mill and can give us some guidance," Jeff added.

"Is there anything else anyone would like to add?" Jeff asked.

One of the outlying ranchers said, "Could we have these meetings on a regular basis? It felt good to be included in the discussion and decisions of the town. Even though we don't live in town, we rely on the town for our supplies and for information about what's going on in the area."

George answered the rancher, "I see no reason why we can't have a town meeting two or three times a year or more often if needed. Even if there is no real business to talk about, it makes for a good social get-together." Someone else shouted out, "How about a Friday night dance?" Everyone clapped in agreement. Someone else brought up the idea of a fair showing animals and having prizes and ribbons for baking and canning.

"All of these are great ideas. Let's see about getting a committee together to plan some of these events. Because of the harvest and the colder weather beginning soon, we probably would not be able to get anything going before Spring. Thanks so much for coming tonight. There are refreshments at the back of the room. Have a safe trip home," added Jeff.

Fiona was standing at the front of the room. Several of her students brought their parents up to meet her. She was very glad they did. In some cases, meeting them answered questions she had about their attitude towards school and learning. Some of the fathers felt that it was not necessary for their children to go to school beyond the 6th grade. They were only going to be farmers; what did they need more schooling for?

Fiona had her work cut out for her. She had to figure out a way to teach the children that they were worthy of more education and that it would be useful in their later life. Young girls needed to know how to add fractions if they wanted to double or triple a recipe. Young men needed to know if they were being paid fairly for a crop. If the price of corn is $1.50 a bushel and they have 8 bushels to sell, how much are they going to get? They won't always be able to rely on the honesty of the merchant.

Fiona had to devise practical lesson plans for both the boys and the girls. Somehow, she was going to involve the parents also.

One Saturday when Fiona was going into the dining room for lunch, she saw Susan with her mother come into the lobby. "Hello, Mrs. Lewis, Susan," greeted Fiona. "It is good to see you again." Mary excused herself to go to her room for a few minutes. "Susan, do you suppose I could talk to you for a few minutes?" asked Fiona.

"Certainly. Mama and I were just going to have lunch. Will you join us?" asked Susan.

When Mary returned, the three of them went into the dining room and sat at a table near the back so they could talk. Each of them ordered a bowl of chicken soup with bread. Fiona explained to Susan her dilemma with the continued schooling of some of the farmers' children.

"First of all, you need to understand that those children will miss a lot of school days. In the Winter, the weather will prevent them from getting to school. In the Spring, they are needed to help with the births of the baby animals and planting. In the fall is the harvest and they are needed to help with that. That leaves the summer and school is not in session then. If the farmers want a crop brought in at all, they need their children's help. With so few days left, they are not expecting to learn very much. Their parents don't expect it and therefore, neither do they. It is a hard life for those kids. They start working very early in the morning and work late into the evening," Susan explained. "Part of your job will be to change the parents' mindset, not the child's. The children will do what their parents tell them to."

"How am I to teach them?" questioned Fiona.

"You cram as much knowledge into them in a short amount of time as you can. You send assignments and papers home with them that explain the work they are doing, and you praise them every chance you get. Some of them get very little of it at home and they do crave it. Even if they are dirty and tired, praise them for making the effort to get to school that day. Give them special little jobs, make them feel needed and important in the classroom," Susan said. "You have to make them want to come to school. I went through this same thing with my students in Laramie," Susan explained.

"Thank you, Susan. You have given me a lot to think about. Now I have to make a lesson plan that will give them as much practical information as possible in just a few weeks."

The harvest was already in full swing and the students who needed the extra help were not in class. Hopefully after the harvest, the weather would not get too bad, and the students would be able to get to school.

Fiona made charts for the girls on dry and wet food measurements and how to read a recipe and increase or decrease the ingredients. For the boys, she made charts showing how much 1 bushel of corn was worth, then showing how to double or triple that amount depending on how much they were selling. She wanted to make it easier for the students to figure out if they were being paid what was owed to them. She also wanted to impress on them and on their parents that an education was valuable to them in any job they would be doing.

CHAPTER 14

Steven and Jane's twins were crawling now and getting into things all the time. Their parents had to be on guard all the time so that they would not get hurt. Jane was working at the hotel desk again and usually took the boys with her to work. Steven had an area set aside in his office for them and Grandma Mary took them to her room for their nap in the afternoon.

All of Mary's grandchildren were growing and doing well. Anna, Irene, and Charlotte were all doing well in school. Anna still had problems with her attitude and would slip up and get in arguments with her mother and sisters and brother sometimes. Irene still had her nose in a book most of her spare time. She was like her Papa and Aunt Susan when it came to reading. Charlotte was still prone to tantrums when she did not get her way, but she was growing up and realizing that the tantrums got her nowhere. She was growing out of her obsession with Freddie also.

She still watched out for him and made sure that he was safe but was not as possessive about him.

Marie was feeling much better with this pregnancy than with any of the four previous ones. She was able to do all the sewing and needlework that she had done before along with helping George in the kitchen when she was needed. She was looking forward to having this baby now. She knew that her family, except for Anna, was excited about having another baby in the household and so was she now. Anna resented anything that was not centered around her. The whole family had tried to give her a sense that everyone in the family was important and should be respected for who they are, but Anna did not seem to grasp that idea. Unfortunately, George and Marie spoiled her terribly when she was a baby, and she was used to getting what she wanted. They were trying to treat all of the children equally and Anna did not like it. She felt that since she was the oldest, she should have the most and the best. Her family was getting used to her tirades and just ignored her. She did not like that at all, but so far, she had not retaliated. They were all expecting something to happen, but they didn't know what or when.

Steven's job as postmaster was not a demanding job, but he was kept busy doing the books for the hotel, and restaurant. He continued to do all the ordering for both the hotel and dining room.

One evening after he closed the store, Clyde went to visit Steven and Jane. They had just finished their supper and Jane was putting the boys to bed when Clyde knocked on the door.

"Hello Clyde," Steven said surprised to see him at his door. "Come in. It's cold out there. What can I do for you?" inquired Steven. "I have something to talk over with you and something to ask," Clyde said. Jane came into the room at that time and was also surprised to see Clyde standing there. "Hello Clyde. Please have a seat. Would you like a cup of coffee? It's pretty cold outside," Jane asked. "Yes, please," Clyde answered uncomfortably. He was embarrassed talking in front of Jane. "I'm having a hard time keeping up with the ordering and the books at the store. I was wondering if I could hire you to take over that part of the business. I honestly don't understand the ordering that well and am not good at keeping up with the paperwork. I understand you take care of the ordering and the books for the hotel, dining room and Ray's blacksmith shop and livery. Do you suppose you could find the time to help me out?" begged Clyde.

Steven looked at Jane and she gave him a slight nod. He had been wanting to build up a business as an accountant and this was a good addition.

"Clyde, If I were to do this for you, I would require a complete audit of your books to date before I could begin." "But I haven't done anything wrong, I just can't keep up," Clyde questioned. "I am not accusing you of doing anything wrong. It is just good business practice. I would require this of anyone I would accept as a client. An audit is a starting point. It is a protection for both of us."

"As far as the ordering is concerned, I can do that for you. Just give me a weekly list of what you need and where you order from, and I will add it to the orders that I make for the hotel and dining room. You will receive an invoice with each order, and it is due in five days from receipt of the merchandise. It will be your responsibility to add the goods to your inventory list," Steven explained. "Every business must have a process of checks and balances. The audit and the inventory are part of that process."

"Thanks Steven. I will get you the information you need for the audit. You will have complete access to my books, although you might find them a bit confusing. I am not an accountant, nor did I do well in Math at school, so I won't profess that the books are in good order," reiterated Clyde.

"I want you to know that the results of the audit will determine if I take the job and what I will charge you for my work. I am not inclined to clean up drastic mistakes that you have made. It will be up to you to take responsibility for what errors there might be," Steven said.

"I understand and thanks Steven. I will have everything ready for you. Thanks, Mrs. Taylor, for the coffee. Good evening," said Clyde appreciatively.

After Clyde was gone, Steven looked at Jane and said, "I'm afraid this job will become more complicated as time passes. I will be interested to see his inventory and ordering habits. I know Susan had a hard time getting him to order some books that she wanted, and I know he has run out of items in the store that should always be in stock. We'll see!"

"Sweetheart why don't you open a business doing accounting. You already have the hotel, restaurant, blacksmith, and livery. Now it looks like you will have the store," asked Jane.

"I will have to hire an assistant if I take on more work. Ordering alone will become a full-time job with the addition of the store," mused Steven.

"Maybe there is a young student in school who is proficient in math who would be interested in working after school and possibly on Saturday," Jane thought out loud. "You wouldn't have to pay them as much and you would be giving someone an opportunity to learn a trade," Jane added.

"That is a great idea. I will talk to Fiona about getting a student helper," said Steven.

"You might also talk to Susan. She probably knows some of the students' abilities a little better," Jane commented.

"I will do that and thanks for the great suggestion," Steven said as he put his arms around his wife. Just then, one of the twins started to cry and they both knew that if one started, then the other would follow. "Never fails!" they both said in unison as they chuckled and went to tend to their crying child.

The holidays were quiet this year. The weather was terrible with wind and snow making the roads almost impassable. School was closed until the weather cleared enough for it to be safe for the children to get to and from classes. Clyde's business suffered. There were very few people coming into the store. It was well into the new year before he saw a customer from one of the outlying ranches.

Steven finished the audit and inventory of Clyde's books. All was well, except for a few small errors and they would have to be addressed. He figured out a price to charge for his services and felt it was reasonable and fair. The ordering of supplies would have to be separate, and he would have to set up a system so that each person ordering supplies would get a separate bill, even though the orders would go in together. There could be times that the orders for the store would be the same as the orders for the dining room. He would have to set up a system that would be easy to teach to a part-time helper.

Steven talked to both Fiona and Susan about a young student who would be capable of working part-time and be qualified to do the bookwork involved in ordering supplies. He would prefer a young boy as there would be heavy lifting of boxes and crates. Both Fiona and Susan recommended the same young boy. He was 15 years old, strong, and very good at numbers. He lived just outside of town on a small farm his father owned. He had two younger brothers and an older sister. His mother was dead, and his father was trying very hard to keep the family together. They could use the extra money. His name was Leo Gregory. He was very excited to work for Steven and learn a new business. Farming was not his favorite thing to do, and he did not want to be a farmer for the rest of his life. He had dreams of seeing far-away places when he grew up. Leo's father thought that this might be a change of luck for the Gregory family.

Jane was excited about the extra income Steven's business would bring into the family. She and Steven wanted to add another room to their small home, but they could not afford it. This increased income would help them to save faster for that addition. Jane was still working part-time at the hotel desk. She enjoyed the work and meeting the people who came into the hotel, but she wanted more time at home with her boys. Mary watched them a lot during the day, but Marie would have another baby soon and possibly Susan would become pregnant. Jane knew that her mother's time would be spent helping with new babies. This additional income from Steven's business would hopefully make it possible for her to quit working altogether and stay home with her boys.

George had hired a young boy just graduated from high school to work the night shift at the front desk. His name was Jake Leoni. The last train coming into Rawlings was the 8:45 PM train coming from Lewiston on Monday, Wednesday, and Friday. There were often passengers who would need a hotel room for the night. Jake worked those nights when the train came in.

Ray Clausen had a small room behind the post office and if anyone needed assistance on nights Jake did not work, Ray was always there to help.

Mary Lewis was getting tired. She was glad she had her own room at the hotel, but it didn't give her the privacy she was hoping for. Her girls still needed her to help with the grandchildren and it seemed that she had one or more of them with her all the time, day, and night.

She was coming up on the 10th anniversary of Fred's death. It was hard for her to believe it had been 10 years. She still mourned him daily. She had had several suiters throughout the 10 years, but she spurned them all. In her eyes, no one could compare with Fred Lewis.

Mary was forever grateful to George for asking her to join him and Marie on their move to Portland and then to Rawlings. It was very scary for her. She had never lived outside of Cheyenne. The trip itself was scary for her, but she was with her family and that was all that mattered. She was immensely proud of her daughters. They were married to fine men who had careers that they loved and took excellent care of their wives and children. She knew that Fred would be pleased with them as well.

CHAPTER 15

Jeff was still looking for someone to run a grist mill. He had advertised in all the large papers on the West Coast. He had only one response from a man in San Francisco who said he would be willing to learn the business, then asked what a grist mill was. He would have to start advertising again, but in Boise, Cheyenne, Denver, and points East. He didn't want to proceed with construction until he had someone to run it who knew what a grist mill was.

In the meantime, the running of the ranch, even with Earl as a very capable foreman, was a full-time job. The winter weather had been so bad, and he was worried about his pregnant cows. Earl and the hands had herded them to a fenced area behind the barn where it was easier to watch them, but Jeff was still out every day with the rest of the hands making sure that the animals were safe from predators and were being given enough feed. He had found the remains of two pregnant cows while riding near his property line. It looked like they were killed by wolves. Because of the depth of the snow, the animals were probably stuck and couldn't get away. It hurt Jeff to lose any animal for any reason, but he did understand that it was the natural progression of life and he had to accept it.

Jeff wanted to make a trip to the Palouse Indian village as soon as the weather permitted. He wanted to purchase four more horses from them and to take some meat and supplies to them. He wanted the additional horses to build up his herd and to have extra mounts for the cowboys in case their horse would come up lame. He was also looking for a special horse for Susan. He had wanted to get her one for Christmas but could not find the perfect horse for her.

Susan was having fun decorating their home. Some of the furniture that they had ordered on their honeymoon was finally starting to arrive in Rawlings. Since most of the pieces that they ordered had to be custom made, they had taken a long time to arrive. She was having fun arranging and rearranging the furniture to see what looked best. Jeff never knew if the place would look the same as the day before.

"It's a good thing I am not blind," teased Jeff. "I would trip and fall over furniture every time I walked into the house. Hopefully, the rest of the pieces we ordered will be in soon and I can get everything in its proper place."

"It had better be delivered soon because I am not going to be able to do a lot of furniture soon," Susan said with a contented look on her face.

Jeff looked at Susan with a worried look, "Are you sick?" Jeff asked worriedly.

"No, but we are going to have a baby in about 8 months, and I probably won't be able to move anything very large," Susan declared.

Jeff got a huge grin on his face, gave a great war whoop, and picked her up and spun her around. He gave her a big kiss, set her down and said very forcefully, "You are not to move anymore furniture by yourself. I don't want you to hurt yourself or the baby."

"I won't hurt either one of us. I will be very careful," promised Susan.

Jeff was smiling most of the time now. Even when he was out feeding the cattle, he was smiling. His ranch hands had heard the news and thought the boss was a little addled but were happy for him. All the hands liked working on the JSJ Ranch. They liked Jeff and appreciated his fairness to all of them. They had good working conditions and a good, warm place to live and plenty to eat. Jeff never asked them to do anything that he wouldn't do himself.

Susan was feeling sick in the morning and didn't get going on her daily chores as early as she usually did. She found that if she ate some bread right after she woke up, she wasn't as sick. She knew from her sisters' experiences that the sickness would pass.

One Sunday morning Jeff and Susan were headed into town on Sunday morning for church and dinner with the family. They had not made the announcement about the baby yet and were planning on telling them at dinner.

Susan woke up feeling especially sick that morning. She couldn't keep any food down and only wanted to go back to bed. Jeff was worried about her and sent one of the hands into town to let George and Marie know that they would not be there for church or dinner. "Do not say anything to them about the baby," admonished Jeff. "None of the family know yet. Just say she is not feeling well."

"Okay boss!" answered the ranch hand.

As the cowboy rode into town, he saw Marie standing on the porch of the hotel. He stopped and told her the Jordan's wouldn't be in town. "The Missus is not feeling so good and is staying home," he told Marie. Marie thanked him and went inside to gather her family together to walk to church. She worried about all her family when they did not feel well but wasn't overly concerned about Susan.

After Jeff spoke to the ranch hand, he went back to Susan, "Are you feeling any better sweetheart?" he asked her lovingly.

"A little, but only when I'm lying down. When I sit or stand, I get a dizzy feeling and a backache," answered Susan. She dozed off then and Jeff sat with her for a while.

Suddenly, Susan woke up with a gasp of pain and she was bleeding. She knew she was losing the baby. Jeff yelled down the stairs for someone to ride into town and get Susan's mother and sister and bring them out to the ranch.

He got some towels to try to stop the bleeding, but it did not slow down. Susan was very weak and was crying between the pains.

The bleeding had finally slowed down a bit and Susan was sleeping lightly. Jeff never left her side, wiping her forehead with a cool cloth and telling her he loved her.

Almost an hour had passed before Mary and Marie came rushing into the bedroom. Jeff explained to them what was happening, that Susan was pregnant, and she was bleeding badly.

Mary shoved Jeff out of the room then and turned to Marie who was checking on Susan. Susan knew she had lost her baby. "Oh Mama, I lost it before I could even tell you," Susan cried. As Marie was cleaning her up, Mary was washing her face and trying to soothe her, but Susan was bereft. "Mama, I waited so long after Gerald died and thought I would never love again. Then Jeff came into my life and my world changed completely. Mama, I so wanted to give him this baby," Susan sobbed.

"Hush my daughter," Mary said gently. "You will fill this house with children. I know you wanted this one and you will mourn it always, but there will be others."

Mary and Marie had cleaned her up and changed her bedding when Susan finally was able to go into a deep sleep. They left when Jeff came back into the room to sit with Susan. He sat up on his side of the bed and just held her with tears streaming down his face. He too would mourn the death of his first child.

Mary and Marie went into the kitchen to prepare some broth for Susan. Marie also prepared some supper for Jeff. Earl came into the house at that moment and Marie explained to him what had happened. Earl assured the ladies that he would make sure Jeff ate and let him know to make Susan drink the broth and plenty of water. It was necessary that she have plenty of liquids now. Earl again assured the ladies that he would see that Jeff had their instructions. He found a ranch hand to take them back to town. They went back in to say goodbye to Jeff and check on Susan and found him sitting up on the bed, holding Susan and sound asleep with tears streaming down his face.

It took Susan about a month to get back to her feet and be able to do her daily tasks. She mourned the loss of her baby but knew she could not live her life like she was dead also. Jeff took her for rides in the buggy, explaining what he was doing around the ranch and what his dreams were for the future of the ranch. He made a conscious decision to include Susan in all the plans he was making and get her opinion on it all. She was going to be an equal partner in the business as well as in his life.

"I would like to plant a vegetable garden. Do we have a small spot of ground that I could use?" asked Susan.

"We can find you a spot close to the house so you would be able to have better access to it," answered Jeff. "I can have one of the boys plow it up for you, then you can do with it as you wish."

"I would like that. When I first moved here, Mama, Marie and Jane canned some fruit from the trees by the hotel. I want to learn to do that. I know that with the proper equipment, I will be able to can the vegetables also," Susan explained. "Maybe if there is extra, I can share it with other families in the area," Susan mused.

They rode along the creek for a while when Jeff announced, "I have been thinking about calling another town meeting. I think that because of what happened to you, we need to investigate the possibility of getting a doctor to set up his practice in Rawlings. What do you think?" Jeff asked.

"I'm not sure a doctor could have done anything for me, but I do think a resident doctor is becoming a necessity. I know of two children who have permanently disfigured arms because of improperly set bones. I know of families who take the train to Dayton to see a doctor and I know of some who do not have the funds to do that and go without any medical care at all," explained Susan.

"If we did have a doctor come here," commented Jeff, "we would have to make it very enticing for him."

"What about building a clinic," asked Susan. "I think that would be a big enticement for any doctor. To have his own clinic with patient rooms and a separate office and living quarters on premises would be a dream."

"I will talk to George and arrange a meeting date and time," said Jeff.

The next day, Susan was stunned to see a wagon drive up with crates of baby furniture that they had ordered for the nursery. The sight of the crates brought to the surface all the hurt and ache of losing their baby. Jeff had all the crates taken to the barn and stored there.

The next Saturday, the Jordan's were making their first trip into Rawlings since they lost their baby. They were having supper with the family and spending the night at the hotel so they could attend church in the morning.

Marie was only a month away from delivering her 5th baby. She was concerned about how Susan would feel seeing her 9 months pregnant and knowing that she had lost her baby. She was still in mourning for that baby.

Marie was large and uncomfortable but managed to get her daily chores done and tend to the children. Irene, Charlotte, and Freddie were a great help to her. They took care of their own things, cleaning up after themselves and taking their dishes to the sink after dinner. Anna was indifferent to her mother and always had to be reminded to pick up her things. She would come home from school, change her clothes, and leave them on a chair, her bed, or on the floor. She thought that her mother should take care of them for her. George heard Anna yelling at her mother one day about not being a good mother because she did not care about Anna or the way she looked. She was yelling that all she cared about was the thing in her stomach. Marie was standing in front of Anna totally stunned at what she was saying. George came storming into the room, grabbed Anna by the arm and said to her, "You are coming with me." Anna started to protest when George said, "not another word out of you, young lady. Not another word!"

George was livid! He said to his daughter, "You will never speak to your mother like that again. She has given you everything and you criticize her by calling her a bad mother. You are a willful, disobedient, spoiled child. That is the fault of your mother and me, but no more. This is going to be your schedule from now on until I say it is different. You will get up one half hour earlier, get dressed, make your bed, and tidy your room. You will eat your breakfast, take your dishes to the sink, wash them and stack them in the dish drainer. You will go to school. When you get home, you will change your clothes and come into the hotel kitchen to work with me until supper. You will help your mother with supper, and you will wash the dishes and put them away. When I get home after work, I expect the table to be set for supper and you and your sisters to set the food on the table. After you have completed all your chores, you may do your homework. When that is done, you will check to see if your mother needs anything before you go to bed. Now, you will go and apologize to your mother for the way you talked to her. Do you have any questions?" George asked. Anna was stunned, just shook her head and went off to her mother. She knew that there was no gain for her in arguing with her father. He had been angry with her before, but never like this. It was all the fault of that baby in her mother's stomach. After the baby was born, she wanted nothing to do with it at all.

CHAPTER 16

Jeff talked to George about setting a date for another town meeting. He explained his concern about the town not having a doctor. It was decided that they would schedule a meeting for the last Saturday in April. "I agree about the need for a doctor, Jeff. Marie is about to have our fifth child and so far, we have been very lucky and have had no accidents or illnesses. I am surprised because of how much we have moved around, but God has been good to us. I do know that, that good luck could change in an instant."

Hopefully spring planting and calving will be over by the meeting date, Marie will have already had the new baby by then. Jane walked into the dining room at about that time and said, "Why not have a Spring Dance on the same day. Have the meeting earlier in the afternoon and the dance in the evening. We haven't done that before and it would be a good way to celebrate the season." "Great idea Jane," George and Jeff said at the same time. "Why don't you be the head of the dance committee?" Jeff suggested with a grin on his face.

"Me and my big mouth," Jane moaned.

George and Jeff continued the discussion about the need for a doctor after Jane left the dining room. Jeff mentioned the need for a clinic for the doctor to practice. George said that he had a small parcel of land that he owned behind the hotel that he had no use for. It was not big enough for a home to be built on. There would be no land around the house for a yard or garden. "Let me discuss it with Marie, but I see no reason why we could not gift the land to the city for a doctor's clinic. It could also have a second story home for the doctor."

Jeff was grateful for George's input and said, "Thanks George. You are the greatest."

Marie totally agreed with George and Jeff about the need for a doctor in town. Because of the way Rawlings was growing, the need for a doctor was becoming a necessity.

A notice was posted at the General Store, the Hotel and Post office, the Livery Stable and the train station announcing a town meeting on Saturday, May 21, 1887, followed by a spring dance. With the date over a month away, it should give the distant ranchers a chance to plan to get into town. It would also give George a chance to plan for extra business at the hotel and restaurant.

On the 4th of April, Valerie Ann Seevers was born to George and Marie. She was small, but perfect. Grandma Mary was thrilled with a new granddaughter, Freddie was disappointed it was not a brother, but conceded that she was kind of cute. Irene and Charlotte were thrilled to have a new sister. George was over the moon about her. Anna was the only one not thrilled with her new sister. She put on a good front, but George could tell by her expression that she was not happy with a new baby in the household.

Marie was depending on the girls to give her some help while she was recovering. Anna very reluctantly agreed to do some of the chores around the hotel, but she would have nothing to do with the baby. George had also hired some part-time help to carry bags from the train across the street to the hotel. All the part-time help was paid a small wage. In many cases, it was the only money coming into the household until they could harvest and sell a crop.

Marie recovered quickly from Valerie's birth and was up and about by the date of the meeting and dance. She and George did not want to expose such a young baby to disease, so Grandma Mary stayed behind to care for Valerie. George was very tired from an extra busy day, but he was determined to stay until the bitter end. He had adequate staff in the dining room to take care of some of the late customers.

It was a cool but clear day and the schoolhouse filled up quickly. People were curious about what was going to be discussed at the meeting. It was pretty much a consensus that Jeff would lead the meeting since he was the one who called for it.

"I'm glad to see you all here today," said Jeff. "I have a topic I want to discuss that could be of great importance and benefit to all the residents of the surrounding area. I believe that this town needs a full-time resident doctor. With Rawlings growing as fast as it is, the potential for serious injury or illness is great," explained Jeff. "George, why don't you explain the situation."

"I completely agree with Jeff about the need for a doctor, but we will have a hard time convincing a doctor to come here without some place for him to practice medicine. I have a small piece of land behind my barn that my wife and I are willing to donate for use as a clinic, office, and as a home for the doctor. The plot of land is not big enough for a home and yard for a family, but with a second story, would be okay for an office and home. I will donate the lumber for building the clinic if we can find someone in town who can supervise the building."

"Why are you being so generous with your land George?" Someone from the back of the room hollered.

"Because I see a need," answered George. "My wife and I are the parents of five children. So far, the Lord has been good to us and none of them have been hurt or ill to the point of needing a doctor, but I know that some people have had to go all the way to Dayton on the train to get medical care. That is over 50 miles and several hours away and that is unacceptable where my children are concerned. I am sure that other parents feel the same. What better way to use our land than to build a doctor's office that could possibly make our town a safer place to live," explained George.

Jeff interceded, "Let's advertise for a doctor and see what response we get. There might be none, then again, we might get the perfect fit for our community."

Most of the people agreed with Jeff and George about the doctor. Most of them had families that could possibly benefit from having a doctor close by. Some of the outlying farmers and ranchers admitted that they put off seeing a doctor because it took too much time away from their land to travel to see one. If a doctor would come to them, it would be ideal.

The idea of the grist mill was brought up, but Jeff admitted that he had no response from the ads he placed. He would try again to advertise in other cities. The townspeople were still in favor of the mill and agreed that Jeff should continue to try to find someone to run it.

The meeting ended with much discussion about a doctor in town. They all agreed that it was exciting to see their town growing the way it was. As the people were leaving, some of the men were moving chairs and tables out of the way, getting ready for the dance due to start in about an hour. The men with their instruments were setting up. The ladies were in the back setting up a table with punch bowls full of lemonade and coffee pots ready for hot coffee and tea. Plates of cookies were being set out and it was hard to keep the children away from the plates.

The residents who stayed in town were mostly at the restaurant eating a light supper until the dance started. Everyone was eager for some social time. They all worked long and hard on their land and a little time away and visiting with friends and neighbors was needed and appreciated. It was a beautiful, clear evening when the dance ended, and it made for an easy ride home for everyone. There were three families who lived too far to drive home so they stayed over at the hotel. There were also several of the single men who wandered across the street to the saloon to spend what was left of the evening.

George walked over to the railroad depot the next morning to talk to Gus, the telegrapher, about sending notices advertising for a doctor. He wanted them to go to newspapers in some of the larger cities in the East, Denver, Omaha, Chicago, even Boston and New York. "Let's send a wire to Cheyenne and Rapid City as well. We might as well hit all the areas at once," said George. He handed Gus a written advertisement for him to send.

"I will get as many out as I can today. You know, railway business is a priority," said Gus.

"I know Gus. Thanks for doing this for us. Jeff Jordan will probably be in to see you in a couple of days to advertise again for a grist mill operator. We still want to build one," said George.

"Okay, I will do what I can," answered Gus.

As George was walking back to the hotel, Clyde stopped him to complain about Steven. "He keeps wanting information from me about inventory and sales figures. I don't have time for all that paperwork," Clyde complained.

"Clyde, if you don't take the financial part of your business seriously, you will be bankrupt very quickly. If you don't want Steven to do it for you, then do it yourself and see where you are in six months. You won't have a business and will have lost everything because it will have to be sold to pay your debts. Steven is only trying to help you and the town. We need a general store and would like you to have a profitable business," commented George.

Clyde walked back to the store grumbling under his breath about all the paperwork. George heard him grumbling, "Okay, okay" as he walked back across the street.

Within two weeks, George received a wire from a Doctor Blake Stephens from Cheyenne, expressing interest in relocating to Rawlings and practicing medicine there. He explained in his letter that he practiced medicine in Cheyenne, Wyoming with his father, but was interested in going out on his own and working and living in a small town. He said that he went to medical school in Boston but did not want to practice in the east.

George was very excited about the letter. He almost ran to his house to show the letter to Marie. Dr. Blake Stephens was the son of the doctor who treated George when he was assaulted by the drunk cowboys in Cheyenne. He and Marie sat down and composed a letter to the doctor inviting him to visit the town and see for himself what they had planned for a clinic for him.

George wanted to talk to Jeff but could not leave because the restaurant would be busy for supper, and he was the one cooking tonight. George knew that Jake, the night clerk, was sitting in the lobby of the hotel reading and he asked him to ride out to the JSJ Ranch with a note to Jeff. Then George sat down and wrote that note telling Jeff about Dr. Stephens and that he had invited him to visit Rawlings. Jeff answered George's note asking to be present when the doctor comes. He would like to meet him.

Construction had started on the clinic. Most of the men in town were willing to work on the building. They wanted Jeff and George to know that they were grateful that a doctor was coming to town.

Jeff had said that he would ask Earl if he would come into town and supervise the work on the clinic. Jeff knew that it would get done much sooner than if someone else did the work. Earl seemed to be a master carpenter and his work was always top quality.

The next day Earl came into town to plot out the clinic on the plot of land George had designated for the clinic. He would supervise the building of the clinic and had four men from town helping him. He figured it would take a month to get the building to the point of moving in. The supplies for the clinic would have to be ordered after the doctor arrives. He would let them know what he needed and where to order them.

Dr. Blake Stephens was busy getting ready to leave Cheyenne. He had some equipment that he would box up and take with him. His father had some duplicate supplies that Blake would be able to use. He would arrive in Rawlings in about a month and would have several crates of supplies and equipment with him. He would have one crate just full of medical books. He was looking forward to practicing medicine in a small town.

CHAPTER 17

There were several men in town who were helping with the construction of the clinic. The building was changing every day with the walls going up and the second story being put up within a week of the main floor walls being raised. Earl was pleased with the work the men were doing. He was very good at praising good work and the more praise they got, the better and faster they did the job. Everyone in town was eager to have the doctor there.

The ladies were busy sewing curtains for the windows in both the clinic and the doctor's apartment. They had gathered pots and pans, dishes, and utensils for his use. One of the outlying ranchers had a table and four chairs that he was not using. He fixed two of the chairs, painted the set and brought it into town for the doctor's use. Someone else donated an easy chair. George remembered that there was an old desk that had been in the room that they cleaned out for Grandma Mary. It needed some repair work and a couple of coats of paint. It would make a fine desk for the doctor's office. Jake volunteered to get the desk out of storage, do the repairs that he could and paint it. George was proud of him for wanting to do that.

The clinic itself was whitewashed on the outside so it would stand out among the other buildings. The inside walls were also painted white. There were two examination rooms and temporary beds were put in both. Each room had a bowl and pitcher to wash and had a small wood stove for heat. The walls of each room had shelves and a cupboard for storage of supplies.

Earl assumed that the doctor would have books with him, so he built shelves in the office for them.

Doctor Stephens sent a wire to George advising him of the date he would arrive and that he would need transportation to the hotel. He had no idea the hotel was just across the street and that it was just a quick walk.

The finishing touches were being put on the clinic and apartment on the day the doctor was to arrive. Marie realized that he would need a bed and dresser in the apartment, so they were taken to the clinic from the hotel. Jane hurried and made up the bed in anticipation of the doctor being tired when he got there and possibly wanting to rest a while. There were still items of furniture that would need to be purchased, but it looked very nice and clean for the doctor to start work.

George and Marie, Jeff and Susan, Steven and Jane and Clyde and Fiona were all at the station when the doctor's train arrived. When Blake Stephens stepped off the train, he was overwhelmed at the reception he received. All were in a festive mood and so excited to have him there. After the greeting he received, he just hoped that he could live up to their expectations.

Doctor Stephens walked across the road towards the hotel with George and Jeff, still stunned at the reception he received. "We have reserved a room at the hotel for you this evening doctor, then you will be able to move into your clinic tomorrow morning," explained George. "All your luggage and crates will be taken directly to the clinic. Would you like to see the clinic before you settle in at the hotel?" asked Jeff.

"I certainly would," answered Dr. Stephens.

"Right around this way," said Jeff, leading him around the side of the hotel and up to the front step of the clinic. Blake was in awe of the look of the building. It really stood out as a special building in the town. No other building was white. There was even a metal bracket on the front for him to hang his shingle. Roy had fashioned the bracket at the blacksmith shop.

George opened the door and handed Blake the keys. "Doctor, these are the keys to the clinic. This other set are the keys to your apartment. There is a separate set of stairs in the back as well as a set of stairs inside for your easy access to the clinic from your apartment."

"Gentlemen, when we are together with no patient around, please call me Blake. Around patients, Doc, Doctor, or Doctor Stephens is appropriate, but between us, Blake is good. And this building is incredible, and a lot more than I expected. I can't thank you enough for all of this and for such a nice place to live. I am looking forward to getting to know the town and the people," Blake commented. "There is one more thing I will need for the office. I will need a cupboard that will be locked, preferably in a space that is not visible to the public. I will have some drugs that are narcotics, and they always need to be locked up. My father had some problems with people coming in and stealing them. They can be lethal if taken incorrectly," explained Blake. Earl had stepped into the room and heard the conversation.

"I will get on that immediately," he said.

Blake turned around at the sound of his voice when George said, "This is Earl Jansen, Blake. He is a master carpenter and supervised the construction of this building. He is also the foreman of the Jeff's ranch, the JSJ Ranch."

"I am very glad to meet you, Earl. You have done an incredible job with this building," Blake commented.

After his visit to the clinic and settling in at the hotel for the evening, Blake walked around the area close to the hotel to get a feel of where things were. He walked past the general store, and past several empty buildings waiting for business to occupy them. There was a lot of potential in the town.

After walking back towards the hotel, Blake saw the blacksmith shop and livery stable behind the hotel. He stopped to introduce himself to the blacksmith. "Hello, my name is Blake Stephens. I am the new doctor in town. I want to thank you for the work you did on the bracket to hang my sign on. It is outstanding work."

"Thanks Doc! I'm Ray Clausen. I enjoy doing work like that. It is a break from shoeing horses. Good to meet you and welcome to Rawlings. I would shake your hand, but mine are dirty right now. I have been working on cleaning up the hoofs of this horse and putting new shoes on him. He was in bad shape."

"Ray, can you tell me where I can buy a horse and buggy. I will need a reliable buggy trained horse to make calls to outlying farms and ranches."

"This horse I am working on is a buggy trained horse. He is a good horse, just not well taken care of by his previous owner. He was left here yesterday, and the owner left town without him. He would be available as soon as I am finished with his hooves, and he has a good washing and rub down. He will probably be ready tomorrow morning. As for a buggy, I have three of them here. Two I must keep for hire, but the third you could purchase for a small sum. You can stable your horse for free and park the buggy out of the weather in an area where it will not be blocked in by anything else. I am sure there will be times when you will need quick access to both horse and buggy. This horse is also saddle trained if you prefer traveling that way. If this horse does not suit you, I have others available that are both buggy and saddle trained," Ray explained.

"I have my own saddle and tack coming with my other belongings, so I will not need that, but a horse I will. It looks like the one you are working on will do me fine. He is a good-looking animal. When he is all cleaned up, he will be perfect. Do you have a designated area for tack?" asked Blake.

"Sure do! You are welcome to leave it here anytime," answered Ray.

After leaving Ray, Blake decided to walk back to the general store to meet Clyde Rodgers, the owner of the store. As Blake walked in, he saw a man, most likely Clyde Rogers talking to a lovely young lady. He did not want to interrupt, so he looked around to see what was available. When the lady was finished talking, she whirled around and started out the door. She stopped abruptly and looked at Blake. "Do I know you from someplace?" she asked.

"I am not sure. I just got in on the train from Cheyenne. My name is Blake Stephens. I am the new doctor in town."

"My goodness," exclaimed Fiona. "My name is Fiona MacGregor and I am the school teacher in Rawlings. I was visiting some friends in Cheyenne just before I came here. I believe you made a house call to my host in Cheyenne, Mr. Harold Walls. He was having some heart problems."

"Yes, I remember Mr. Walls. Fortunately, his heart problem was minor and could be easily taken care of with a change in his medication," commented Blake.

"It's a small world, isn't it Doctor?"

"Yes, it certainly is Miss MacGregor," answered Blake. "It's Mrs. MacGregor, doctor. I am a widow.

And please call me Fiona except in front of the students. Then I am "Mrs. MacGregor.""

"And I am Blake, except in front of a patient." They both laughed at their explanations. "May I escort you someplace Fiona?" Blake asked.

"I was just headed over to the hotel and the restaurant for some supper." "I have not had my supper yet. Would you join me?" Blake asked. Fiona nodded and they walked back toward the hotel.

All Blake's luggage and boxes and crates were delivered to the clinic the next morning. After he had a light breakfast, he walked back to the clinic to start unpacking and moving in. He worked hard at putting things away in his office and in the clinic rooms, making good progress on emptying the crates. He came to the crate filled with his medical books, but decided to wait on those for a while until he had the rest of the clinic in order. He needed to take a break and since he realized that he did not meet Clyde Rodgers yesterday, he decided to walk to the store and purchase some things he needed. Before he left, he picked up his candy jar to take with him. He intended to fill it with lemon drops for the kids. Hopefully, Clyde had lemon drops. He couldn't imagine a general store without them. They happened to be his favorite and he was hard pressed to keep his hand out of the jar.

As he walked into the store, he noticed that it was very busy and some of the ladies were lined up at the counter waiting to pay for their purchases. A lot of the conversations stopped when he walked in, and the women stared at him and wondered how a man could look that good and thinking about the possible embarrassment at having him treat them. They all knew that he was the new doctor in town.

Clyde stopped waiting on the lady in front of him and went to Blake, introduced himself and asked what he could help him with. Blake noticed the angry look on the lady's face and said, "I can wait my turn. These lovely ladies were ahead of me."

"Oh, they can wait. They have nothing pressing to do, I am sure. They rarely buy anything anyway," Clyde said.

"Well, I notice that each one of them has something in their hands to purchase. I will wait my turn in line." Clyde whirled around and asked the lady at the counter what she wanted. He had a surly tone in his voice and was not pleasant to her at all. Blake noticed his attitude right away and pegged him for a man who didn't like women very much.

Blake looked around the store, picked up a few things he wanted to buy, mainly a good-sized coffee pot, coffee, sugar, and flour. He had brought some basic cooking ingredients with him, mainly things he liked and wasn't sure he could get here without special ordering them. He also bought some eggs, potatoes, and some sausage so he could fix himself a decent breakfast in the morning. Clyde finally helped him get some canned goods down off a high shelf, took his money, and boxed up his purchases. Suddenly, Clyde wasn't very friendly to him.

As Blake walked back to the clinic with his purchases, he was stopped by several of the ladies he saw in the store. They wanted to thank him for his kindness in the store by waiting his turn for help. "You are very welcome, ladies. My parents trained me well," acknowledged Blake.

"We want you to know that Mr. Rodgers will always try to serve the men before he does the ladies," said one of the women.

"I'm sorry to hear that, but I want you to know that unless it is truly an emergency, I will always take my turn in line and not take advantage of you ladies."

Blake said goodbye to the ladies and walked back to the clinic. As he approached the door, he saw a little boy sitting on the step. He was crying and holding his knee. Blake set his purchases down and hunched down to talk to the boy. "What is your name?" Blake asked him.

"James," the little boy mumbled.

"Well, James, what are you doing crying on my doorstep?" questioned Blake.

"I fell down and hurt my knee," James explained. "Where is your mama, James?" Blake asked.

"She's off gettin' another baby. Pa told me to get the hell out of the house. I was afraid he would slug me again and I ran out and fell on the rocks in front of our house," James said.

"Is your knee hurting bad?" asked Blake.

"Yes, but that is not the big trouble. I got blood on my pants and Pa's going to be real mad. Because of the new baby, Ma won't be able to do the washing for a while and my sister will be too busy cookin' for Pa, so he won't let her do it and I am too dumb to wash out my pants."

Blake told James that he could probably remedy both problems. He could clean and bandage the cut on his knee, and he could wash the blood out of his pants. "Why don't you come in and we will see what is available to clean and bandage your knee. I haven't unpacked all my supplies yet, but I think I will be able to find what I need."

James got up and walked into the clinic. Blake noticed that he was limping. "How old are you, James?" asked Blake.

"I'm five," said James very proudly.

"Do you have any brothers or sisters?" queried Blake. "Yeh. Lots of them. I have a little sister Margaret and a bigger sister Josephine. Then there's Bill and Daniel and Seth, my older brothers. Pa says he hopes this new baby is a boy. At least he will grow up to work. Pa says girls are only good for cookin' and breedin', whatever that means," said James.

"What happened to your leg? Why are you limping?" Blake asked James.

"Pa says I was born defective. He doesn't like me because I can't work on the farm very well. He likes my brothers better because they do what he tells them to," James explained. Blake noticed that James was not afraid to talk about his father. The treatment he got must have been habit for him. He was used to it.

When James took his pants off, Blake noticed how dirty he was and that he smelled bad. He also noticed that he had bruises all over his legs. "When was the last time you had a bath?" Blake inquired.

"I don't remember. Not for a while. Pa says it's too much trouble haulin' the water in. None of us washes much," James said. Blake was horrified that a parent would treat their child like that.

Blake bandaged James' knee and washed out his bloody pants. He hung them up in front of the stove so they would dry quickly. In the meantime, he made a sandwich for James and one for himself. James said, "I am not supposed to eat other people's food. Pa says we do not take charity from anyone."

"This is not charity. I am hungry and I asked you to join me. It would not be polite to eat in front of you without offering you something," Blake answered.

"Thank you," said James. He took one bite and then put his sandwich down on the plate. "I usually must share my food with my brothers. They need to eat more because they work on the farm and need extra energy. Pa says I don't deserve more food. Do you mind if I take this home to them? Josephine is cooking tonight, and she is not very good at it. Pa complains about her cooking."

Blake really wanted James to finish the sandwich but knew he couldn't force him. When his pants were dry, and he dressed again, Blake walked him home. He wanted to come in and introduce himself, but James quickly said "NO!" with a very fearful expression on his face. Blake didn't want to cause James any trouble with his Pa, so he left him at his doorstep. He would meet those parents later. "Goodbye James. I was very glad to meet you. Take care of that knee."

James answered with a very quiet "Thanks. See ya later."

Blake returned to the clinic very troubled about James. He would have to talk to George about him and see if there was anything that could be done for the little boy.

He continued to unpack his crates of supplies brought from Cheyenne. He had both personal and professional supplies and decided to get the clinic set up first. George had thought of everything he would need in a clinic. The two patient rooms and an office for his own use. There were shelves in the office for his medical books and an old, battered desk George had found. It would work very well for his current needs. Someday, he would like to have a large executive desk with a comfortable chair, but that was in the future. He did make a note to himself to order a comfortable rolling desk chair.

After unpacking and organizing the clinic rooms, Blake went into his office to write letters to the hospitals in both Portland and Spokane. He wanted to be able to establish a relationship with the hospitals if he ever had to send a patient there. He also needed to have a source for ordering supplies and hospitals were the best place for country doctors to get supplies.

After finishing up his letters, he locked the front door of the clinic and went upstairs to his rooms. He had a lot of work to do up there to make the area his home. First and foremost was to get his clothes put away and get his toiletries arranged. He needed to be ready to dress quickly in case of an emergency in the middle of the night. The ladies had done a fine job of organizing the kitchen items they had donated. He had brought a lot of kitchen equipment of his own and wanted to put things away where he knew where they were. He would ask Marie Seevers about returning any items that were duplicate to what he had brought with him.

Blake's mind kept going back to James and his family. He wasn't sure what his responsibility would be in keeping the boy safe. James did say that his mother was having another baby. Maybe once she was back on her feet, things would be better for him.

Fiona MacGregor was busy getting ready for school to start in September. She was cleaning up the classroom and putting charts and pictures on the walls. The desks were scrubbed, and some supplies were put in them. She put readers at each desk appropriate to the age. She put paper in some of the desks along with a lead pencil.

Lesson plans were made for each grade level and when those were done, she finally felt like she was ready for school to start. This would be her second year in Rawlings, and she was looking forward to a good year. She knew that it was still harvest season and she would only have part of her class there. The older ones would still be working in the fields. She didn't like that they were not able to come to school, but she understood why. Their families depended on them to help bring in the harvest.

She was especially concerned about the Kingman children. She should have had four of them in class, but Josephine, the 7-year-old daughter was the only one who came, and it wasn't often that she was there. Sometimes she would bring her five-year-old brother with her. He was too young to be in school, but Josephine said that he had nowhere else to go. Their father wouldn't let him stay at home unless he could work in the fields and because of his limp, and being unsteady on his feet, it was not safe for anyone else. It sounded to Fiona like the father didn't want his son around.

The first day of school was an exciting and anxious day for the students. Exciting for the ones returning and anxious for the first-time students.

Fiona stood on the porch and rang the bell for the students to come into the classroom. As they entered the room, she asked them to line up at the back of the room and she would give them desk assignments. "The first, second and third grade students will be in row one. The fourth, fifth and sixth grade students will be in row two and the sixth, seventh and eighth graders will be in row three. The high school students will be in row four. There will be some activities that we all do together, but the actual schoolwork will be divided into grade levels. I hope that you will all reach your full potential. Please take a seat in the row assigned to your grade level. That will be your permanent seat for the school year," Fiona explained. There were still students standing in the back. It seems that no one wanted to sit in the front row. They all grumbled when asked to sit down but they finally did.

Josephine Kingman held her little brothers' hand while she made her way to the front of the class. She asked Fiona where James would sit. Fiona looked at her and at James and told Josephine, "Well Josephine," Fiona said, "James is too young to be in school yet. He really should be home with your mama. Since he is here with you today, you will have to share your seat with him. There are no extras now."

"Pa says he can't stay at home because he is useless. Ma got a new baby, and both are sick," explained Josephine.

"I am sorry to hear that, but we have no more seats, so I guess he will have to sit with you."

Not much schooling was done on that first day. The students talked about their summer activities and Fiona started reading "Moby Dick" by Herman Melville to the class. She explained that she would be reading a little at a time.

James Kingman came to school every day with Josephine. Fiona noticed that during lunch, they would sit off by themselves and never would bring lunch to school. Josephine would sometimes have a slice of bread and would share a bite or two with James, but James never had anything of his own. Fiona offered them both a sandwich that she brought, but they were very reluctant to take it. Josephine said, "Our Pa doesn't let us take food from someone else. He said we don't take charity."

Fiona answered, "This isn't charity. I made more than I can eat, and I really hate to waste it." They finally shared half of the sandwich, but that was all they would accept. Their hunger always got the best of them.

Josephine came to school one Friday and announced that she wouldn't be coming to school anymore. Her Pa told her it was not necessary for her to get an education, all she was good for was cooking and breeding. Josephine also told Fiona that her Pa didn't approve of the teacher reading crazy stories to them about a giant whale.

That same Friday, Dr. Stephens was in the classroom talking to the children about the importance of washing their hands after they use the outhouse and before they eat a meal. He was talking to them about keeping clean for their health.

While Dr. Stephens was there, Otis Kingman stormed into the classroom yelling, "There ain't no such thing as a giant whale. She's lyin' to you."

"Sir, please leave my classroom. You are scaring the children," Fiona stood and admonished Otis. Otis ignored her and grabbed both of his children and dragged them out of their seat.

"No kid of mine is going to sit here and listen to lies!" Otis hollered.

Josephine was in tears, but James was stoic. He had no expression on his face at all. He was blank, like nothing had happened. "And lady, you don't ever give my kids food again. Kingman's don't take charity," Otis yelled. He stormed out of the room screaming and cursing at his kids.

Fiona stood there in stunned silence, as did Dr. Stephens. One of the students stood and said, "Mrs. MacGregor, Mrs. Kingman just had another baby, and both are sick. Mr. Kingman don't believe in doctors, so they don't get any help. Nobody at their place is fixin' food for them so they are all hungry."

"Thank you. Let's all sit down and take a deep breath, then we will get back to work. First, I want to explain to you the difference between fiction and non-fiction. Fiction is a story that is made up in the author's head. Non-fiction is a true story. For instance, if you were to write a story about Thomas Jefferson writing the Declaration of Independence, that would be non-fiction because it is a true story. If I was going to write a book about Dr. Stephens and how he got to Rawlings, it would be called a biography. But, if I was going to write a book about how I got to Rawlings, it would be an autobiography. So, we have four forms of writing: fiction, non-fiction, biography, and autobiography. Moby Dick is fiction. Melville made the story up in his mind. It is not true, but it is a good story. Are you enjoying listening to it?" asked Fiona.

"YES!" the class said in unison.

"We only have about 15 minutes of class left before lunch, so why don't I read to you." The students all expressed their pleasure. They were all excited to hear more about Moby Dick.

The next day James came to school by himself. "Where is Josephine?" asked Mrs. MacGregor. "Pa wouldn't let her come. He said she don't need no more schooling for now. She needs to learn to keep house and breed," explained James. Fiona was shocked at what James said, but asked why he was here without her. "Pa says I can't stay around during the day. He says I'm defective and can't work so I'm no good to him," explained James. Fiona had tears in her eyes after hearing what he said.

"James, I am going to let you come to school every day. You may sit in Josephine's seat for now. If you are able, you may do the work the same as the other students and I will give you credit for that work."

Dr. Stephens was scheduled to come and speak to the class again. He had a young patient from one of the outlying ranches who died from a rattlesnake bite, and he wanted to explain to the students how important it was to be aware of where they were and what was around them. He also wanted to explain to them what to do if they or someone they were with was bitten by a snake or anything else.

When the doctor walked into the classroom, Fiona introduced him as he approached the front of the room. "Children, you remember Dr. Stephens, He is here to talk to us about a very important subject." As Blake looked around the classroom, he noticed James sitting there by himself. He knew that James was too young to be in school but didn't say anything. He talked to the students about snake bites and bug and lizard bites. Some of them were poisonous and some were just a nuisance. He answered some questions that the students asked and started to leave. Before he left the room, he whispered to Fiona, asking her for a short meeting after school. Fiona nodded and thanked Dr. Stephens for taking his time to inform them of the dangers of snake bites.

As the doctor walked out, he stopped at James' desk, put his hand on his shoulder and said, "Good to see you again James." James proudly said to the doctor, "I'm an official student now." He had a huge smile on his face.

Blake left, and the students were dismissed. Everyone left but James. Fiona went over to him and told him school was out and it was time for him to go home. James got a very sad look on his face but put his coat on and started to leave the building. Just then the doctor walked back into the room, saw James, and said to him, "James, why don't you walk down to the clinic and wait for me on the step. I will be there right after I talk to Mrs. MacGregor." "Okay, see you there," James answered with a big grin on his face as he went bounding out of the classroom.

"Why is James in school?" asked Blake. "Isn't he too young?" Fiona proceeded to tell Blake the whole saga of yesterday when Otis Kingman came into the class very drunk and pulled his children out. She explained that she had let James stay because he had nowhere else to go. His father didn't want him at home because he limped. Blake in turn told Fiona about the day he met James, the skinned knee, his fear of his father finding out he had blood on his pants.

"I know Kingman beats him up," said Blake. "He mentioned something about not wanting to make his father mad because he would slug him again," related Blake.

"I think he is a very smart little boy. He is very verbal for a five-year-old and answers questions in class like he's been doing for years. When I read to the class, he sits there in rapture almost. He is so concentrated on what I am reading. James is probably the smartest one in the family. The others have been put down so much and for so long, they don't know anything different. I have not met the other children. Josephine is the only one who ever came to class," Fiona explained.

"I would like to help Mrs. Kingman and the baby but am reluctant to approach them since he has not asked for my help. James indicated that his Pa doesn't believe in doctors. He's a good-sized man and he could cause a lot of harm to his family if he is riled. Let's keep an eye on James. He is not afraid to talk about his family, so we might ask him a question or two about his mama and the baby," Blake said.

Blake went back to the clinic after his talk with Fiona, thinking of James, but also thinking what a good-looking woman Fiona was. Maybe he would ask her to supper some evening.

CHAPTER 18

The JSJ Ranch was amassing a good-sized herd of cattle. Jeff had a field prepared to plant wheat and alfalfa in the Spring. This first year he would use his harvest as feed for his animals. He had a good group of cowboys who were ready and willing to spend the winter out on the range keeping the cattle safe. He was taking every precaution he could think of to protect his animals.

Jeff had also purchased more horses from the Palouse, had broken them to the saddle and taken them in to Ray at the livery stable. There were times when someone would need a horse and ask to rent one.

In November 1887, Susan discovered she was pregnant again. Jeff was determined that she would be under Blake Stephens' care this time. Her stomach acted up a bit in the morning, but she got over it quickly if she ate something. One of Susan's favorite activities was riding out on the range with Jeff while he did his inspections. Doctor Stephens said that that activity had to stop. It was too dangerous for the baby. So, Jeff bought a buggy so that he could take her with him. Blake figured the baby was due in late May or early June. He wanted her to walk as much as she could and get plenty of exercise. He felt that women who were pregnant needed to use common sense.

Jeff was still anxious to build a grist mill but didn't have any response to his ads. He opted to try one more time with advertisements in smaller papers in the central part of the country. He figured putting ads in the area where wheat is grown would generate more interest. At least people living there might know what a grist mill was. So, he went to the telegrapher at the depot to place ads in papers in Ohio, Iowa, Missouri, Kansas, and Nebraska. Maybe some response would come from those areas.

After sending the wires, he and Susan walked across the street to the hotel. He surprised George and Marie. Jeff said that they just wanted a family dinner. Marie looked at Susan and said, "Are your pregnant again?" Susan nodded her head yes. Marie grinned and hugged her sister, then went to find the girls and her mother and ask them to the restaurant for supper. She found Jane and Steven in the lobby with the twins and asked them to come to supper with the family. The minute they walked into the dining room and saw Susan and Jeff there, they knew what the big announcement was. Everyone was excited about the new baby. Everyone except Anna. She stood up, stomped her foot, and shouted, "I don't know why everyone is so excited about a stupid baby. All of it is a big bother, a lot of mess and noise. You are all stupid for thinking it is a great idea." The family sat there in stunned silence.

George rose from the head of the table, walked around to Anna, took her arm and in a very calm voice and said, "Please come with me." He led her back to the kitchen and outside the back door, past the livery and blacksmith and around to the back of the clinic. He did not want anyone to hear what he was going to say to her. All the time they were walking back there, he had a tight grip on her arm. He shoved her down on a bench and looked at her with such a disappointed look on his face and there were tears running down his cheeks. George proceeded to tell Anna what he was going to do. He was going to put her over his knee and take the flat of his hand and paddle her good.

Anna looked at him and said, "You can't do that."

George answered, "Oh yes I can!" He sat down, pulled her across his knee and proceeded to spank her hard. He spanked her through her dress and petticoats, so it didn't sting at all, but the humiliation was almost more than Anna could take. After he had paddled her, he said, "You will go back in and apologize to your Aunt Susan and the rest of the family. You will sit there quietly until we are finished with our meal, then you and I will walk home, and you will go directly to bed. If you do not do exactly as I have said, you will get another spanking, this time in front of your brother and sisters, and this time without the padding of your dress and petticoats. Do you understand?"

"Yes Papa." Anna answered very quietly.

They walked back into the dining room. Anna very quietly apologized to Susan and Jeff and sat down in her chair.

She did not eat anything else but sat there very quietly. Just as everyone was finished and started to rise from the table, the door burst open and a very drunk Otis Kingman came stumbling in the room yelling, "Where is that teacher? I'm going to get her for what she is teaching my girl. She's telling them stories that are lies."

Susan spoke up and said, "Otis, she's reading a story to them. It is called Moby Dick. The story is not meant to be true."

"She's a bitch and she's lying to those kids," he yelled as he pulled out a pistol from his waist band and started waving it around. Jeff was standing slightly to his left and lunged at him. He tackled him by the lower legs, knocking him down. The gun went flying. Otis yelled profanities at everyone. Jane ushered the children out of the room with the babies crying and Marie took charge of the older girls and Freddie. Grandma Mary stood up, stepped forward and covered the gun with her skirt.

"Let's get him over to the locked room in the depot before he hurts someone," George ordered. "What happened to the gun?"

Mary quietly said, "I have it." And she lifted her skirt to show them.

George took one arm and Jeff the other and almost had to drag Otis across to the depot. He was screaming and yelling the whole time, screaming for another drink. After Otis was locked up, Jeff sent a wire to the county sheriff in Dayton, briefly explaining what had happened.

Steven walked over to the clinic to let Blake know what had happened. Blake thought that this was a perfect time to visit Mrs. Kingman and the children. She needed to know that he was going to be in jail for a while. He was drunk and was swinging around a loaded pistol in the restaurant. "We are concerned about Mrs. Kingman and the children. Apparently neither Mrs. Kingman nor the baby are doing well."

"Thanks Steven. I will ask Fiona Mac Gregor to go out there with me. She knows both Josephine and James."

Blake walked over to see Fiona and to ask her to ride out to the Kingman's farm with him. Once he explained what had happened, she got her coat and they left. As they approached the Kingman house, Blake had a strange feeling. He was very uncomfortable about going into the house. He warned Fiona to be very vigilant. They walked onto the porch, knocked on the door and waited. No answer! They knocked again and a third time before Josephine got up to answer the door. The children were sleeping on the floor with only one blanket apiece to keep warm. Josephine was lying with James cuddled up close to her. Margaret was lying close to them, and the older boys were across the room, one of them trying to keep the meager fire lit.

Josephine got up and opened the door. She looked scared when Blake and Fiona stepped in. Fiona recoiled and stepped back out. The smell in the house was horrible. "Where is your mama, Josephine?" asked Blake. Josephine pointed to a closed door. Blake knocked on the door and opened it. Virginia Kingman was lying on a filthy bed with her dead baby lying beside her. She was alive, but not really aware of what was going on around her. It didn't look like anyone in the house had eaten anything in days.

Blake took the baby, wrapped it in blankets and took him to his buggy. He needed to be buried as soon as possible. Fiona took the other children back to the hotel in Otis' wagon. They needed a good meal, and she was sure that George and Marie would take care of them. They were all so hungry that no one protested about leaving the house. "Pa will be very mad when he gets home. We haven't finished our chores but were cold and needed to get a fire going before we could finish," Seth explained. Seth was the oldest and tried to look out for his younger brothers and sisters, but his Pa would stop him with a beating if he caught Seth helping them. They were to do their chores by themselves.

Marie was horrified at the sight of these six children coming into the restaurant. She had them all go to the back to wash up before they sat down to eat. George had fixed some good hearty chicken soup for supper that evening and there was plenty for everyone, along with plenty of fresh bread.

In the meantime, Blake was tending to Mrs. Kingman. Mary had joined Blake to help him get her cleaned up. Mary had also brought some chicken soup for her. She needed sustenance. It looked like she hadn't eaten in days. After cleaning her up and putting clean bedding on her bed, Virginia Kingman ate some soup. "Where are my children?" she asked Mary.

"They are at the hotel and eating some of this good soup. Please don't worry about them. My daughter and son-in-law will take good care of them," answered Mary.

"Otis will be so angry; he will beat them again. They are not to leave our property unless he says so. James is the only one he doesn't care about," Virginia stated.

"Virginia, I must tell you that Otis is locked up at the railroad depot. He was drunk and stormed into the restaurant looking for Mrs. MacGregor. He was waving a loaded gun around and there were small children in the room. Someone could have been seriously hurt, so we locked him up. We have wired the county sheriff to come and investigate the incident, but with what happened to you and your baby, I have a feeling that Otis will go to prison."

Virginia looked visibly relieved at the news about Otis. Blake explained to her that because her husband had withheld food from her, she was not able to produce any milk for her baby and the baby starved to death. He would probably be charged with child abuse, spousal abuse, and manslaughter.

Finally, after she had been cleaned up and had something to eat, Blake and Mary bundled her up and took her to the clinic so that he could properly treat her. The children would stay in a room at the hotel tonight and would each sleep in a bed instead of on the floor. George had a room set aside for railroad workers that had 6 beds in it. The room was not being used tonight, so it would be ideal for the Kingman children.

Grandma Mary stayed at the clinic with Virginia while Blake went to the hotel to check on the children and to talk to George about Otis.

Blake filled George in on what went on at the Kingman farm. George wanted to go over to the depot and beat Otis senseless, but he restrained himself and listened to Blake. George agreed that he should be charged with manslaughter and child abuse, but he had not heard of anyone ever being charged with spousal abuse. But why not? If it would keep him in prison longer, that would benefit Virginia, the children, and the town.

Blake walked across the street to send another wire to the county sheriff updating him on Otis and the circumstances of the death of his baby son and asking the Sheriff to come to Rawlings as soon as possible. After he sent the wire, he went to see Otis and update him on his situation. Otis was storming mad at Blake for removing his family out of their home. "You had no right to come into my home and disturb my family," Otis yelled. "They are my family, and it is my decision what happens to them."

"Killing one of your children by neglect is my business and it's the business of the law. I have wired the County Sheriff to come to Rawlings. He will determine if you stand trial for murder or not!" said Blake.

"I didn't murder no one!" Otis railed.

"You murdered your newborn son because you failed to provide food to your wife, and she was not able to provide nourishment to your baby."

"Where are Seth, Daniel, and Bill?" asked Otis. "They must work on the farm. They must feed the stock. I made sure that they ate so they could work. That's only fair," Otis stated.

Blake explained to him, "Someone is feeding your animals, but your children and wife are not there. Virginia is at the clinic recovering from a horrendous ordeal, no thanks to you. Your children are at the hotel under the supervision of George and Marie Seevers. From the looks of their legs and back, you made them work for things other than food. Those bruises are evidence of abuse."

"Those are my kids, and I can do what I want with them," Otis said firmly.

"No, you cannot!" Blake said firmly. "The county sheriff will come, and you will probably stand trial for manslaughter along with some other charges. You will stay here until a trial date has been set. Get used to this place. You will be here awhile." "You didn't even ask about your wife," Blake said.

"She's always wantin' something. What now?" Otis said with disgust.

"All she wants now is some rest, good food and a little peace and quiet. She just lost a child and is in pretty poor health herself, no thanks to you," stated Blake.

CHAPTER 18

November and December of 1887 were busy months in Rawlings. The weather stayed mild through the middle of December, then it started to snow, but not heavily.

The county sheriff came to town, listened to the evidence against Otis Kingman and transported him to Dayton to stand trial for manslaughter and child abuse. Dr. Stephens and Fiona MacGregor both had to go to Dayton to testify against Otis. Otis remained defiant though the whole process. He was found guilty and sentenced to 5 years in the new Walla Walla state prison.

Virginia Kingman was recovering from the birth and death of her infant son. She was afraid for the future of her six children. Without Otis, she had no way to take care of them.

George, Marie, Jeff, Susan, Steven, and Jane all got together for supper one evening to discuss the situation with Virginia and see if there was anything that they could do to help. Marie suggested that they might hire Virginia to work in the hotel. They needed someone full-time to handle the maid service. Grandma Mary was doing more than her fair share of changing beds and cleaning rooms. They employed several young girls on a part-time basis to do laundry and do some of the cleaning, but they needed a supervisor and Marie thought that Virginia would be the perfect person.

Jane said, "All of the children will be in school except Margaret, and she can hang out with the boys."

Jeff added, "Since the older boys have not been in school at all, maybe it would be an embarrassment for them to start school at their ages. What if they work at the ranch during the week and maybe if Susan is willing, she can work with them in the mornings. Seth and Daniel are old enough to work with the animals and Bill could work in the house doing chores, or work with Susan in the vegetable garden while she is pregnant. It would help her out a lot, I'm sure."

"Josephine and James would be in school during the day and with Virginia in the evenings," Susan added. "Of course, all of this would be subject to what Virginia wants to do. We are planning her life for her, and she isn't even here to have a say," George commented.

The family decided to bring Blake and Fiona into the conversation. They both happened to be having supper together in the dining room. They were at a table in the corner having an intense conversation, but Marie decided to interrupt them anyway. "Would you two lovely people like to join us for a few minutes? We have an idea and would like your input."

Blake and Fiona looked at each other, then got up and followed Marie over to the family table. Jeff explained the plan that they had come up with and asked for their ideas. "If Virginia agrees, I think it is a great idea. She does need the work. She has no income at all and does not have the resources to even feed her children. She is a proud woman and does not want to ask for help," Blake said.

Fiona added, "The idea of the older boys working on the ranch is perfect. I am afraid it would be too hard on them to attend a regular school at this point. Susan, if you could give them the basic reading, writing and arithmetic skills it would be great for them. If they are anything like Josephine and James, they are smart kids. And working at the JSJ Ranch will give them a positive work experience instead of the terror they have been working under for years."

"I know that several of the ladies in town went to Virginia's home while she was at the clinic and with

Josephine's help, did a thorough cleaning of the place. They threw away the ragged sheets and some of the blankets and replaced them with old, but good ones from here," Marie added. "Some of the men in the area cleaned up the yard around the house. It had been neglected for a long time. It looked like Otis just threw his garbage out the front and back doors of the house. Some of the men repaired the roof and the chimney. They also filled the wood box."

"Blake, would you make this proposal to Virginia?" asked George. "You have been around her more than we have, and she might not think of it as charity if you approach her. Emphasize that we really need help here in the hotel. Mama is working too hard. She needs to rest."

"Sure, I will talk to her. I think it will be a perfect solution for her. She needs to have some interaction with other people anyway. Otis kept her completely isolated," Blake said.

Blake presented the whole idea to Virginia the next day and she was overwhelmed. She was especially grateful that her older boys would be able to learn to read and write along with being able to work on a real ranch.

Blake wanted Virginia to wait another two weeks before she started working at the hotel. She needed the time to get her strength back. She also wanted Bill to stay home with her to help with some of the chores at home. He had always expressed a desire to go to school, even at his age now.

Virginia was feeling so much better now and just the fact that she would have the resources to feed her children was a big relief to her. Now she had to decide what to do about her marriage to Otis. She had not loved him for a long time. She feared him, not only for her safety, but for the safety of her children. She never knew what he was going to do. Because he was in prison, she would be able to divorce him without much trouble. She had to think about her future and the future of her children.

CHAPTER 19

During all the activity with the Kingman family, Jeff received a wire from Jesse Chamberlin of Lincoln, Nebraska. Jesse worked in the grist mill in Lincoln and wanted to move West. He has no attachments to Lincoln and wanted the adventure of living in the Northwest.

Jeff was excited about finally getting a reply to all his advertisements. He wired back to let Jesse know that he was very interested in meeting with him, but they still had to build the mill and depending on the weather, it would be Spring before it was ready to begin operation.

Two days later, Jeff received a wire from Jesse saying that he would be interested in coming out and helping to build the mill. He was also an accomplished carpenter and might be able to lend a hand. Jeff was stunned at his good luck and talked to Earl about the possibility of having someone else work on the mill too. Earl wasn't sure how much time he would be able to spend on the construction. Since he was foreman of the ranch, his duties had increased, and his time was taken up with ranch business. Earl was pleased at the possibility of someone else helping who knew how to wield a hammer.

Jeff wired Jesse back and told him to come out as soon as he could. They would really appreciate his help and his knowledge of the construction of a grist mill. He would also be able to guide Jeff in ordering the right equipment for the mill.

Susan was doing well with her pregnancy. She was a little sick in the mornings but managed to make it through without too much discomfort. With the responsibility of teaching the two Kingman boys and feeding the ranch hands, she was busy most of the time. With the added men building the mill, the bunk house table was full at every meal. The men were good about fixing their own breakfasts and making their own lunches to take out on the range with them, but they did appreciate a good hearty meal after a hard day's work.

One evening when Susan finished cleaning up after supper, she mentioned to Jeff, "I could sure use some help fixing the meals. I am so tired, I could sleep for a week."

Jeff gave her a hug and said, "I need to hire a bunk house cook and add a kitchen onto the building. I am sorry you are so tired sweetheart. Maybe we can ask your Mama if she would be willing to come out and help just until I can find a cook. I can ask her when I take Seth and Daniel in to see their mama tomorrow if that is okay with you."

"It is okay with me. At this point I would accept anyone who can boil water," Susan moaned.

On Friday, after leaving the boys at the Kingman farm, Jeff went to the hotel to see Mary. "Hello, Mama," Jeff greeted Mary with a hug.

"Hello, Jeff. I usually don't see you on Fridays. What's happened?" asked Mary.

"Nothing happened but I have come to ask your help before something does happen. Susan is so tired after cooking for all of the hands and I'm afraid she will lose this baby if she tries to do too much. Would you consider coming out to the ranch just until I can find a cook?"

"Certainly, I will help. Susan needs her rest, especially now," answered Mary. "Do you want me to pack a few things and go with you now? I can let Marie and Jane know that I will be gone for a while."

Mary went to find both Marie and Jane to let them know that she would be with Susan. Susan needed her help. Both Marie and Jane relied on Mary to help with their children but realized that Susan needed her Mama now. Susan had always been the more self-sufficient of the three girls and didn't depend on others for help, but she needed help now.

When Jeff pulled up to the front door of the house, Susan was resting in the living room before the fire. She was so tired, she didn't have the energy to get up to bed. She cried when she saw her mama come in the door. Mary went to her and said, "Hush now. I am here to help."

It was the beginning of December and Christmas would be here soon. The children were getting excited because Fiona was working with them on a Christmas Pageant to be performed in front of family and friends. George and Marie were busy baking treats for Clyde to sell at the store and of course, George was planning special meals throughout the holiday season.

The weather had been cooperating so far with only rain and a very few snow flurries that did not stick to the ground. Everyone was hoping the good weather would hold until after the pageant. It made traveling to and from town much easier. Doctor Stephens appreciated the milder weather. It made house calls easier to get to. Clyde appreciated the weather. More people came into the store and sales were up. Fiona was happy with the weather because it wasn't preventing the students from coming to school. She had a full classroom. With the addition of Bill Kingman, who had never been to school and some of the other students who only came occasionally, she was very busy. It took a lot of organization to make sure each student had enough of her time.

The children were anticipating the arrival of Santa Claus. They were sure he would arrive the night of the pageant. There was a rancher at one of the outlying farms who would make an appearance every year in his red Santa suit. He was naturally rotund and had a long white beard. His name happened to be Nickolas and he smiled and laughed all the time.

With Mary staying at the ranch with Susan, Marie was extra busy taking care of 9-month-old Valerie, helping in the diner when needed and supervising the staff of the hotel. She also had to give time to Anna, Irene, Charlotte, and Freddie. Jane was still working at the front desk along with keeping an eye on the twins. The trains brought new people to town every day. A lot of them stayed over for one or 2 nights waiting for a connecting train. George had set aside a room with six beds in it for transient passengers, usually railroad workers who had to spend the night. It was full most of the time now. Jane was hoping it would slow down when people went home for Christmas.

Steven was getting busier all the time with his accounting business. He had Leo working for him and he was doing a very good job. He was good with numbers and could add a column of figures without writing down the totals each time. He was a big asset for Steven's business. Steven not only kept the books for the restaurant and hotel, but Clyde's store, the blacksmith and livery and now Jeff and Susan. They did not have the time or knowledge to keep the books accurately. He would also keep the books for the grist mill when it became operational.

George had not given up on his dream of seeing the Pacific Ocean. Life had just gotten in the way. Travelers would come through town and stay at the hotel or stop at the restaurant for a meal and he would hear them talk about the ocean and what a magnificent place it was to visit. The pull was very strong, but the pull of wife and children was even stronger. He had too many responsibilities to up and take a trip to the ocean. He pictured the ocean in his mind but couldn't see the colors of the sea or land around it. He still dreamed of it and believed that someday he would see it.

Christmas of 1887 proved to be a very happy time for all of the Seevers, Taylors, and Jordans. The weather was mild and allowed them to all be together. Susan and Mary arranged a Christmas celebration and dinner for all the ranch hands. Jeff gave them each a bonus for a Christmas present. On Christmas morning, they took Mary and the two Kingman boys into town to celebrate with the rest of the family.

Virginia Kingman had all her children around her this Christmas, and it was a happy time for them all. It was the first happy Christmas that they could remember. She liked working at the hotel and having other people to talk to. She and Marie and Jane had become good friends. She had never had a good friend before.

Virginia never heard from Otis. He was in prison in Walla Walla, but she had no word as to how he was. She missed the idea of being married, but certainly did not miss him or the abuse he heaped on her and the children. Seth and Daniel loved living at the ranch during the week. They spent two hours every morning with Susan learning to read and write and the rest of the day was spent working with the animals or doing odd jobs around the grounds close to the house. They were helping Mrs. Jordan as much as they could. Jeff gave them strict instructions to not allow her on a ladder to hang pictures or do any type of work that would be too strenuous for her. They spent their weekends with their Ma and the rest of their brothers and sisters. They would do some of the small chores around the farm, but with no animals left except a few chickens, there wasn't much to do. They enjoyed being able to relax with their family and not having to look forward to a beating for some infraction of a rule that they did not know about.

Bill, Josephine, and James would spend their days in class and their evenings with Virginia and Margaret. Being considered a family gave them security for the first time that they could remember.

With the very generous help of neighbors, Virginia's small bit of land was maintained. She had no animals to take care of, only a few chickens who would lay enough eggs to give the family a decent breakfast. She was earning wages working at the hotel and was able to buy food and other essentials that the family needed. She did not have a running bill at the store, because she never knew if she could pay it.

Clyde Rodgers was becoming accustomed to living in a small town and running the general store in a fair and friendly manner. He still wasn't overly friendly with Doctor Stephens or Fiona, but he was trying. He was learning to give Steven the information he needed to maintain the books accurately. Steven was pleased with the information he was receiving.

The Kingman children had never celebrated Christmas before and were fascinated by the decorations at the hotel. They had never had a tree or hung stockings.

CHAPTER 20

Jesse Chamberlain arrived in Rawlings the 3rd week in December, just as the holiday festivities were in full swing. He was a tall, good looking young man with huge muscles in his arms, but soft spoken and very polite and courteous to everyone he met. Jeff was excited to finally have him in town and to get started on the mill.

Jesse walked from the depot over to the hotel, looking around the town as he walked. He was pleased so far with what he saw. He met Jane as he walked into the hotel. She was at the desk with two little boys playing at her feet. When he introduced himself, Jane looked up at him and said, "Welcome Mr. Chamberlain. We have been looking forward to you coming. My brother-in-law, Jeff Jordan is in the dining room. I believe you have been corresponding with him. Please follow me and I will introduce you to him. Just let me get these little monsters corralled." Jane took the boys by the hand and led them to the dining room and Uncle Jeff. They approached Jeff's chair, and the boys broke loose, and each jumped onto Jeff's lap. Jane laughed and said, "Jesse Chamberlain meet Uncle Jeff Jordan." Both men laughed, shook hands around the little boys.

Jeff handed the boys back to their Mama after a big hug and sloppy kisses from both boys. "Off with you fella's," he said, laughing at their sad faces. They had thought they were going to get to spend some time with Uncle Jeff.

"Good to meet you, Jesse. Welcome to Rawlings. You will find if you hang around the hotel long enough that the place is swarming with kids. My brother-in-law, George Seevers and his wife Marie own the hotel and run this restaurant. George is the chef and a darn good one. Another brother-in-law, Steven Taylor is the postmaster and owns an accounting business. His wife Jane is the lady you met at the front desk with the twin monsters. My mother-in-law rounds out the adults in the family. Normally, she lives here at the hotel, but she is residing temporally at the ranch. My wife is pregnant, and Mary is helping with some of the cooking chores," Jeff explained. "George and Marie have five kids, Steven and Jane have two. Virginia Kingman is the supervisor of the housekeeping staff, and she has little Margaret with her most of the time.

It is a big noisy group when we get together for family meals."

"The town looks very friendly. I am looking forward to meeting the people and settling in," said Jesse.

"I have a place for you to live on my property that is close to the mill site. My foreman is willing to share his cabin with you. It is big enough for 2 people. He is also a master carpenter. He is the one who built the ranch house, the bunk house and the barn and corral. His name is Earl Jansen. If you do not want to live there, there is always room in the bunkhouse."

"I am sure the cabin will be perfect. It will be nice to have company, especially someone that I have something in common with," Jesse said.

Jeff and Jesse made arrangements at the depot for Jesse's belongings to be sent out to the ranch. He also had some very heavy equipment for the mill that would be coming soon. His former employer had some spare parts for the mill and sold them to Jesse for a very reasonable price.

"Fortunately, the weather has cooperated with us so far and we have not had our usual heavy snow and freeze. It is fairly easy to get back and forth to town. There have been years when we weren't able to get down to the main gate," Jeff explained.

Jeff got Jesse settled into the cabin. Earl was there to greet him, and they immediately liked each other. Jesse thought the "cabin" looked more like a little house. There were two bedrooms, a kitchen area with a large square table and four chairs along with a huge fireplace, big enough to stand in. Earl often cooked his whole meal in the fireplace and didn't use the stove at all. He said that it made him feel like he was out in the woods, camping.

Jeff helped unload Jesse's luggage from the wagon and went up to the house to see Susan. She had not been feeling well in the morning, but thought it was just a bit of nausea from the pregnancy and didn't think much of it. Jeff was concerned enough that when he was in town to pick up Jesse, he saw Blake Stephens and asked him to come check on Susan.

Blake arrived shortly after Jeff got home. He checked on Susan and the baby. He was concerned about the way the baby's heart was beating and told Jeff that she should be on bed rest. That meant no climbing stairs, no lifting anything and spending her time in bed. She needed to have her feet up for a minimum of 16 hours a day. Blake told her that if she wanted to deliver a healthy baby, she must rest with her feet up higher than her heart.

Being on bed rest meant no cooking meals for the ranch hands. Mary was helping, but she could not do it all herself either. Jeff knew that he had to find a cook for the ranch hands and a housekeeper/cook for the house.

George had mentioned at one of the family suppers that he knew a man in town who was a cook and had applied for work at the restaurant. George did not need extra help at the time and did not pursue employment for the man. His name was Joe Morrison.

Jeff asked around town if anyone knew him. Clyde said that he and his wife had come into the store a couple of times. "They are renting a small house just on the east side of town. Mr. Morrison has been getting temporary work on some of the ranches and farms around the area," explained Clyde.

"Thanks Clyde. I will go talk to them," said Jeff.

Jeff found the house that the Morrison's were renting. Both Mr. and Mrs. Morrison were at home and greeted Jeff with smiles and handshakes. Jeff noted that even though the inside of the house was sparsely furnished, it was clean and neat. "What can we do for you Mr. Jordan?" asked Mr. Morrison.

"My brother-in-law, George Seevers, told me that you were looking for work as a cook. I am looking for a full-time cook for my ranch hands. My wife has been cooking suppers for them, but she is pregnant, and the doctor says she must have bed rest, so she can no longer cook for them. I am also looking for a housekeeper/cook for the house. You two would be perfect for the job if you would like to have it. There are two rooms off the kitchen that could be made into a small apartment for you," explained Jeff.

Gus and Cora Morrison followed Jeff to the ranch in their wagon. To them, the offer of a job for both of them was like a gift from heaven. They were from the Northeast part of Oregon, up in the Wallowa Mountains. Their children were grown, and they wanted to have an adventure.

As Jeff was riding back to the ranch alongside the Morrisons, he was hoping that he did not make a mistake in offering them the job. He knew nothing about them, but when he walked into their house, he had a feeling that they were good people.

Jeff introduced Joe and Cora Morrison to both Susan and Mary. Then he took Joe down to the bunkhouse to introduce him to Earl. Both Susan and Mary were impressed by Cora. She was a very happy lady with a smile on her face most of the time.

Joe and Cora were ready to leave. They had talked about the jobs offered to them and agreed that it would be a good opportunity to settle down in one place again.

"Mr. Jordan, we would like to accept the jobs that you have offered us. We would be very happy here and the rooms that you have for us are perfect as long as we can use the kitchen for our personal use also," said Joe.

"Welcome to the JSJ Ranch then," Jeff commented with a big smile on his face.

Joe and Cora Morrison moved into the two rooms behind the kitchen at the JSJ Ranch and were a great help to Susan and Jeff. Joe was a very good and creative cook, and the hands loved his food. He was up early and down at the bunkhouse kitchen to fix them a good hearty breakfast before they started their busy day. While they were eating their breakfast, he put together sandwiches for them to put in their saddlebags for lunch. A good substantial supper was usually ready for them when they got in from the fields. Depending on what Joe was cooking, sometimes it was a little late, but always very good and worth waiting for.

Cora worked very well under Susan's instructions. She was meticulous in her cleaning, making sure that everything was dusted, and the floors swept every day. "Mrs. Jordan," Cora asked, "May I request that the men take their boots off before they come into the kitchen?"

"First, please call me Susan. And yes, you certainly may request it. In fact, I will ask Earl to make a bench on the back porch for the men to sit and remove their boots. Good luck in your efforts to get them to remove them. Maybe a sign on the door saying "DO NOT ENTER WITH YOUR BOOTS ON" would do the trick." Both ladies laughed.

After Mary knew that Susan would be okay with the new housekeeper and cook, Jeff took her back to her rooms at the hotel. George, Marie, Steven, and Jane were very glad to see her, and the children crawled all over her. She loved being with Susan and Jeff but was glad to be with the rest of her family and in her own room with her own bed.

The Spring of 1888 was a busy time in the city of Rawlings. The weather had stayed moderate all winter and people were not confined inside their homes.

Between harvesting and planting, the students attended school on a regular basis. Fiona finished reading Moby Dick and started on Little Women by Louisa May Alcott. Even the boys were interested in the comings and goings of the March sisters.

Clyde's store was doing a booming business. He had turned a corner in his own attitude towards his customers and the store was operating with a profit now, which gave Clyde more confidence in his ability to run a business.

Virginia Kingman was working hard at the hotel and loved her job. She was earning her own money and did not have to answer to anyone except herself and her children. She had obtained a divorce from Otis and was given full and complete ownership of the farm. Otis had signed it all over to her.

Virginia and Jane were having a cup of tea together one afternoon and Virginia mentioned her dislike for the house and farm. It had so many bad memories and she couldn't seem to get past them. Even her children had mentioned it. "Why don't you sell it and move closer into town? I've noticed several houses for sale near here," mentioned Jane.

"I didn't even think about selling. Now that I own it outright, I suppose I could sell," mused Virginia.

"Why don't you talk to Steven about it. He is knowledgeable about finances and property values," suggested Jane.

"Thanks, I will," Virginia answered.

The next day, Virginia walked into Steven's office to speak to him about selling the farm. She was very nervous talking to Steven. She had never dealt with the finances before and wasn't sure of what he was doing. "Good morning, Virginia. What can I do for you this morning," Steven asked.

Virginia stammered and said, "Jane suggested I talk to you. I want to sell my farm and buy a place in town. The farm has bad memories for me, and my children and we would like a fresh start. I know there are a few that are for sale."

"Have you seen one that interests you?" asked Steven.

"No, I haven't even looked yet. I can't buy anything until I sell my farm and know how much money I will have. I don't make enough money to make payments, so I must buy it outright."

"Okay, has anyone approached you about selling?" Steven asked. "No, but Otis once said that the neighbor was interested in expanding his farm. Otis got into a big argument with him and told him that he would be shot if he stepped foot on his property again," answered Virginia.

"I will visit him and see if he is still interested in expanding and if he is, how much he would offer for the piece of property," Steven said. "I will let you know as soon as I do."

"Thanks Steven. I appreciate your help," answered Virginia.

Bruce Williams was interested in purchasing the Kingman Farm. Virginia's children were all in favor of selling. The place held too many bad memories for them also.

Within two months, Bruce Williams had paid more than a fair price for the Kingman farm and Virginia had purchased a lovely little white house with a white picket fence around it with a very neat and tidy yard. There was a large tree in the front yard to give shade in the hot summer months and plenty of room in back for a small vegetable garden. The house had three bedrooms, one on the main floor and two on the second floor. The room on the main floor would be Virginia's and the others would be for the boys and girls. With Seth's decision to stay on at the JSJ Ranch, he would bunk with the boys when he was home.

The sitting room was very spacious with a large fireplace and room for a sofa and several occasional chairs. The kitchen was adequate. It did need some upgrades, but there was a pump that brought water directly into the house. No more hauling water to wash. An enclosed back porch ran along the entire house with some clothes lines strung there as well as some outside. There was also an area alongside the house to stack wood. The boys would not have to go so far in the winter to bring wood inside for the fire.

The Kingman children were very happy with their new home and to be closer to school and their friends. When their Pa was at home, they were not allowed to have friends, so it was a new experience for them to have someone their own age to talk to. The younger three children acquired nicknames: Josephine became Josey, James became Jimmy and little Margaret became Maggie. Even Mrs. MacGregor called them by their nicknames.

Virginia Kingman and Clyde Rodgers were becoming friends. Clyde thought that she was so brave for surviving the ordeal of losing her baby and the abuse that Otis heaped upon her. He was learning to like her children. He found Josey and Maggie enchanting little girls and Jimmy was a very smart little boy. Bill was still a little distant, but always very well-mannered and polite. Seth and Daniel were only with their mother on the weekends and sometimes not even then. They were busy working on the ranch and loved living there. Virginia missed them and always let them know that they had a place at home, but she also understood that they wanted their independence.

The grist mill was almost finished. Jesse was getting ready to install the final workings of the grinding wheel. The wheel had been delivered and installed and now the final gears were ready to install. Jesse Chamberlain proved to be a master carpenter indeed. He did a great job on the mill and the waterwheel. Jeff thought it was a beautiful sight. He couldn't wait to see the first wheat milled into flour.

CHAPTER 21

George received a letter from Isaac Sorenson wondering if there was an opening at the Rawlings bank for his oldest son Jacob Sorenson. Jacob was married and had two children. He was 32 years old and wanted to raise his children away from the big city.

George answered his letter immediately explaining they did not have a bank in Rawlings, that they went to either Colfax or Dayton to do their banking. A series of letters and wires passed between Isaac, Jacob and George and the result was the decision of Jacob and his family to move to Rawlings and open a bank. It would be a branch of the Citizen's Bank in Portland.

There was a building on the railroad side of the street that would be perfect for a bank. It would take a lot of modifications to make it serviceable, but it was possible.

Announcements were sent out and the citizens of Rawlings were ecstatic about a bank in town. The trip to either Colfax or Dayton was a great inconvenience for them. Jacob Sorenson and his family would be another great asset to the city of Rawlings.

In July of 1888, Susan safely delivered a beautiful baby boy named Jeffrey Charles Jordan Jr. He was the pride of the entire ranch. Every one of the ranch hands came to see Jeffrey and bring him a little gift, most of them handmade.

Cora Morrison proved to be a godsend to both Susan and Jeff. She took such good care of Susan during the last month of her pregnancy and during her labor. She was there with Susan until Marie and Mary got there.

Susan recovered very quickly from Jeffrey's birth and was so very happy to have her baby in her arms. It was hard for her to put him down, but between Cora, Marie, and Mary, she was learning to not hold on so tight. She was able to go back to working with the Kingman boys for three hours every morning. They were very intelligent boys that had never been given a chance to learn. Now their minds were like sponges, soaking up every bit of knowledge that they could.

George still had dreams of the Ocean. It was still his fondest wish. He had recently read an article in a magazine about a salt works not too far from

Astoria. It was here that Lewis and Clark boiled down sea water for the salt to preserve their meat. George wanted so badly to see this, but it would have to wait.

Life continued peacefully in Rawlings. Businesses were flourishing and new residents were moving in a lot. Everyone seemed to be happy and contented.

The years passed quickly. People were taking advantage of the services that were available in town. The hotel was busy most of the time with the railroad bringing in new people almost every week. George had turned one of the second-floor rooms into a dormitory room with 6 beds. Railroad workers that had to stay over, or steamship crew members that needed a place to sleep away from the ship were able to have a comfortable, warm place to sleep. The railroad or steamship line paid for the bed and George supplied hot water for a bath for them to clean up.

In 1894, Anna Seevers turned 17 years old and was out of school. She refused to work in the hotel or the restaurant. She wanted adventure and to be independent and out of Rawlings. Without her parents' knowledge, she signed up to be a cook on a steamboat going down the Columbia River to Portland. She told no one of her decision to leave Rawlings but left her mother and father a note the day she left.

She left the house very early one morning after her parents had gone to the hotel to prepare for the breakfast crowd. She only had a small bag with her extra clothes in it and some personal items.

She was told by the steamship line that she would have a two-day layover in Portland and then turn around and come back to Rawlings.

George and Marie did not see the note that Anna left until they got home that afternoon. She was already well on her way down the Snake River by that time. Both were horrified that she had done something so stupid without discussing it with them. Marie was in tears at what she felt was the loss of her first child. George questioned Irene and Charlotte to see if they knew anything about her leaving, but they seemed to be as surprised as their parents.

George went to the steamship office next to the railroad bridge across the Snake River and got some information about the route the steamship was taking and where it was going. The name of the ship was the Chinook. George then sent a wire to his friend Isaac Sorenson in Portland, letting him know that Anna would be on the Chinook stopping in Portland in a few days. George asked him to meet her and make sure she was okay. Isaac wired back that he and Julia would be at the dock when the ship came in.

Anna was very busy on the boat. She and one other older woman cooked for the crew and the passengers. On this trip, there were four Palouse Indians on board who were going as far as Celilo Falls to fish for Salmon. The Indians did not pay for their passage. The steamship line let them ride for free.

While she was on an afternoon break, she met a crew member, Will Jones. He took a liking to Anna and she to him. During their off time, they were always together. Will was Anna's first boyfriend, and she was falling in love with him. He spoke very little about his past or his family, only that he wanted to sail on the big ocean-going ships and travel to exotic places. That's what Anna wanted too.

"Let's get married and work our way across the Ocean to China," exclaimed Will.

Because she wanted to be with him, Anna answered, "Yes!"

The steamship did not dock in Portland but kept going down the Columbia River to Astoria and docked there. Will asked the captain if he would marry them and he agreed. They were married onboard the ship between Portland and Astoria.

When the ship did not arrive in Portland, Isaac inquired at the company's office as to what happened. He was told that the ship was never scheduled to stop in Portland on the West bound trip. They were going directly to Astoria, then would stop in Portland on the way back upriver.

Isaac wired the news to George. George and Marie were devastated not knowing where their daughter was.

After three weeks of not knowing where she was or if she was safe, they finally received a wire from her. She was in Astoria, living in a boarding house near the docks and working in a restaurant. She said a letter was coming later.

George finally received a letter from Anna two weeks later. She told him about getting married to Will Jones onboard the ship and docking in Astoria. Unfortunately, the company did not need her for the return trip up the river. She had a job at a diner along the waterfront and was living in a boarding house nearby. Will had signed on to be a crew member on a large Ocean-going freighter headed for China. He promised her he would be back in three months and then they would be together.

"I am okay, Mama and Papa. I am making enough money to pay for my room, and I get a free meal every day, so I am not going hungry. Papa, the food is not as good as yours, but it fills me up," wrote Anna. "I will post this letter now. I don't know how long it will take for you to get it but know that I am okay. I will wait here until Will gets home. I do love him with all my heart."

Irene was in the post office sorting the mail when she saw the letter from Anna post-marked Astoria, Oregon. She dropped all the mail and ran to the kitchen to give the letter to George.

He sat down, opened the letter, and read it. He turned white, then very red and then he cried. Irene had never seen her Papa cry before. He handed the letter to Marie to read, and she had the same reaction. They were both angry, hurt and very concerned about the welfare of their daughter. "What are we going to do George?" cried Marie.

"I don't know. We can't leave here now. There is no one capable of taking over the hotel. Freddie wants to run it, but he's not ready and he's still in school. I will hire another cook. That way someone will be trained." George was muttering to himself as he and Marie put their arms around each other and cried for their daughter.

Irene picked up the letter off the floor where Marie had dropped it. She read the letter and grew rigid with anger. She did not understand how Anna could have done that to her parents. She would have hit her if she had been standing there.

Marie was afraid to tell her mother what Anna had done. Mary's health had been fading lately and she spent most of her time in her room or sitting on the hotel porch in the nice weather. She did not have the energy anymore to take care of the little children. Marie was afraid the news of Anna would push her over the edge.

Mary was stoic when Marie told her about Anna and read her the letter. "Silly girl" was all Mary said. She waited a few minutes and then told Marie that she was tired and going to take a nap. Marie left after making sure her mother had everything she needed and was comfortable. Marie was hesitant about leaving her alone, but Mary assured her that she was alright, that she just needed to rest.

George was devastated by the news of Anna. He had wanted so much more for his children. Here she was married, living in a rooming house in Astoria, Oregon and working in a diner on the waterfront. And to top everything off, she was married, and her husband was on a ship headed for China.

That evening, George and Marie sat down and composed a letter to Anna, telling her that they would pay for a train ticket home and to get on the first train she could to Portland. Isaac and Julia Sorenson would meet her and make sure she would get onto the train east.

As soon as Anna got the letter, she wrote back that she promised Will that she would wait for him in Astoria, and she was not leaving and did not want to come back to Rawlings.

George was beside himself worrying about Anna and there was nothing he could do to help her right now. He did get a letter from Isaac and Julia saying they were going to Astoria, find Anna and take her back to their home in Portland. They would convince her that she could wait for Will in Portland and be in a lot more comfort than if she stayed in Astoria. She would also be a lot safer in Portland.

Isaac and Julia arrived in Astoria, checked into a hotel, and changed their clothes. They did not want to wear clothes that would announce that they had some money. They rented an old wagon with a horse that looked like it wouldn't go one block without falling apart. They made it to the dock, tied the horse to a rail and started looking in every diner for Anna. They finally found her at the last diner on the waterfront.

They sat down at a table and waited for Anna to come to them. When she did, she did not recognize them at first. "Hello Anna," Isaac said quietly.

Anna jerked her head up and gasped, "Mr. Sorenson, Mrs. Sorenson! What are you doing here?"

"We have come looking for you and to take you back to Portland with us. Your parents are very worried about you and are scared for you being here alone."

"Anna!" the cook yelled. "Get busy, you have orders to deliver," Anna ran off to deliver the food orders, then went back to the Sorenson's' table, always keeping an eye on the man behind the counter.

"I am off in 20 minutes. Please wait for me outside. I can't afford to lose this job," cried Anna.

Isaac and Julia walked back to their wagon and brought it down in front of the diner. When Anna came out, Isaac climbed down and said they would take her to the boarding house to get her things, then they would take the next train to Portland. "I can't go! I promised Will I would be here when he got back," exclaimed Anna. Isaac explained that she could wait in Portland just as easily. They would leave a note with the shipping company office telling Will where she was.

Anna started to cry, "But I promised him!" Isaac said to her very quietly, but firmly, "Anna, Will could be gone up to a year or more,"

"Oh no – he said that he would only be gone three months," cried Anna.

"Let's at least gather your things and take you back to our hotel. You can have a nice long bath, a good meal and sleep in a clean bed tonight," Julia said soothingly. They packed what little she had in her case and Julia led her out to the wagon where Isaac was waiting.

After a nice hot bath, a good meal and a good night's sleep, it was refreshing to see Anna smile the next morning. Isaac had gone to the shipping office and left a message for Will Jones that his wife was waiting for him in Portland. The shipping company had Sorenson's address so Will would be able to find her. Isaac also inquired about the length of time the ship would be gone. The clerk said it could be up to two years, maybe more depending on where cargo needed to be shipped. This trip that Will was on would be about two years. After China, it had a load going to Australia. "It will be a long time before that ship is back in Astoria, if it ever will be," said the clerk. He explained that all the crew had been informed about the length of time the ship could be gone. "Mr. Jones pulled a fast one on the little lady," the clerk said. You know, bad weather could delay them even longer. Isaac thanked him for the information and left the office for the hotel to pick up Anna and Julia and head for the train station.

At the last minute, Anna agreed to return to Portland with Isaac and Julia. Once she was convinced that Will could find her, she was willing to go. Isaac had decided not to tell her about the length of time the ship would be gone and the fact that her new husband lied to her. He would wait until they got home before breaking the news to her. When they got home, he would discuss it with Julia, and they would decide when and how to tell her.

The next morning the three of them boarded the train for Portland after Isaac assured Anna for the fifth time that he had left a message for Will on the board at the shipping office as to where she would be waiting for him. The train took six hours to get to Portland. Anna slept most of the time. She did wake long enough to have some lunch, but dozed back off until they arrived in Portland.

Anna was nervous about staying with the Sorenson's. It had been a long time since she had seen them, but they had remained good friends with her parents, and she did feel safe with them.

Isaac had arranged for a buggy to be available to take them home from the depot. They had a lovely home in the hills above Northwest Portland. Anna was amazed at the view of the city and the river.

Julia showed her to the guest room and explained that it would be her room while she was with them. The room was done in soft blue with white curtains and cover over the four-poster bed. Anna stood in the middle of the room and cried when she saw how beautiful it was. This is the room she had wanted all her life.

"I will have Anita draw a bath for you," said Julia.

"Who's Anita," asked Anna.

"Anita is our housekeeper. She is a lovely lady and very much a part of our family," answered Julia.

Julia left to find Anita and ask about the bath. "Anita, could you possibly scrounge in some of the old clothes we have and see if you can find something for Anna to wear?" requested Julia. She noted when Anna was packing in Astoria that she only had one other dress and it was badly soiled, probably from serving food at the diner.

Anna sank into the hot bath with a sigh. It felt good to bathe in a tub. She had only been able to wash in a basin and very rarely with hot water. She laid her head against the back of the tub and wondered how she was going to tell the Sorenson's that she was going to have a baby. She had missed two of her monthly's and she was usually very regular. She so wanted Will with her. She ached for him.

Mr. Sorenson told her it could be up to a year, maybe more, before Will was home. Will had promised her that he would be home in three months. She really wanted to believe him, but she also knew that Mr. Sorenson would not lie to her. She did not know what to believe, only that she was going to have a baby in about seven months, and she was not happy about it. She did not even like babies. How could this have happened to her?

Isaac went to the bank when he got home. He wanted to wire George right away and let him and Marie know that Anna was safe with them in Portland.

CHAPTER 22

Mary Lewis died in June 1894. She had not been well for some time and her memory was fading. She had a hard time remembering her daughters and her grandchildren. Marie, Susan, and Jane were all with her when she passed, and they all hugged each other and thanked their mother for a good life.

It seemed like everyone in town came out for the funeral. There was a reception at the hotel after the service. When Mary's husband Fred died, there was no body to bury, so Marie, Susan and Jane added his name and dates to Mary's stone. It seemed only fitting that they should be together again.

After many years, Doctor Blake Stephens and Fiona MacGregor were married. Fiona moved into Blake's apartment above the clinic. The school board gave her permission to continue teaching after she was married. She was a good teacher and the students loved her.

Clyde Rodgers and Virginia Kingman also got married in 1894. Virginia kept her job as head housekeeper at the hotel and Clyde moved into her home. Virginia's children were very pleased that their mother was happy. The three older boys all worked at the JSJ Ranch and lived in the bunkhouse. They thrived on the open air and the trust that Jeff and Susan had in them. Clyde had grown to love Josephine, James, and Margaret. They had become like his own children. He knew that Virginia could have no more children and he was okay with that. He had a good family.

Irene Seevers had graduated from high school and received her teaching certificate. She had been offered a job as a teacher's assistant at Whitman College in Walla Walla. She was excited about the opportunity to teach college age students. She wanted to work towards an advanced degree in education.

Charlotte, Freddie, and Valerie were still in school and worked part-time at the hotel. Charlotte was learning from Jane how to greet people and check them into the hotel. Freddie would spend most of his spare time in the kitchen with his father. He was like a sponge when it came to learning to cook. He loved experimenting with different foods and tastes. Valerie was a very busy seven-year-old. She had many friends and in the good weather, they could usually be found at one end the hotel porch playing with their dolls. She sometimes was called upon to help clean tables in the restaurant, and she always did it willingly.

Steven and Jane's twin boys liked nothing better than to be at their Uncle Jeff's and Aunt Susan's ranch galloping across the fields. Before they could saddle their horses though, they had to clean out the stables. It was their job in exchange for being able to ride the horses.

Jeff and Susan doted on Jeffrey Jr. He was being home schooled, but occasionally went into town to stay with Aunt Marie and Uncle George. Then he would attend school with his cousins. There was only one year difference between Valerie and Jeffrey, and they were in the same grade. Susan and Fiona were using the same lesson plan, so Jeffrey was not confused or behind when he attended school.

Except for the difficulty with Anna, George and Marie were very happy with their family and their life in Rawlings. The only problem George had was his continued desire to see the Pacific Ocean. He had the yearning for so long and it would not go to the back of his mind. It was always there – the Pacific Ocean. Sometimes he could put the immediate desire out of his head, but something would happen, and it would come back in full force.

In November 1894, George and Marie received a letter from Anna informing them that she was going to have a baby sometime in May or June. She assured her parents that she was fine, and that Will would be home for the baby's birth.

Marie was heartsick that her little girl was going to have a baby without her husband being there to support her. But not knowing Will Jones, she did not know how much support he would be. George was just plain mad. He was mad at Anna for getting herself into this situation and he was mad at Will for going to sea and leaving her stranded and pregnant.

Julia Sorenson assured Marie that Anna was physically fine. She had taken her to a doctor to confirm the pregnancy. She did tell Marie that Anna still thought that Will would be home before the baby's birth. It seemed that no one could convince her otherwise. She didn't even believe the clerk at the shipping office and was convinced that Will would be home when their baby was born. He promised her and she believed him.

Marie was terribly concerned about Anna but knew that Julia and Isaac were taking good care of her. She just hoped that Anna was behaving herself. Meanwhile, Marie had four more children to see to and a husband who needed her attention also. She still got up early and baked bread for breakfast at the restaurant. She helped George as much as she could with food preparation and serving. Along with what she did at the restaurant, she needed to supervise her children's homework. Charlotte was about ready to graduate, and Freddie had two more years. Valerie was seven years old and just starting school, so Marie was looking at six more years of homework.

With all of Marie's responsibilities, she found time to do some sewing. Clyde was carrying a lot more fabric in the general store than he used to, and Marie was fascinated by some of the fabrics and the patterns. Many of the women in town knew that she was an excellent seamstress and asked her to make them new dresses. She could have a very good business if she had the time.

This was the first Christmas that Grandma Mary was not with them, and everyone missed her. Apart from Anna, who was in Portland, the family was all together for Christmas. As usual, they had a huge family meal at the restaurant. There were thirteen family members and this year they invited Blake and Fiona and Ray Clausen to join them. It was a festive time for all of them, but they all missed Anna and Grandma.

The weather cooperated through Christmas day and then it started snowing and didn't stop for six days. The roads turned icy, and it became very dangerous to be outside. Jeff, Susan, and Jeffrey stayed in town for 3 days before they could get back to the ranch and even then they were not sure that they would make it. Jeff was worried about his stock and the ranch hands but knew that Earl could handle any problems.

Once home, Jeff and Susan were not able to go back into town for another month because of the icy roads and snow piling up. The hands had managed to move the cattle into holding pens closer to the homestead where it was easier to feed them. The pregnant cows were isolated in another pen until they gave birth. Even though they could not go off the ranch, it was a busy and exciting time on the JSJ Ranch.

Time was dragging on for Anna. She was uncomfortable now and she couldn't go out because she was obviously pregnant. She began questioning whether Will told her the truth about anything. It had been 6 months since she had seen him, and she had not gotten one letter. She had thought when they made port, he would post a letter to her.

Maybe Mr. Sorenson was right, and it would take a lot longer for him to get home. She didn't know anything about cargo liners or how long their trips were. She really wanted to believe Will but was beginning to question. She was seven months pregnant and wanted this baby out of her.

Anna was a good seamstress. That was the one domestic activity that she enjoyed doing with her mama and grandma, but she was not interested in making anything for her baby. She should have been making little shirts and rompers and blankets, but her heart wasn't in it. All she wanted was Will and the baby out of her.

On April 16, 1895, Anna received a wire from the shipping company that the cargo ship "The Independence" had gone down in a typhoon in the South China Sea. There were no survivors.

Anna screamed when she read the wire. Isaac was beside her immediately and eased her into a chair. She sobbed, "He promised he would be home. He promised. He promised me."

The wire also stated that Will Jones had left some personal property in a locked box at the shipping office, and they had his final pay available, pending information on where to send it.

After sending for the doctor and making sure Anita was with Anna, Isaac took the buggy to pick up Julia at her weekly card game and go to the telegraph office to send a wire to the shipping office notifying them of the address in Portland to send Will Jones personal property and a wire to George and Marie telling them about what had happened.

When they arrived home, they saw that the doctor was with Anna. He was concerned that she would go into labor, and it was too early to deliver the baby. It needed at least another two weeks before making his first appearance. "At this point, she needs complete bed rest," the doctor told them. "She needs to eat good, nutritious food and get plenty of sleep, and definitely no stairs." "We will see to it," answered a worried Julia.

When George received the wire from Isaac about Will's death, he felt so sad for his little girl. He knew she was deceived by Will and now she would have to raise his child by herself.

"Marie, I think it's time we made the trip to Portland to bring Anna and our grandchild home," announced George as he handed the telegram to Marie to read. After reading the wire Marie cried, "Yes please! I want my daughter home."

It was Wednesday and George contacted the rest of the family for a family meeting on Saturday evening. He also included Blake, Fiona, Virginia, and Clyde in the meeting. They would be affected by George and Marie's absence also.

On Saturday evening after supper, George got up to speak. "Please let me finish my thoughts before any of you speak," he commented. "We received a telegram from Isaac Sorenson yesterday about Anna. Her husband Will Jones was on the cargo ship "The Independence" when it went down in a typhoon in the South China Sea. There were no survivors. Anna's baby is due next month, but the doctor has put her on complete bed rest. Marie and I feel we need to go to Portland to be with her and bring her and the baby home as soon as they can travel."

Heads were nodding in agreement. George continued, "But we need to make sure all of you are okay. I am not worried about the restaurant. Jim Barnes is a very good cook and will handle the restaurant very well. The hotel is not a worry. Steven, between you, Jane, and Virginia, I have no worries."

"Thanks George! We will take care of things here," answered Steven.

George continued, "It's you Irene that I am worried about. We could be gone for up to six months. I fully intend to get to the Pacific Ocean while I am there. I have had this dream and desire to see the Ocean since I was a boy and I want to fulfill it."

"Papa, I will be leaving for Colfax in July, but in the meantime, I will help Virginia here at the hotel,"

Irene said. Steven said that he and Jane would oversee the running of the hotel and restaurant with Freddie to help.

"He is welcome to stay with us," said Jane. Susan said that Valerie could stay with them at the ranch. She would check with Fiona about any class work needed and she would take care of it.

"Then if all of you are okay with these plans, we will leave as soon as we can. We will take the train to Portland next week. And I want you all to know again that I fully intend to go to the Pacific Ocean on this trip. It has been my dream for so long and this might be the last chance I have to see it."

George and Marie boarded the West bound train on Thursday. The train went down the Washington side of the Columbia River to Kalama, then the passengers who were going to Portland were ferried across the river to Goble to get on another train to Portland. The trip was made longer by stopping in Kalama instead of Vancouver, but the ferry from Vancouver to Portland was not working so they had to go through Kalama. At least the train at Goble was waiting for them and they had no layover.

Isaac was at the depot to meet the Seevers and was so pleased to see them. It had been a long time. "You two look great," he said after giving a big handshake to George and a hug to Marie. "Julia is at home with Anna and is anxious to see you. Anna knows you are coming and is very nervous about seeing you. She is afraid you will not have anything to do with her or the baby. She has been in tears a lot during the past few months."

"We love her and sure, we are angry at what she did, but she is our daughter, and we would never reject her or our grandchild," Marie declared.

Both Seevers noticed the growth in Portland and the fact that the Sorenson's had moved into the hills of Northwest Portland. Their home was beautiful with a view of Portland and the Willamette River.

As they walked into Anna's room, they were shocked to see the condition she was in. They could see that she was badly depressed. She had not taken care of herself. Her hair was not groomed, she had obviously not done any exercise because she was badly overweight, even being pregnant. Anna cried when she saw her mama and papa. She gave them each a hug but was quite reserved around them. "I'm sorry to cause you this worry. You really didn't have to come this far," Anna mumbled.

"We wanted to see you Anna," George told her.

"Papa, mama, would you mind talking later? I am tired and the doctor said I needed lots of rest. We can catch up when I wake up." Anna said rather forcefully. Both of her parents were surprised at what she said. They had just gotten there, and she was dismissing them already. But both gave their assent and left her room.

As they left the room, Julia was there to greet them and show them to their room. It was next door to Anna's. Marie was shaking when she walked into the room. "What has happened to her?" Marie cried.

Julia explained, "The doctor says that she is in a deep depression and needs bed rest, so she doesn't have the baby too early. I don't agree with him. I think she needs to be up and active right now, but Anna agrees with the doctor and wants to be waited on. I must force her to get up and bathe. She has no desire to do anything. She doesn't even read. She just lays there and cries or sleeps. I have tried every enticement I can think of. I must tell you, she has done nothing to prepare for the baby. I have purchased a few things that she will need right away, but she seems to show no interest at all."

George had gone down to talk to Isaac. Marie took Julia's hand and said, "Anna has never liked the idea of being around babies. When Jane's twins were born, she was resentful of the attention they were getting. When Susan had Jeffrey Jr., she was terribly rude to her, and she will have nothing to do with Valerie. She does not acknowledge Valerie as her sister, so I am not surprised that she has done nothing to prepare for her child. But I will go into her room and lay down the law to her. She will get up, bathe, and come downstairs and eat with us. I also do not agree with the doctor. She needs exercise." Marie added, "Julia, I cannot thank you enough for going to Astoria and bringing her to your home and taking care of her. I am sorry she has been such a handful. For some reason Anna thinks that the world revolves around her and that she should always have the best. She was a terrible bully in school. We tried everything we could to turn her attitude around, but obviously, it did not work."

At that, Marie got up and walked out the door and went into Anna's room. Anna was not sleeping but staring up at the ceiling. She looked awful. She was lying there in a soiled nightgown. She had not bathed or washed and combed her hair, nor had she thought to smile and greet her mama. She only had tears running down her face.

Marie said very forcefully, "Anna, you get out of that bed, and go into the other room and take a bath. It is ready for you. And while you are bathing, wash your hair. Then you will get some clothes on and come downstairs and have dinner with us. Your days of lounging around in bed are over."

"I cannot do that," Anna replied in a surly tone, "The doctor says I need complete bed rest and I am not to walk up and down stairs. My supper is brought to me."

"Well, the doctor is wrong! You are going to get up if your Papa and I must drag you out of that bed. You will not take advantage of the Sorenson's hospitality any longer." Marie pulled the covers off Anna and pulled her up. Anna grumbled, but she did as her mama said. She did admit to herself that it felt good to sink into a warm bath. She washed her hair, then got out of the tub and toweled off. Marie had laid out a clean nightgown and put her robe out for her. Slippers were waiting at the foot of the bed. She put the robe and slippers on and went out into the hallway, headed for the stairs, and slowly descended. Her Papa was waiting at the bottom of the staircase for her. He escorted her into the dining room. Isaac, Julia, and Marie acted like she was there every meal. Marie explained to Isaac and Julia before Anna came down that she craved attention and wanted to be the center of attention on every occasion, even family dinner.

After dinner, George and Marie went back to Anna's room with her to talk. Anna told them about

Will, how he said that he loved her and wanted to spend the rest of his life with her. She explained that the captain of the Steamboat "The Chinook" married them. "I was surprised Papa when we went to Astoria and didn't stop in Portland. They told me that I would go to Portland, lay over a couple of days and then return to Rawlings on the same boat. When we got to Astoria, they said they didn't need me anymore. Then Will went and signed on as a crew member for a cargo ship headed for China. I didn't want him to go, but he said the money was so good and we would only be away from each other for three months."

"He found me a room to live in and said that he had read a sign on a diner window that they were hiring waitresses for the second shift. I worked hard Papa, I really did. The owner of the diner was also the cook. He yelled a lot and threatened, but he never hurt me."

"Will promised me that he would be home in three months, and I believed him mama. Why would he tell me that if it was not true?"

"I don't know Anna," answered her mama.

"Isaac said something about a box of his belongings that would be coming from the shipping office in Astoria. What is that about?" asked George.

"Apparently, he left a box of his stuff at the office in Astoria. They have a place for crew members to store some of their belongings they can't take with them. They are also sending his final paycheck. I don't suppose it will be very much," Anna mumbled as tears ran down her face again.

After Anna went to bed, George and Marie sat with the Sorenson's for a long time. "I tried to get Anna to get up, bathe and take care of herself, but she flat out refused. She also refused to see the doctor again. The only reason he put her on bed rest was that she was so distraught about her husband. He thought some bedrest would calm her down," Julia explained.

"I hate that word husband when it comes to my daughter and that man. I would throttle him if he were alive," declared George.

The two couples finally went to their respective rooms for the night. They were tired after a long day. About 2:00 A.M., Marie was awakened by a loud cry from Anna's room. Julia had also heard the cry and was on her way to Anna's room. They found Anna standing by her bed in a pool of water. She was in pain, begging her mother to make it stop. Marie cleaned her up and put her back into bed while Julia went to get Isaac up so he could fetch the doctor.

Marie realized very quickly that this would be a difficult birth only because Anna was not going to cooperate and listen to advice to make it easier. Marie had been through childbirth five times and knew the stages well. Anna was going to make it difficult on herself and everyone around her.

Marie was right. Anna hated everyone in the room including her and especially the doctor. She screamed and yelled for almost the full 20 hours of labor. Finally, the doctor had to threaten her with surgery and a scar on her stomach if she did not listen and push when he told her to. Finally, she pushed the baby out. It was a beautiful baby boy. The doctor estimated his weight at a little over 9 pounds.

Unfortunately, Anna wanted nothing to do with her baby. She did say his name would be William Henry Jones Jr., but that was all the interest she had in him. She wouldn't hold or cuddle him and would not feed him. She thought that was nasty. Both Maria and Julia were astounded at her attitude. The motherly instinct did not appear to be there at all.

After a month of recovery, Marie refused to let Anna have her meals in her room. She had to get up, bathe, dress and come down to the dining room to eat with everyone else. When she finally did come to dinner, she would only answer questions with one-word answers and would not join in any conversation.

George was thoroughly disgusted with her. One evening after dinner, she got up from the table, excused herself and headed for the stairs up to her room. George stopped her saying, "You and I are going to have a conversation young lady, right now." They went to the living room and sat before a fire. "I want to talk to you about your future and the future of your son. You know Anna, I grew up in an orphanage and not a very pleasant one. I worked from the time I was two years old and have never stopped. It was hard work for a boy of my age and if I did not do it to the satisfaction of the headmaster, I was whipped. Is that what you want for your son? He deserves more from you. Just because his father disappointed you, doesn't mean that you can take it out on an innocent baby. He didn't ask to be born. That was your decision when you married his father."

"So, from now on you will live by my rules. Number one will be, you will tend to your own child. You will hold him, bathe him, change him, and feed him. You will not push your child's care off on your mother or anyone else. You will get up at night with him. I cannot force you to love your own child, but you will take care of him."

"Papa, I am too young to be tied down to a child," cried Anna.

"You should have thought of that before you laid down with a man," George answered her angrily.

"Now you go back to your room. Your son will be in his bed in your room. Anita is there with him, but she has had a long day and is tired. She works hard and needs her rest."

Anna went back to her room and saw William there. Anita left and Anna was alone with her child. She looked down at him and saw Will and cried for both of them. How was she going to love this baby of hers when his father hurt her with his lies. She finally got ready for bed, crawled in and was asleep in minutes only to be awakened a short time later by William's cries. She reluctantly got out of bed, fed him a bottle that was waiting there, changed him, and put him back to bed. He still whimpered and occasionally cried out loud. She got back out of bed, picked him up and put him to her shoulder and paced the floor. He finally let out a loud burp and promptly went to sleep on her shoulder. She put him back in his bed, went back to hers and promptly went back to sleep, only to be awakened four hours later to go through the whole process again.

When she went downstairs in the morning, Marie asked her how her night went. Anna gave her a detailed account of her night, between yawns. Marie's only comment was, "Welcome to Motherhood."

The day after her talk with her papa, Anna received the box of Will's belongings from the shipping office in Astoria. She also received a draft for $38.00 which was his final pay.

The box was large enough to need help getting it up to her room. She was nervous opening the box, not knowing what could be in it. She opened it slowly but found only clothing on top. Most of it was old and torn and of no use to anyone. There was a bedroll with a pistol and bullets wrapped inside it. George took charge of it right away. There was $10.00 in cash in an envelope and two packets of official looking papers. The first contained Will's certificate of birth. It showed that he was twelve years older than she was. The second packet contained a certificate of marriage to Shirley Branson of Virginia City, Nevada. Anna screamed when she read it and threw it at her papa to read. George didn't swear very often but swore now. Anna had dropped the rest of the papers and Isaac picked them up. "Here, look at this! It is a divorce decree dissolving the marriage of one William Henry Jones to Shirley Branson."

Marie and Julia said at the same time, "Thank God!"

CHAPTER 23

As George and Marie were lying in bed that night, George said, "Marie, if we do not go to the Pacific Ocean now, we might never get there. Please, let's plan the trip now and leave soon."

Marie answered him with a big hug, "Yes!"

Marie was awake a long time that night. She watched George sleeping and thought that she had never seen him with such a contented look on his face. He was finally going to fulfill his lifelong dream.

The next morning, George told Isaac and Julia what they were planning while Marie told Anna. The Sorenson's were very happy for them. They both knew of George's dream and were thrilled that he was finally going to realize the end of his quest. Anna was not as enthusiastic about the idea. She wasn't sure about being left alone with William, but Marie assured her that Julia would be there to advise her, and Anita was available to help occasionally.

Within the week, George had rented a wagon and two horses and Marie had purchased necessary clothing and food items. Julia had supplied them with bedding and necessary cooking utensils for camping. Isaac had mentioned to George that there were great camping areas along the coastline. George wanted to sleep under the stars and experience the coast from outside, not inside a building.

They gave Anna a hug and Marie hugged her grandson, said goodbye to Julia and Isaac and were on their way. They went down the Columbia River towards Astoria and they were like two little kids out on a new adventure.

When they came to Astoria, they went in search of the waterfront area that Anna had lived in. They were horrified at the area and at where Anna lived and worked and were forever grateful to Isaac for getting her out of there.

They camped just South of Astoria for the night. They were not near the beach, but the air smelled different, and George's mood lifted. He knew he was breathing sea air.

The next morning as they rode a little further down the coastline, George saw the Pacific Ocean for the first time. He stopped the wagon, handed the reins to Marie, and got down. He walked to the sand like he was in a trance. He walked further down to the water line, got down on his knees and cried. He scooped up some water in his hands and tasted it. It was indeed very salty. He looked out at the waves rushing into the shore. He was getting very wet from the water rushing over his legs and feet.

He reluctantly got up and walked back to the wagon. He was wet and was covered with sand, but he was a happy man. He got into the back of the wagon and changed to dry clothes and shoes. Marie was very happy for him and knew that his emotions were racing now. She decided not to ask him any questions now.

As they started out again, George whispered to Marie, "I finally have seen it. I am a contented man right now." All Marie did was put her arm through his and give him a hug.

The next day, they saw the fort where Lewis and Clark spent the winter of 1805-1806. From the fort, they went south to an area where the explorers hauled sea water to be boiled down for its salt. They used salt to preserve the meat that they hunted for.

From the salt works, they were going to head back to Astoria when another camper told George about a huge rock just South of where they were now. He had never seen a rock this big. The camper told him about this very wide beach alongside the rock and how beautiful it was. Marie thought that they could take the extra time to see this huge rock. She wanted to be able to tell the children at home about it. George agreed to take the extra two days and go see this rock.

They rode through tall trees to get to the sandy beach. There was a good-sized camping area near the beach and George decided to stay there. Once they had the wagon and horses secured, they walked the trail to the ocean. They got to an opening in the trees and saw the beach and the enormous rock. They were both stunned at the size of it. Neither one of them had seen anything like it before. They were entranced by the view. They sat down on a log to watch the waves pound against the rock. The sun was going to be setting soon. The sky was orange and the waves looked pink as they were coming onto shore.

George slowly rose from the log and started walking towards the water. As he got to the water line, he put his fists in the air and thanked God for allowing him to fulfill his dream. He would return to Rawlings with his wife, daughter, and grandson, but would always remember the majesty of the Pacific Ocean.

Milton Keynes UK
Ingram Content Group UK Ltd.
UKHW020642041223
433752UK00017B/787

9 798890 913401